LEADING PHILIPPI

Paul's Patrons Series: Book 1

JENIFER JENNINGS

Editor: Jill Monday
Interior Map: BMR Williams

Scripture quotations and paraphrases are taken from The Holy Bible, English Standard Version, Copyright © 2001 by Crossway, a publishing ministry of Good News Publishers.

This book is a work of historical fiction based closely on real people and events recorded in the Holy Bible. Details that cannot be historically verified are purely products of the author's imagination. Any resemblance to actual persons, living or dead, or actual events is purely coincidental.

ISBN: 978-1-954105-46-1

For Angela,
May God continue to move you around this world,
spreading His light wherever you go.

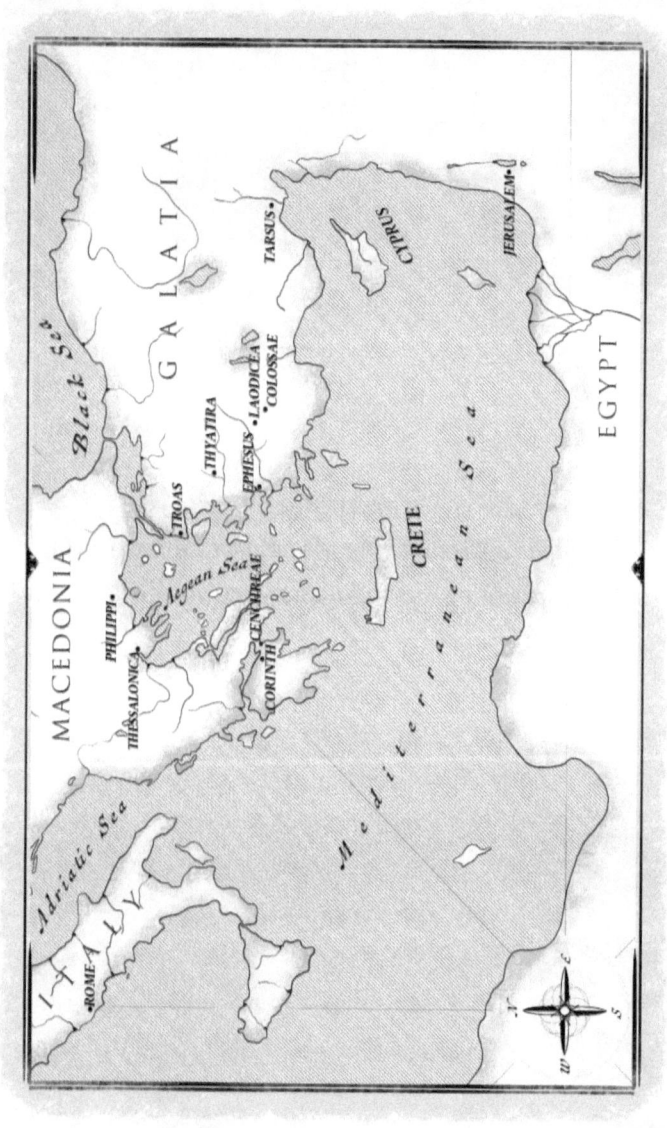

"So receive [Epaphroditus] in the Lord with all joy,
and honor such men,
for he nearly died for the work of Christ,
risking his life to complete what was lacking
in your service to me."
-Philippians 2:29-30

*And Samuel said, "Has the Lord as great
delight in burnt offerings and sacrifices,
as in obeying the voice of the Lord?
Behold, to obey is better than sacrifice,
and to listen than the fat of rams."*
1 Samuel 15:22

AD 37, Paphos, Cyprus

Epaphroditus darted through the turquoise surf
lapping the Paphos shore. The sea tugged at his
ankles and splashed his calves, each wave coaxing
him further. After a week confined to the creaking
belly of the ship from Philippi, his ten-year-old legs

ached for freedom. His mother granted him a brief reprieve while she directed the unloading of their belongings.

When he tired of sprinting, he slowed, scanning the area for a sea pebble. This was his first visit to the Sanctuary of Aphrodite, and he needed an offering worthy of the goddess.

Sunlight glazed the shoreline, igniting a path of scattered stones. Some gleamed white, others gray, and several shimmered with flecks of green and blue, mirroring the sea. He crept along the shore, eyes sharp, fingers trailing just above the stones. A gull cried above, swooping low before vanishing toward the harbor rocks.

Then he saw it.

A large, smooth stone with bluish-green veins poking out of the wet sand. He knelt to retrieve it just as a wave broke against the shore, frothing over his arm. Tiny bubbles danced on his skin, fizzing and vanishing, as if the goddess born of sea foam had kissed his hand.

He enclosed the stone in his palm, the weight of it anchoring his choice. "This one."

Turning, he ran back toward the path, his fist clenched tight. Sand clung to the soles of his feet as he kicked up grit.

He dashed toward his mother, brandishing his fist in the air. "I've got one!"

Neda glanced up as he approached, her sun-lined face softening into a smile. She brushed her hands on her cream-colored toga before holding her palm out. "Let's have a look."

He placed the stone in her hand.

"Ooh." She tilted it in the light, inspecting the stone before returning it to him. "That's a beauty. Aphrodite will be pleased."

Epaphroditus pressed the pebble to his chest. "Do you think so?"

"I know so." Her hand rested lightly on his back, nudging him toward the inland path. "Since this is your first pilgrimage, I need you to understand how important this is."

"Yes, Maia." He gripped the stone tighter.

As they walked the dusty trail, Neda recited expectations for the temple visit, clean speech, respectful tone, eyes lowered at the altar. He whispered them back under his breath like a chant, determined not to shame her, or the goddess after whom she had named him.

Epaphroditus stole glances at the stone in his palm, now dry and warm. Would the goddess notice it among the other offerings? He imagined Aphrodite rising from the foam, towering and radiant, her gaze sweeping over her worshipers. Would she pause for him? Would she speak?

Olive trees swayed above him, their silvered leaves whispering like voices just out of reach. They reminded him of home, though the air here carried a different weight.

The path wound upward, flanked by flowering shrubs that spilled their perfume into the air. Bees hummed between thick petals. A lizard darted across the packed earth, tail flicking behind. The deeper they walked, the more the world shimmered before him.

Cyprus.

His mother had spoken of this island since he was small, of its temples and warm winds, of their beloved goddess. But no story matched the living color before him.

They crested a hill, and the trees fell away. Ahead, the Sanctuary of Aphrodite gleamed in the morning sun. The temple's white stone walls glowed against the slope, wrapped in gardens that spilled like paint across the terraces. Flowers of every hue bloomed—blush roses, violet cyclamens, golden narcissuses—bursting from clay jars and baskets nestled between columns. The columns themselves soared upward, wrapped in crawling deep green ivy.

Worshipers moved in and out like waves on a tide. People in finely dyed tunics, some with gifts balanced in outstretched hands, others leading children or bearing garlands, all gathering inside the marble structure. Voices rose and fell with music from within, like the heartbeat of the sanctuary itself.

Epaphroditus hesitated at the edge of the

courtyard. No temple or altar in Philippi ever shimmered like this.

"It's wondrous, isn't it?" Neda's voice dropped low. Her fingers slid into his, warm and secure. "I'm so glad I finally get to share this with you."

He nodded, his chest too full for speech.

As they approached the entrance, Epaphroditus caught glimpses of the temple's sacred women. Their sheer robes whispered against tanned legs. Gold glinted from the braids wound through their hair. Eyes, sharp and lined with kohl, flicked toward him with practiced precision.

His mother's hand stiffened, her fingers firm, pulling him forward.

Inside, the air grew thick. The scent of burning incense mingled with crushed petals and oil. Mosaics shimmered beneath their feet, scenes of the goddess rising from the waves, flanked by dolphins and doves. The altar stood ahead, draped with embroidered cloth. Offerings crowded its surface. Painted statuettes, bowls of figs and almonds, and tiny amphorae sealed with wax.

Neda found a spot and arranged her offerings, leaving a space among them. "Go ahead," she whispered.

Epaphroditus stepped forward. He placed the pebble gently among the other gifts, then closed his eyes and recited a prayer. The words filled him, as natural as breath, spreading warmth from his chest to his fingertips. They were the same words his mother whispered over him during storms, before meals, and as he drifted to sleep. He rehearsed them repeatedly, hoping Aphrodite would hear his small pleas.

When he finished, Epaphroditus opened his eyes to take in his mother's approving smile. She clasped his hand again and turned to lead him out.

Before they reached the columns of the courtyard, a figure stepped into their path.

A woman stood before them, motionless and tall, her presence so striking it appeared sculpted rather than born. Her robe glittered with gold thread, catching every shaft of light. Gemstones studded her collar and wrists. She fixed her gaze on Epaphroditus.

"Priestess Arianna." Neda's breath caught. "I didn't see you."

Arianna didn't answer her. She lowered herself to Epaphroditus's level, the folds of her robe pooling like tidewater. Her ruby lips curled. She raised a single finger and placed it under his chin and tipped it upward.

Her eyes were unlike any he'd seen, deep brown but with flecks of gold, as if the sun had sunk into them and stayed.

"Such a handsome boy," Arianna said, her voice smooth as a calm sea.

His mother's fingers tightened around his, her

fingernails digging into his skin.

Arianna leaned closer to him. A thick braid fell over her shoulder, studded with glittering stones.

Epaphroditus stared at them—white, green, blue—the colors of the sea. His hand hovered, longing to brush against the polished gems.

When his eyes returned to hers, he froze. Her pupils twitched, unblinking. The darkness overtaking the flecks of gold. A strange dizziness swirled in his gut, like the ship's sway all over again.

Then she spoke, "Death waits for you across the Great Sea; your life will be Aphrodite's fee."

Neda shifted, stepping forward. "What did you say?"

Epaphroditus didn't breathe. The words etched themselves deep inside him, like a brand pressed to flesh.

Arianna blinked once, twice, as if waking from a trance, and rose to her full height.

His mother stepped between them. "Arianna, what did you say?"

The priestess's gaze sharpened. "Aphrodite has spoken."

Epaphroditus stood still. He didn't fully understand the meaning of her words, but the message struck clear. Cold prickled along his neck. Something inside him recoiled. He wanted to flee, to run down the path, back to the boat, no, not the boat.

His mother's grip squeezed harder. Pain flared in his knuckles.

Why had she brought him here?

The women's voices rose, sharp and urgent. But their words drifted, muffled and indistinct, as if he slipped into a tomb with the stone door sealed shut.

He thought of his father's merchant vessel and all that waited for him at his father's side. And now, death? That wasn't what the goddess was supposed to offer. Not to him.

He turned his head, just enough to look past the priestess. His sea pebble still sat nestled among the other offerings.

Was it not beautiful enough? Had he chosen wrong?

*Immediately an angel of the Lord struck
[Herod] down, because he did not give
God the glory, and he was eaten by
worms and breathed his last. But the
word of God increased and multiplied.*
Acts 12:23-24

AD 45, Philippi, Eight Years Later

Digging a piece of day-old bread into the leftover stew, Epaphroditus lifted the bite to his mouth. The cold meal broke his fast, though a part of him longed for a warmer start to the day.

His younger sister, Calliope, dashed into the room. Her eyes sparkled with mischief and curiosity, full of restless energy that seemed to fill the space around her. She threw herself onto his arm, jostling his bowl.

"Careful, Calli." He pressed the bowl to its proper place.

She kissed his cheek. "What are we doing today?"

"*We* are doing nothing." He shoveled the last bite of stew into his mouth. "*I'm* meeting Luke at the Theater."

Calliope crossed her little arms, huffing. "You told Maia you'd look after me while she was gone."

"I have been. Mother will be back from Paphos soon. Luke invited me to join. I'm sure Uncle Rufus won't mind if you help him for the day." He ran his fingers through her tangled curls, his hand disappearing in the storm of her wild hair.

"I don't like the dirty olive grove." She batted his hand away. "It smells funny, and Maia will not be happy with you if I get into trouble."

"Then keep out of trouble." He rose from his seat, filled his bowl with a smaller portion of cold stew, and set it on the table. "Eat up."

Calliope's face twisted. She plopped on one of the embroidered pillows, causing the gold lunula around her neck to bounce against her chest. "It's not even warm."

"Sorry." He grabbed an empty pouch and filled it with dried fruits and nuts. "I'm late as it is."

"I can't wait until I'm old enough to go with Maia to Paphos."

Epaphroditus's chest constricted, and every muscle stiffened as if the gods had turned him to marble. Arianna's wild gaze flashed in his mind, her voice echoing like an old wound reopening.

What would Aphrodite say about Calli?

He glanced over his shoulder at his younger sister. She was the daughter their mother didn't know she was carrying on that fateful trip to Paphos. Since then, their mother had returned to her homeland occasionally, bringing offerings in an attempt to sway the fickle goddess. Since his return, Epaphroditus had not boarded another boat. Much to his father's disappointment.

Watching Calliope break her fast, he silently prayed she'd never set foot on those cursed shores.

He dreamed of them almost every night, of foaming waves and a temple glowing white in the sun. The scent of incense, the hush of whispered prayers, and Arianna's voice curling like smoke through his thoughts. No matter how many years passed, the memory clung to him like sea salt in his hair.

"Here." He tore off a sizable chunk from a loaf and placed it beside her bowl. "When you're finished, rinse your bowl and find Uncle Rufus. I'll be back later."

"Please, can I come with you?" Calliope clasped her hands. "I'll be good."

"Not this time." He tied the pouch inside his tunic. "If you're good, I might bring you something from the market."

She sank into the pillow. "Promise?"

"Promise." He kissed her smooth cheek and headed for the door.

The rising sun warmed Epaphroditus in a way his meal hadn't. He walked north toward the Theater, crossing the Via Egnatia that split Philippi in two. The semi-circular building stood proud in the shadow of the great hill.

Luke waited by a curved archway, arms crossed but relaxed, a leather satchel slung casually over one shoulder. His eyes, bright and attentive, skimmed the passing crowd with the quiet alertness of a physician used to noticing small details. A few days' stubble softened the sharp angles of his face, and the faint crease between his brows spoke of long hours spent studying.

"You're late."

"Had to make sure Calli ate."

He gave a knowing nod. "When is your mother expected?"

"Any day now."

The two walked through the arch and toward the upper-class seating. Music and drama had already begun on the stage below, though several members of the audience continued chatting among themselves. People made or lost many business deals while actors retold stories of gods and goddesses.

Luke picked an open spot and dropped onto the cool stone bench. "Did you hear about Herod Agrippa?"

Epaphroditus sank down beside him, one knee propped casually. Politics wasn't exactly his favorite subject, but it was Luke's, and judging by the gleam in his friend's eye, the play wasn't the real draw.

"He died," Luke blurted, barely containing his eagerness. "During the Games at Caesarea."

"Assassinated?" he asked, brow raised.

Luke's gaze wandered to the stage as if the answer might be hidden in the painted backdrop. "Not by human hands."

Epaphroditus shifted. "What's that supposed to mean?"

He spread his hands slightly, palms up. "The Jews think it was their god."

"The Jews think their god is responsible for everything." Epaphroditus gave a dry laugh, reclining slightly on the stone with one arm braced behind him. "How did he die?"

Luke pulled his cloak tighter, settling in as though preparing for a long tale. "There's some debate about that."

He flicked his attention to the stage, then back to Luke. The pantomime before them paled next to whatever drama his friend was about to unravel. He nudged Luke with his shoulder. "Go on."

"You've heard about the troubles Herod had with the people of Tyre and Sidon, right?"

"Father has mentioned it."

"Well, on the second day of the festival, Herod went out to address the people... wearing his royal robes." Luke hesitated.

"What's so special about a king giving a speech in his robes?"

He held up a finger. "Ah, but these weren't just any robes. They were sewn entirely of silver."

"Silver?" Epaphroditus leaned toward him, skepticism heavy in his tone. "Really?"

"The witnesses say the sunlight reflecting off the strands of silver was so dazzling that it struck fear into everyone who looked upon him." Luke glanced around to see if anyone was listening. He leaned closer, lowering his voice, "As Herod spoke, the people shouted, 'This is the voice of a god.'"

"And?"

Luke straightened, lifting his hand. "The Jews say since Herod didn't praise their god, one of his divine messengers struck the king."

"So, he died from being struck?"

"Not immediately." Luke's gaze dropped for a moment. "He died in agony. Took five days."

Epaphroditus caught the shift in the physician's voice, more clinical than theatrical.

"Afterward, they found the cause," Luke said slowly. "Worms."

His stomach churned. "Worms?"

"Internal worms." Luke cast his attention to the stage. "The man's insides were full of them."

"And the Jews think their god is to blame?"

"That's what they claim." Luke lifted a shoulder, unconcerned. "I've heard Rome has already annexed

Judaea and made it a Roman province."

"Sounds like Rome thinks the Jews' god is to blame too," Epaphroditus muttered, allowing his gaze to return to the actors below as he digested the story. Would someone write a play about the silver-robed king and his belly full of worms?

"I grow tired of this play." Luke huffed.

Epaphroditus smirked. "Perhaps you should write a better one."

"I might just do that." He straightened his back. "A grand story that everyone will want to read."

Epaphroditus gave his friend an amused scoff. Luke was a talented storyteller, an even better physician, but could he write a tale the entire empire would read? An insurmountable feat, even for someone like his dear friend.

Luke fidgeted. "Want to visit the baths afterward?"

"I promised Calli I'd get home soon." Epaphroditus rubbed the back of his neck. Aches he'd ignored crept forward. "Though a soak sounds good."

"When does your father return?"

Epaphroditus shrugged. "'Trade doesn't follow the whims of the merchant,'" he said, deepening his voice in a fair imitation of his father.

Luke chuckled. "Speaking of voyages, I'll be traveling to Troas soon. You should come with me this time."

Epaphroditus's stomach tightened. "Sounds like you need a seafaring wife."

"I'm serious." Luke nudged him with his elbow. "You should come. It would do you good to get out of your family's groves for a while. Physician's orders."

"Oh, yes." Epaphroditus nodded in mock agreement. "All that fresh air and sunshine can't be good for a man."

Luke jabbed him in the ribs. "Some sea air and foreign lands might loosen up your sense of humor."

"Not this time."

"You say that every time."

The tightness in Epaphroditus's stomach climbed into his throat as the stage drama reached its climax.

For all the years he'd known Luke, he kept the deepest part of his life private, the trip to Paphos and the haunting prophecy. Though Luke was only a few years older, he carried himself like a much older man, no doubt because of his hours spent studying and tending to others' ailments.

"I've been thinking about it," Luke said, breaking Epaphroditus's musings.

"About what?"

"A wife." Luke grinned. "Besides"—he shoved Epaphroditus—"I can't spend my life hanging out with you."

Epaphroditus snickered. "Maybe we should

marry sisters, so they'll let us still have our outings together."

"Not a bad idea." Luke stroked his shaved chin. "Not a bad idea at all."

Epaphroditus cast him a look of feigned defeat. "Well, if you find two who are willing, you know where to find me."

"In the olive groves," Luke teased.

Better than aboard a ship bound for death.

She makes bed coverings for herself;
her clothing is fine linen and purple.
Proverbs 31:22

When the play ended, Epaphroditus stretched his legs, trying to shake the ache from the stone bench that had bitten into his bones for the last hour. "I promised Calli I'd bring her something from the market. Want to join me?"

"I don't have any better offers today." Luke groaned as he stretched his back.

"Maybe today's the day you'll find that wife you're dreaming about."

"They've got everything else a person could want."

They filed out of the theater with the rest of the crowd, turning west toward the Macellum. The rectangular building that housed the common market buzzed as usual, the air thick with the noise of merchants and shoppers. People from all social classes filled its porticos.

Passing through the colonnade, Epaphroditus heard the clatter of bone dice hitting marble slabs as various games of chance played out around them. Carvings of circles and squares marked shaded areas where gamblers wagered, either for fun or gain.

"Epaphroditos!" Shouts rang through the portico.

On his first trip to the market, he'd asked his mother why the people shouted what sounded like his name. She explained people yelled, "Favored of Aphrodite!" before their roll, hoping to invoke the aid of the goddess of gamblers.

Epaphroditus climbed the worn marble steps leading to the market. Passing between two Corinthian columns, he and Luke entered the peristyle courtyard. Flanked by shops on all four sides, the courtyard was a place for people to socialize and shop. Several statues and honorary monuments dotted the space, memorials to those who achieved great deeds. Altars and talismans to Sylvanus, Dionysus, and many other gods and goddesses filled the area. It was truly a place one could find just about anything their heart desired.

Snippets of his father's wisdom rattled in his head as he drifted past the vendors. *Don't look eager. Don't pay full price. Never buy from the first man who offers.* The older merchant had taught him the art of buying and selling. Though he wasn't hunting for a deal today, he'd be no seller's fool either.

His gaze landed on a familiar face. Lydia stood with effortless poise, her robe of rich purple draping around her like liquid silk. Her eyes lit with recognition, and her warm smile unfolded at his approach.

"Greetings, Epaphroditus."

"Greetings," he answered with a familiar ease, his posture relaxing at the sight of her.

"Good to see you well." She bent around him. "And you, Luke."

The physician gave a polite nod to her and tapped his fist to his chest.

Lydia stepped out from behind her booth and moved toward Epaphroditus. "How's your father?"

"Well enough," he said, eyes drifting over the fabrics. "Still at sea."

"Pass along my greetings when he returns."

"I will." He continued to inspect the merchandise. "How long are you in Philippi this time?"

"You know me." She waved her hand around dramatically, mimicking the wind. "I travel when I get bored."

Epaphroditus chuckled. "I don't know how you manage a home and business both in Thyatira and here in Philippi."

"Both keep me busy." She grinned. "Anything catch your eye today?"

"Perhaps." He tapped his fingertip on the edge

of the table. "I owe Calli a gift."

"Ah." Lydia stepped deeper into her booth. "I might have something that would interest you." She pulled out a dark purple veil and laid it gently across her arms. "Freshly dyed. This color would suit your sister well."

Epaphroditus rubbed the soft fabric between his fingers. "It's lovely."

She didn't need to voice her agreement; her pride clung to the fabric like the dye itself.

He knew better than to let on. Lydia's dyes were unmatched, but so were her prices. "I think Calli would like it, but..." With his father's sly tone, he offered a price even he knew was not acceptable for such craftsmanship.

Lydia's face soured, but she recovered quickly. She adjusted the veil and spoke her counteroffer, emphasizing the prolonged process of dyeing the fabric. "And I'll put it on your father's account, so if Calli doesn't like it, you can return it."

Epaphroditus resisted the urge to grin. She offered a fair bargain, but he didn't know if it was because of his trading skills or Lydia's partnership with his father. "Agreed."

With a delicate touch, Lydia handed him the veil. "She'll look striking."

"I'm sure." He carefully rolled the material and tucked it into his belt.

Lydia's gaze flicked to Luke. "Anything for you

today?"

Luke brushed his fingers over a hanging strip of linen but made no move to choose one. "Nothing today."

"Then I need to head home." Epaphroditus turned away. "Calli will be waiting."

"Come see me anytime," Lydia called. "I'll be here until the wind changes."

A flicker of amusement rose as he matched Luke's stride. "See anything interesting?"

Luke let out a breath through his nose. "Same crowd. Different day."

As they walked between the columns, Epaphroditus ran a hand along one of the stone pillars. "Were you serious about finding a bride here?"

Luke's face warmed with sudden color.

"Trust me"—Epaphroditus clapped his friend's shoulder—"you won't find a good woman in a market stall."

"They've got to be somewhere." Luke shrugged off his hold and continued forward.

"I'll keep an eye out," Epaphroditus chuckled, following after him.

Out in the open street, a commotion interrupted their teasing.

Someone screamed, "Help!"

Both men turned toward the sound. Luke was the first to react, rushing toward the source of the panic. Epaphroditus followed, heart quickening. They pushed through the gathering crowd until they reached the scene.

A boy, not much older than Calliope, lay in the street, blood pooling from a gash on his head.

Luke dropped to his knees beside the boy. "What happened?"

"A donkey." One man pointed down the street. "It got away from its owner, dragging the cart behind it. Ran over the boy."

Luke examined the injury, his brow furrowed in concentration.

Epaphroditus stood nearby, tension coiled in his gut as he tracked every movement, every shift in Luke's expression, searching for answers the physician hadn't yet spoken aloud.

Luke lifted his attention to the crowd. "Does anyone know this boy?"

"He was playing with some other kids," the man answered. "They ran off. I hope to search for his family."

"Epaphroditus." Luke looked at him. "Get over here."

Obeying the command, Epaphroditus knelt on the other side of the boy. He didn't have his friend's training, but the seriousness of the situation was obvious even to him. "Luke, he does not appear to be awake."

"I know." Luke searched through his bag. "I need

something to stop this bleeding."

Epaphroditus's fingers flew to his belt. "Here." He pulled out the purple veil. "Will this work?"

Luke hesitated. "It should."

"Then take it." He shoved the material into Luke's hand. "I'll get Calli something else."

Luke wrapped the boy's head carefully. "That'll hold for now." He gently opened the boy's eyelid, blocking the sunlight with one hand, then allowing it to shine on him again. "He needs proper care, but I can't do any more here in the street."

A woman's shrill cry pierced the air. "Felix!"

Epaphroditus turned to see a woman running toward them, her face streaked with tears.

She fell over the boy, her sobs wracking her body. "Felix!"

Luke put a hand on her arm. "Are you his mother?"

"I am." She patted the boy's face. "What happened to him?"

"A cart ran him over."

She pressed herself to her son's chest. "Is he alive?"

"For now." Luke jerked his chin toward Epaphroditus. "But I need to move him somewhere I can better tend his wound."

The woman's wails filled the air.

Luke bent near her ear. "My father's house is not far."

Her head came up with a jolt.

"We've got to move him."

She looked down at her son and nodded.

Epaphroditus bent and lifted the boy, arms tense beneath the limp weight. He hadn't carried someone this small since Calliope was little. Following Luke, he gripped the boy close to his chest.

As they neared the house, Luke called out, "Melody!"

Luke's sister appeared in the doorway, her dark braid swinging over one shoulder, concern already tightening her features. Though younger than her brother, Melody carried the same calm urgency. "What's happened?"

"Grab my supplies and bring some fresh water." Luke pushed past her and disappeared into the house.

Epaphroditus kept just behind him, the boy growing heavier with every step.

Melody gasped as she laid eyes on the injured boy. "Bring him in." She lifted the hem of her toga and rushed inside.

"There," Luke pointed to their low table.

Epaphroditus eased the boy onto it. He stepped back to give Luke room to work.

"Stay close," Luke ordered. "I'm going to need your hands."

"I'm no physician."

Melody appeared with a vessel of fresh water and placed it on the table.

Luke scrubbed his hands, a brief prayer slipping over his lips before he answered, "That may be true, but that doesn't mean you can't assist."

The boy's mother hovered at the door. "Felix?"

"You may wait there." Luke motioned toward a corner of the room with a flick of his chin. "I won't be long."

Epaphroditus watched Luke and Melody's practiced rhythm. How many had bled under their roof? How often had this table seen the razor edge between death and life?

*And Jesus answered them, "Those who
are well have no need of a physician, but
those who are sick."*
Luke 5:31

"Wash your hands," Luke said, nodding toward the washing vessels. "Like your mother's going to inspect them."

A brief smile tugged Epaphroditus's lips. "You've got a wounded boy on your table, and you still have time to jest."

"Humor's one tool among many." Luke focused on the boy's head. "Just make sure you get all that soil from under your nails. It may help your olives, but this boy won't thank you if he gets an infection."

Epaphroditus scrubbed his hands, trying to remove all traces of his labor, though he was certain a speck of dirt would cling stubbornly to his skin.

Luke carefully unwound the veil, now streaked with blood that marred its deep purple hue, and set it aside.

"It's a shame." Epaphroditus lowered his gaze to the ruined cloth. "It was a beautiful veil."

"Don't worry." Luke repositioned the boy to get a better look at the injury. "Melody can get blood out of anything." He winked at his sister.

Her eyes softened as she moved an oil lamp closer.

"Are we going to need all of this?" Epaphroditus waved toward the growing pile of unfamiliar medical instruments.

"I like to be prepared." Luke's gaze lingered on the supplies. "Hand me those shears. I've got to cut away some of his hair."

Epaphroditus followed every instruction, pressing where Luke told him, holding what needed to be held, but a sense of helplessness coiled in his chest. He wasn't suited for this. The boy's skin was cool, his breaths too shallow, and the blood, far too much of it, seeped through Epaphroditus's fingers no matter how tightly he pressed. Luke, on the other hand, moved with calm precision, as if the chaos didn't touch him. His hands were steady, his focus unshakable. It went beyond practice, leaving Epaphroditus to cling to the only thing he could do: stay out of the way.

"A few more," Luke murmured, tugging the fibers taut to close the wound stitch by stitch.

Without warning, Felix jerked upright, screaming.

"Hold him still!" Luke barked.

Epaphroditus's hands trembled as he pressed the fragile boy's shoulders down. "Easy."

"Maia!" the boy screamed.

"I'm here!" The woman's voice quivered from the far side of the room. "Lay still."

"My head hurts," Felix cried.

Luke struggled to keep the boy's hands away from his head. "I'm almost done."

Epaphroditus grabbed Felix's wrists and laid them on his chest, pinning them there. "We're trying to help you."

Tears streamed down Felix's round face, carving paths through the dirt smudged across his skin. "Maia!"

"I'm here," she repeated, her voice soft but firm. "Shh. You need to be brave."

Felix sobbed, his small body shaking under Epaphroditus's hold. "I don't want to be brave."

A hesitant flicker of amusement stirred within Epaphroditus. He met Melody's gaze and sensed her quiet struggle to hold back a laugh.

Luke stitched faster. "You'll only have to be brave for a moment longer."

Epaphroditus leaned in, trying to distract the boy. "Do you know what your name means?"

Felix grunted an uninterested "unh-uh."

"Felix means 'lucky,'" Epaphroditus continued, hoping to distract him. "You've certainly earned your name today."

Luke tied off the last strand with a decisive flick of his wrist. "There." He wiped sweat from his brow with the back of his hand. "Now, we just need to bandage your head, and you'll be back in your mother's arms."

Melody handed Luke clean linens, and he wrapped the bandage with steady hands.

"Finished," he said.

Felix, in a rush, hopped off the table and darted into his mother's open arms.

She kissed his forehead, his cheeks, and his nose. "I was so worried."

Felix reached up and touched the bandage; his face twisted in a quick wince. "My head hurts."

Luke crossed the room toward them and lifted a small vessel from a nearby shelf. "It'll hurt for a while longer." He portioned dried leaves into a small pouch and handed it to the mother. "A little in some boiling water should help with the pain."

She held the medicine close to her chest. "Bless you."

"Keep an eye on that bandage. Any discoloration, come get me."

She nodded, exhaling slowly as relief softened her sharp features.

"The sutures will dissolve with time," Luke continued, bending down to meet Felix's gaze. "You'll probably have a scar, but when your hair grows back, it should cover it nicely."

Felix nestled against his mother's side.

"And no more racing carts, young man." Luke gave him a playful wink.

Felix looked up at his mother. "Can we go home now?"

She shifted her weight toward Luke, a firm grip on the pouch.

Luke gave a gentle nod. "If any concerns arise, be sure to seek me out."

"I will," she promised again, turning to lead Felix out the door.

Epaphroditus watched them go and marveled at his friend's skill. "It's truly amazing." He turned to Melody. "If Luke hadn't been there, that boy would be on his way to being buried. Now, he's on his way home with his mother."

Melody's gaze lingered on Luke, eyes shadowed with something unspoken as she nodded.

Epaphroditus noticed the darkness cross her face. "What is it?"

Her gaze stayed locked on her brother. "The young ones are the hardest on him." Her focus shifted briefly to Epaphroditus, her voice dropping, "He'll need you." She stepped toward the soiled veil and lifted it. "Speak with him. I'll do my best with this."

"What do you mean?"

Melody twisted one of the larger stains on the

veil between her fingers, her expression distant. "I'll let him tell you." She went into the kitchen.

Luke returned to the table, picking up the shears and a clean cloth. "Thanks for your help." He wiped the blades carefully.

"Of course." Epaphroditus ran his fingertips over the table, mulling over the moments before. "Melody seems to think you need me for something else."

"Oh?" Luke paused, looking at him with a raised brow.

"She said, 'The young ones are the hardest on him.' What did she mean?"

He set the tool down with a quiet thud, palms flattening against the table. "Nothing."

Epaphroditus stepped closer. "You know you can share anything with me."

"I do." Luke turned to meet his eyes, his expression tight. "It happened before we met."

"What did?"

"Otho's accident."

"Who's Otho?"

Luke exhaled slowly, his chest rising with the weight of old grief. "My brother."

"I didn't know you have a brother."

"Had." Luke's voice faltered, and he wiped his face. "I had a brother."

Epaphroditus leaned against the table. "What happened to him?"

Luke folded his arms tightly across his chest, his gaze dropping to the floor. "We were playing in the fields. Carefree boys. Then Otho fell. Hit his head on a stone. Blood everywhere." He looked up, his eyes distant. "I ran to get our mother. By the time we returned, he wasn't breathing."

A cold knot formed in Epaphroditus' stomach.

"Mother took him to a physician, but it was too late." Luke wiped tears from his face, his voice trembling. "I couldn't save Otho." He paused. "But I'm glad I could save Felix... and the others before him." He met Epaphroditus's gaze. "Hopefully, a lot more after him, too."

"I bet Otho's proud of your work."

A faint warmth softened Luke's expression. "You think so?"

"I know little Felix is." Epaphroditus gestured toward the open door. "Imagine if we'd gone to the baths instead of the market. I doubt anyone else would have known what to do with his injury."

"I suppose you're right." He stared into the distance for a few more moments. "One thing I've learned is that pain shapes us all... if we let it." He rubbed the back of his neck. "I appreciate you letting me share about Otho. It's nice to talk about him."

"You should've told me sooner. We honor the dead by sharing their memory, not hiding them."

"I know." Luke shrugged, his gaze falling again. "I wanted to tell you when we first met as kids, but the pain of losing him was too fresh."

Epaphroditus placed a hand on Luke's shoulder. "You can tell me anything."

Luke took a steady breath. "That goes both ways."

He let his hand fall.

"I'm a good listener." Luke bumped his shoulder lightly. "It's a skill that comes with my profession."

Epaphroditus dipped his chin in silent agreement.

He helped Luke clean the tools, the weight of the conversation hanging between them. He wanted to share the darkest part of his own life, but the words wouldn't come. Despite his soul bearing the brand of those memories, he held them back. Perhaps one day, he would be ready to speak of them.

He watched Luke, who carefully returned each tool to its proper place.

If only you were a physician of the soul.

*So teach us to number our days
that we may get a heart of wisdom.*
Psalm 90:12

They had finished cleaning the tools and clearing the table when Melody returned.

"I think I've gotten out all the stains." She handed the damp cloth to Epaphroditus. "But it needs to be laid out to dry."

He took the veil and unwound it with care. The deep purple shimmered as if untouched, no sign of injury, no trace of blood.

"I can't believe it," he whispered, reverent. "I would have deemed it beyond restoration."

Her lips curved with quiet satisfaction in her expression. "Very little is beyond restoration."

His eyes lingered on the fabric. "I suppose so." He nodded. "Calli will be very grateful."

"My pleasure."

He rolled the veil with careful fingers and returned it to his belt. "I should head home. Calli will wonder what's kept me."

"I'll see you another day," Luke said, nodding with a lifted chin. "Maybe we can visit the baths next time."

"I look forward to it."

The sun climbed higher than Epaphroditus wanted by the time he left the city and made it to his family's olive groves. Dust clung to his sandals and warmed his skin, but he didn't mind. The breeze carried the scent of pressed olives and ancient trees. He lingered, breathing deep until the olive-sweet air calmed the churn inside him. This land, sunbaked, stubborn, and enduring, had carved its way into his blood, no matter how far his mind wandered.

He found Calliope running circles around Rufus, who was trying, and failing, to work.

She called out, "Epaphras!" Running to meet him, she flung her arms wide, hair as wild as a storm cloud.

Rufus straightened, groaning in frustration. "Thank Aphrodite for your return. I have gotten little done with this one underfoot."

Epaphroditus shot his sister a pointed look. "Were you at least good?"

"I was!" she declared, then turned to Rufus. "Tell him!"

"She didn't get into trouble. Just a distraction." He tousled her tangled hair.

She swatted his hand away and grabbed

Epaphroditus's arm. "That means I get my present!"

"I don't know..."

"Oh, please." She bounced on her toes. "I've been good."

"Peace." He slipped his fingers into his belt and unfurled the still-damp cloth, the fabric cool in his hands, and held it toward her.

She reached out, then stopped. Her fingers hovered, hesitant. "This is really for me?"

He nodded.

"It looks like something a princess would wear."

"Then it's perfect," he said, draping it gently across her arms. "You drive Rufus mad like one."

Calliope's face pinched. "Why is it all wet?"

"It'll dry." He lifted it from her hand and held it up toward the light. "It's from Lydia. Once it dries, you'll see the prettiest purple you've ever seen."

Sunlight filtered through the cloth, casting jeweled patterns across the dirt.

She gasped, eyes wide with wonder. Her gaze locked on the sheen. "But why is it wet?"

"Let's walk back to the house. I'll tell you everything." He turned and dipped his chin toward Rufus in silent thanks.

Rufus nodded. "Was the play good at least?"

Epaphroditus shrugged. "It was entertaining."

"Must've been to keep you half the day."

He ran his fingers over the cloth, stopping at the place where the largest stain had been. "It was worth it."

Rufus returned to his toil.

The sound of the pruning blade was faint as Epaphroditus pressed toward home, keeping Calliope in his sight as they walked.

Olive branches stirred overhead, insects hummed in the heat of the day, but his thoughts turned inward. Felix. Otho. Strange how one turn in the market, one slip of the foot, could ripple through so many lives.

Life was unbearably fragile.

He passed the veil through his hands. Damp. Thin. Delicate. One good tug and it would tear. Blood had nearly damaged the valuable material. Yet Melody, with her quiet resolve, had brought it back.

If only life worked like that.

At the Neapolis Gate, a familiar figure stood waiting beside Calliope.

"Mother," he called as he approached.

Neda brushed her hand through her daughter's wild curls. "I see no one has been helping you with your hair."

A stab of guilt tightened in Epaphroditus's chest. "She wouldn't sit still for us."

Calliope stuck her tongue out at him.

"It's good to see you," he said, ignoring his sister's antics. He took one of his mother's bags and slung it over his shoulder. "How was your trip to Paphos?"

"Long," she sighed.

Calliope walked backward in front of her. "Wait till you see the veil Epaphras brought me!"

Neda's brow lifted.

"It's from Lydia." Epaphroditus held it up.

"Then it's a fine veil indeed." Affection glimmered in her features. Her gaze brushed past the fabric, more interested in the child beneath it. "I'll tame that wild mane of yours, and we'll see how it looks."

Calliope twirled ahead of them. "Epaphras promised to tell me why it's wet."

Neda hesitated. "Wet?"

"It's a long story," he said, rolling it up again.

When they reached the villa, Epaphroditus spread the veil on a sun-warmed stone bench in the courtyard and helped his mother unload her things.

Calliope's bare feet slapped against the stone as she dashed inside, returning with a fistful of combs and leather ties in a breathless blur.

As Neda began combing out the tangles, Epaphroditus recounted the day, the play, Luke's political update, and the boy in the market.

When he described how Luke bound Felix's head with the veil, Calliope gasped. "My veil?"

"It was the closest fabric," he mumbled. "Besides, Melody got out every stain."

Neda's hands moved steadily through her daughter's hair as she braided the luscious strands.

"That Melody could get the stain out of a sailor's soul."

He suppressed a grin, amusement bubbling beneath the surface.

"There," Neda said, patting Calliope's shoulder. "Much better."

Calliope turned eagerly. "Can I try my veil now?"

"It should be dry." He tested it with his fingers. "Dry enough."

He handed it to his mother, who lifted it over Calliope's head, letting it settle over her like a blessing. She showed her a few ways to wrap it, under the chin, across the shoulders.

The purple caught the light, highlighting her cheeks and brown eyes, which danced with delight. It suited her perfectly.

Lydia was right.

"Now"—Neda patted Calliope's leg—"why don't you find me something to eat? I'd like a word with your brother."

"Uh-oh." Calliope grinned at Epaphroditus. "You're in trouble."

"Go," Neda said with a chuckle, swatting playfully.

Calliope dodged her and disappeared inside.

Neda turned to her son. "I saw the state of the kitchen."

"Mother, I can explain—"

She lifted her hand.

He snapped his jaw shut.

"I know it's difficult when I travel." She lowered her hand. "But we all have our duties."

"I've been in the grove with Rufus every day. Luke invited me out this morning, said I needed a break."

"It shouldn't all fall on you." Her gaze drifted over the courtyard, searching for order among the disarray. "Where's Zena?"

"Aunt Zena went to tend her daughter." He looked away, unsure how to meet her eyes. "She lost her baby."

Neda drew in a sharp breath. "How awful."

"Uncle Rufus told Zena to stay with them through the mourning period."

"Of course." She nodded. "But where's your father?"

"Gone again." His voice turned icy. "He took Uncle Tarquin with him."

She closed her eyes and rubbed her temples.

"Said he wasn't about to lose business just because you wanted to make more offerings."

Her eyes flew open. "He left you and Rufus to manage everything alone?"

He nodded.

She reached out, her hand warm on his cheek. "I didn't realize he left so much on your shoulders."

"I've got big shoulders, Mother. I can carry it."

Her eyes misted. "And soon, you'll carry much more."

The words clung to his throat, too heavy to push past the weight in his chest.

"I'll speak to him when he returns," she breathed. "It's time we brought in help. For everyone's sake."

Epaphroditus looked away. Help meant one thing. Slaves. The thought never sat well with him. He found the idea of a person being owned disturbing. Luke's mention of searching for a wife at the market had made him laugh, but beneath the jest, it had chilled him.

Their family once moved as one, each hand knowing its place and the villa was full, men in the grove, women in the kitchen, elders resting in the shade while cousins ran about.

Now their numbers had thinned. The men, dead from wars or illness. The girls, married and gone. The brothers, Tarquin, Rufus, and Epaphroditus's father Kastas, remained in the villa but age was chasing down the former soldiers. By their sides were Rufus's wife Zena, Epaphroditus's mother Neda, himself, and Calliope. Though one day soon, she too would be called to another home.

He could almost see them, spirits of family long gone filling the benches of the courtyard, laughter echoing around them. The emptiness pressed around him.

He looked at his mother; her face was tired but resolute. She knew the truth he didn't want to face.

To survive—no, to thrive—they'd need more hands.

Aphrodite, send us help.

O my dove, in the clefts of the rock,
in the crannies of the cliff,
let me see your face,
let me hear your voice,
for your voice is sweet,
and your face is lovely.
Song of Solomon 2:14

Epaphroditus lingered in the doorway, tapping his foot against the stone threshold as his patience thinned. Morning light spilled across the vestibule, catching in the mosaic tiles. The air carried a faint warmth, olive oil and laurel. "You're wasting light, Calli."

Calliope fussed with her purple veil, squinting into a bronze mirror mounted on the wall. "I've almost got it."

"Why don't you let Mother fix it?"

She twisted the ends once more. "There."

"At last."

Calliope swept past him, chin lifted, sandals

snapping on the stone. "Let's go."

He bowed low with mock gravity. "Your majesty."

She shot him a dry look over her shoulder. "Who's wasting our light now?"

He laughed and matched her stride as they slipped into the street.

Philippi had already awakened. Traders hauled baskets toward the market, craftsmen opened shutters, and Roman officials clattered by, their armor glinting in the sun. Children darted past, kicking up dust and laughter.

Epaphroditus promised Calliope a full day together, doing anything she wanted, a reward for her recent good behavior. She walked ahead; her veil trailing in the breeze. Their first stop was Luke's family home near the Forum.

"Greetings," Calliope called as she stepped into the cool interior.

Melody welcomed them in, drying her hands on a linen cloth. "My"—she pressed her hand to her chest—"that color does suit you, Calliope."

Her cheeks flushed, the color rising slowly under Melody's gaze.

Epaphroditus tilted toward Melody, a grin tugging at the corner of his mouth. "Careful," he murmured. "Keep that up, and she'll be demanding more royal garments."

Melody chuckled. "That veil alone could feed a

family well."

"I got a good bargain," he said proudly. "Let's hope Father agrees. Otherwise, we may have to give it back."

Calliope clutched her wrap. "Never."

"I'm sure your brother is only teasing." Melody sent a playful but warning glance in Epaphroditus's direction.

Epaphroditus looked around the modest room, the warm stone walls lined with simple shelves holding herbs and scrolls. Despite its humble appearance, a calmness he rarely found elsewhere filled the space. This was a place where he could set aside his worries, if only for a moment. A rare flicker of hope stirred within him, sparked by the kindness exchanged in this home. The low table caught his gaze, and he shuddered. Images of Felix's bleeding head struck, but he shook them away. The boy was safe and healing.

He moved his attention toward the rear of the house. "Is Luke ready?"

"My brother will be along in a moment." Melody sighed. "He's got his nose buried in a medical scroll again."

"Greetings to those of this house," a familiar female voice called from the doorway.

Epaphroditus turned to see Felix and his mother standing there. The boy clutched her hand.

"Greetings," Melody said, moving to welcome

them. "Are you seeking my brother?"

"I am."

"I'll fetch him." Melody smirked at Epaphroditus as she brushed past him, her shoulder lightly grazing his. "It's about time he looked up from that scroll. Would you see our guests inside?"

Epaphroditus motioned for the mother and son to enter. "They'll be just a moment." His gaze fell on the linen bandage around Felix's head. "Feeling better?"

Felix leaned into his mother, who gently stroked his hair. His eyes lifted to Calliope and widened. He stepped from behind his mother and pointed. "Purple."

Calliope defensively touched her veil.

Felix stepped forward, fingers reaching for her. "I remember that color."

Epaphroditus crouched to meet his eyes. "You remember?"

Felix nodded slowly. "Just flashes."

"I used my sister's veil to bind your wound. Until my friend could treat you."

Without a word, Felix embraced Calliope, small arms circling her waist.

She shot her brother a baffled look.

He shrugged as he rose, lips twitching.

Luke stepped into the room, wiping ink from his fingers. "Someone called for me?"

Felix released Calliope and retreated, ducking

behind his mother again.

"Felix,"—Luke crossed the room—"any trouble with the wound?"

"No trouble," his mother answered. "I followed your instructions exactly."

"Good." Luke knelt beside Felix. "Still sore?"

Felix touched the wrapping. "A little."

"That means it's healing."

"But the herbs are awful." Felix wrinkled his nose and imitated gagging.

Luke laughed. "Most medicine is."

Felix's mother handed Luke a small coin pouch and a wrapped item. "I've come to make payment for your services."

Luke accepted them with a nod. "How gracious of you."

"It's what's due. You gave me back my son."

Epaphroditus caught Luke's tight swallow and his friend's composure faltered for a breath.

"We'll take our leave now." The woman moved toward the open door. "Come, Felix."

Felix hesitated at the doorway, glancing once more at Calliope before ducking outside.

"Strange boy," Calliope muttered.

Melody's soft laugh floated from the corridor. "I think he's sweet."

Luke tucked the money into his belt and unwrapped the other item, a warm, fresh loaf still fragrant from the oven. "This smells incredible."

"You can enjoy it later," Calliope said with a huff. "I was promised a day of fun."

"And so we shall have it," Epaphroditus agreed.

Luke placed the loaf on the table. "It will be good to walk the city."

"Enjoy," Melody said from the other side of the room, tying her dark hair back with a leather cord.

Epaphroditus approached her. "I was hoping you'd join us."

"Me?" She blinked.

"I'm sure Calli would love having another woman with us. And your brother doesn't let you out enough."

Luke gave him a dry look but said nothing.

Melody glanced toward the kitchen, then back at him, lips pressed into a thin line. "I have a lot to do today."

"Leave it for later. The good physician here will tell you that sunshine and fresh air are healing."

"It's true," Luke agreed. "Join us."

Melody looked at Calliope, who clasped her hands with pleading eyes. "I suppose a few hours won't put me too far behind."

"Finally!" Calliope raised her hands. "Can we go now?"

They strolled the city under the climbing sun, the breeze soft against their skin. They wandered down a narrow cobblestone street flanked by modest stone houses with faded terracotta roofs.

The laughter of children echoed from an open courtyard, while the pleasant scent of roasting meats mingled with the incense wafting from nearby shrines.

Calliope tugged Epaphroditus's hand. "Can we go to the market?"

"It's your day."

"Hope Lydia's there."

"Her presence won't guarantee another expensive purchase," he warned.

"Won't hurt my chances," she muttered under her breath.

The air of the market was thick with the scent of fresh produce: ripe figs, pungent garlic, and the tang of salt from dried fish. Vendor calls echoed, haggling over prices, while the clinking of coins added a rhythmic undertone to the bustle. Bright fabrics fluttered in the breeze from stalls, and the heat of the sun mixed with the earthy smell of dust and mud. Conversations hummed around them, broken by the clank of pottery and scraping of knives on whetstone.

Calliope flitted between booths like a bird searching for a perch.

Epaphroditus lagged behind with Melody. "Enjoying yourself?" he asked.

"It's a lovely day," Melody answered. "And your sister is a gem."

"She certainly thinks she is." He paused. "Uh-oh.

She's found Lydia. Better stop her before she empties the booth."

Epaphroditus quickened his pace. Lydia's wares were tempting, and he knew his sister's stubbornness all too well. If Calliope bought too much, their father's displeasure would surely follow.

"Epaphroditus," Lydia greeted. "Your sister looks stunning in the veil you picked for her."

"I just hope Father approves when he returns."

"If he doesn't, send him to me," Lydia said with a teasing grin.

Calliope giggled, fingering a deep blue fabric.

Melody hesitated by a green palla lying across the table.

"That's a beautiful piece," Lydia said, gliding toward her. "Try it on."

"I couldn't," Melody said, stepping back.

"Come now." Lydia expertly wrapped the palla around Melody's hips and shoulders. "It can be worn like this, or"—she unwrapped it—"like this." She lifted the fabric over Melody's head. "You can pin a fibula here." She pointed to her shoulder.

Epaphroditus watched as Lydia draped the green palla over Melody. The fabric draped around her as if made only for her, catching the light and softening her facial features. It cast a glow that drew out warm olive tones in her skin he hadn't noticed before, or hadn't let himself notice.

An unfamiliar tug coiled in his ribs, catching

him off guard.

He'd seen Melody a thousand times, but never like this. A quiet grace unfolded over her. Then she looked up. His gaze caught hers, and for a breath, the world held still. Just her eyes, steady and bright, holding him fast.

"You're beautiful," Calliope said, the words that stuck in his dry throat.

Melody lowered her gaze to her. "It's not as fine as your purple veil."

"It may be humbler," Calliope replied. "But it's no less lovely."

Melody held up her arm, admiring the fabric. "It is stunning." She began unwrapping it. "But I shouldn't."

Epaphroditus blinked, the trance breaking as the fabric slipped from her shoulder. He stepped in, voice firmer than he expected, "I insist."

Melody hesitated. "I couldn't."

He pulled out his money pouch. "Consider it payment for laundering royal garments."

Pink bloomed under Melody's cheeks as he deposited a generous fee into Lydia's open hands. It was a small price to pay to behold such radiance.

For everything there is a season, and a
time for every matter under heaven:
a time to be born, and a time to die; a
time to plant, and a time to pluck up
what is planted;
Ecclesiastes 3:1-2

AD 50, Four Years Later

Beads of sweat gathered at the nape of Epaphroditus's neck, tracing slow rivers down into his rough linen tunic. The relentless sun scorched the land, offering no mercy. His mouth tasted sour; his throat, dry as cracked clay. He bent low, digging into the earth with calloused hands. The soil slipped easily through his fingers, more dust than dirt, closer to the pale sands that fringed the shore than the rich, dark loam that once nourished his grandfather's grove.

His thoughts drifted to the lush green of Melody's palla she wore when he was near, the vibrant fabric like a breath of life against the dull brown fields. How he longed for such beauty in the land beneath his feet, for a harvest that promised more than mere survival.

But this year's yield was meager, plagued by drought and hardship; the earth had been unkind. Each row he walked reminded him of how much they had already lost, how thin the line was between endurance and despair.

The sun pressed down like a living weight, and his limbs moved slower with each step. A vulture wheeled overhead, too early, too close. He paused to stretch his aching back, squinting toward the horizon where olive trees stood brittle and gray, their branches curled like old hands.

Nearby, his father, Kastas, a hardened Roman soldier turned merchant sailor, stooped over the parched earth, his weathered hands moving methodically among the gnarled trunks of the ancient grove. Years of labor had carved toughness into Kastas's frame, his face set in the stern expression Epaphroditus knew well.

Together with Rufus, the three gathered what little the land and trees grudgingly offered, their movements slow but steady as they prepared to retreat to the villa.

From the kitchen, the clatter of pots and the steady rhythm of women's work echoed through the house. Calliope, Neda, and Zena bent over their tasks.

Neda looked up as the men entered. Her eyes met Epaphroditus's, but he declined with a subtle tilt of his head and moved toward the water jar. Kastas followed him, both men sharing a grateful, indulgent drink.

"I've been thinking," Neda broke the silence. "Perhaps I should take Calliope and journey to Paphos."

Epaphroditus caught the subtle bulge of a vein along the side of his father's neck. That tension always meant Kastas was biting back words best left unspoken.

Her gaze softened as it rested on Calliope. "I'm sure my parents would be delighted to meet her." She cast a wary flicker at her husband and added, "Some offerings might return Aphrodite's favor toward us as well."

Kastas drank deeply before replying, "We cannot afford another of your journeys right now."

"I don't think we can afford for me not to go," her tone was calm but resolute, the kind of certainty that brooked no challenge.

Without another word, Kastas set down his cup and left the room, his footsteps heavy and determined.

Neda watched the empty doorway long after he was gone, exhaling softly in quiet disbelief before returning to her work.

Epaphroditus turned to leave, but Neda called

after him.

"Son."

"Yes?"

"Take this to Tarquin." She pressed a tray into his hands. "He needs tending."

He bowed in acknowledgment, carefully balancing the tray as he moved toward his uncle's chamber.

Tarquin's harsh cough echoed down the hallway before Epaphroditus reached the door. Through the cracked frame, he saw his eldest uncle lying pale and gaunt, baring the lingering shadow of an illness that had stubbornly taken root from his last merchant voyage. The broad shoulders Epaphroditus remembered from childhood, hardened by years of soldiering, were now sunken beneath the rough blanket.

Yet even in weakness, there was a flicker of the old discipline in the tight set of Tarquin's jaw, a quiet stubbornness refusing to surrender. The roughness of a lifetime spent at sea and in battle had faded into fragile skin stretched tight over worn bones, but Epaphroditus still saw the soldier beneath the sickness.

When the coughing fit worsened, Epaphroditus entered and set down the tray to help his uncle sit upright. He reached for the cup his mother prepared. His fingers trembled slightly as he cradled the cool stone, careful not to spill the precious liquid. He lifted it to Tarquin's lips, letting the precious liquid trickle in.

Tarquin managed two small sips, the tea easing the worst of his hacking. "My thanks," he rasped.

Epaphroditus tucked the small vessel into his hands.

Tarquin clutched the cup to his chest, his breath shallow and uneven. "That fit nearly took the wind from my sails."

Epaphroditus dipped a clean cloth in a bowl of water and wiped sweat from his uncle's forehead and neck.

Closing his eyes, Tarquin leaned back, briefly soothed by the cooling touch. "It must be miserable out there in the fields," he murmured.

"Not too bad," Epaphroditus replied.

Tarquin's lips lifted in a weak, weary grin. "Your soaked tunic says otherwise."

"Don't worry about me." Epaphroditus frowned. "We need to focus on restoring your health so you can come back to being miserable with us."

A soft laugh turned into a violent cough, nearly catching Epaphroditus off guard.

"Easy," he urged, pressing the bottom of the cup upward. "Take another sip."

The bitter liquid barely stilled the coughing this time.

Epaphroditus's eyes swept over the untouched bowls of food nearby. "With Mother's remedies, you'll join us soon."

"Perhaps." Tarquin leaned back, exhaustion clear in his eyes and on his face. "I've lived two lifetimes already, one as a soldier and one in the grove and seas." Another fit wracked his body. "Every day beyond my duty to Rome has been a gift."

"Try to rest." Epaphroditus squeezed his uncle's shoulder. "I'll check on you later."

He left the tray and went to the main room, where an almost life-size statue of Aphrodite stood in a carved niche, her marble form radiant and serene. Fresh offerings surrounded her feet, fruit and small bowls of honey glinting in the fading light.

Neda knelt there, renewing the gifts and clearing away what had spoiled.

Epaphroditus came to her side and rested his head on her shoulder.

"How's Tarquin?"

"His cough is worse." He stared up at the goddess with tired reverence. "I wish we could do more."

She sighed, arranging a bowl of souring fruit. "Sometimes there is nothing left but faith."

Faith. The word echoed hollowly in Epaphroditus' chest as his gaze lingered on Aphrodite's calm face. Did she even care that Tarquin was ill? That they were all struggling beneath her distant gaze?

Scents of frankincense and myrrh curled faintly around him, but they couldn't mask the bittersweet tang of the honey offerings at her feet. Faith lodged inside him like a brittle reed, easy to snap under the weight of doubt.

A sudden voice broke the heavy quiet. "Greetings."

Epaphroditus turned sharply, heart lifted at the familiar sound. "Luke?" He blinked, caught off guard. "I didn't expect you today."

Luke shifted the leather strap of his satchel over his shoulder, the worn hide creaking softly. "I had a feeling my friend might need me," he whispered, stepping further inside.

Epaphroditus stole one last look at the goddess, whispering thanks, before rising to grip Luke's extended arm. "I'm glad you came. Would you check on Tarquin?"

He caught the brief flicker of exhaustion in Luke's eyes, the faint shadow behind the thin, practiced smile. The same weariness settled over Epaphroditus.

"Of course."

Epaphroditus led him through the house to the back room.

"I haven't seen you in weeks," Epaphroditus said.

Luke lowered his gaze. "This famine has kept me busy. Food is scarce. Medicine, too." He tightened his grip on the strap across his chest. "Not enough for all."

"We're grateful for whatever you can do."

"I know." Luke's lips pressed together in a tight, tired grin as he followed Epaphroditus down the hallway.

Tarquin's cough echoed from the dim room as they neared.

Luke hesitated at the doorway. "Any change?"

Epaphroditus peered inside. "He hasn't eaten today. Mother has been giving him herbs, but the cough only worsens." He cast a pleading look at Luke.

The physician sighed, then entered the room. "Greetings, Tarquin. Still fighting the same battle, I see."

Tarquin chuckled, a cough overtaking the sound.

Luke knelt by the bed, examining him. "That cough seems to have taken up residence."

"Think you can evict it?"

"I'll try." Luke questioned him carefully and inspected his form. "You've lost weight."

"Lying here hasn't helped," Tarquin admitted between coughs.

"Get some rest," Luke advised. "I'll leave more instructions with the women."

Another cough rattled Tarquin's chest.

Luke stepped out of the room and motioned for Epaphroditus to follow.

"I've always been honest," Luke whispered.

"That cough... it's bad."

"How bad?"

"Bad."

"Is there anything more you can do?"

Luke rubbed his chin. "I can give you herbs to ease his pain, if you can get him to drink."

"Comfort? That's all you can offer?"

Luke held Epaphroditus' unwavering gaze. "In this case, yes."

Epaphroditus took a step back, chest tight. "I don't accept that."

Luke reached to place his hand on his friend's shoulder. "The facts don't change in the face of your denial. Your uncle has days, maybe a week."

Epaphroditus yanked his arm away, eyes burning. "We've given most of our portions to the women," he pressed the words out, voice low and sharp. "Father, Rufus, and I scour the fields and grove for anything to eat. We've prayed, made offerings," his voice cracked. "Tarquin can't die. We need him."

Luke pulled him into a rare embrace, his arms a solid anchor against Epaphroditus' shaking frame.

"I'm scared," Epaphroditus whispered, taking in the scent of medical balm that clung to Luke's skin.

"We all are." He held on for another moment before releasing him. "You've carried heavy burdens. I wish I could lift this one for you. But sometimes, all we can do is wait and hope."

Epaphroditus' heart clenched. Had Aphrodite grown weary of his borrowed days? Was all this suffering the price she demanded for each breath he'd stolen? How much more would she take?

Man is like a breath;
his days are like a passing shadow.
Psalm 144:4

Epaphroditus shook away the nagging questions that plucked at him like scavenger birds encircling a carcass.

"Make him comfortable," Luke said again, as if repeating a prayer against a tide too strong to turn.

The words settled over him like the oppressive heat still clinging to the walls of the house.

Luke moved down the hall and knelt beside Neda, his voice low and urgent as he produced a small pouch from his worn leather bag.

Epaphroditus followed silently, watching as Luke whispered instructions for preparing the herbal mixture.

Neda nodded, gratitude etched on her face, and hurried toward the kitchen with renewed purpose.

Luke straightened and cast a glance at the statue of Aphrodite in her niche. "She's quite beautiful," he breathed.

Epaphroditus came to stand beside him. "As the goddess of love should be," he replied, voice low with reverence.

Luke closed his bag and hesitated. "Could we sit in the courtyard?"

"Not in a hurry to leave?"

Luke's shoulders nearly bowed beneath the weight Epaphroditus could almost see but not touch. He nodded toward the courtyard, and the two walked together into the open air.

The courtyard was a pale echo of its former self, pots of herbs and vegetation withered and cracked from drought, the earth beneath dusty and cracked like old skin.

Luke was the first to break the silence. "Have you been eating enough?"

It was a practical question, though Epaphroditus had already confessed that most of his portions went to his mother and sister. "I get by."

Luke turned and gripped the back of Epaphroditus' arm. "As your physician, I'd say differently."

"And as my friend?"

Luke released him with a heavy sigh. "As your friend, I'm even more worried about you."

"You don't have to be."

Luke stopped walking. "Why is that?"

"Because this famine will not kill me."

His friend's eyes narrowed to slits. "How can you be so sure?"

"I just know." Epaphroditus started to walk away, but Luke's firm grip stopped him, turning him fully around.

"If you know something that can help others survive this famine, you must say something."

Epaphroditus hung his head. "I can't help anyone." Then he met Luke's gaze. "I can't even save myself when the time comes."

"What time?" Luke's face twisted with confusion and frustration.

Epaphroditus's heart beat faster as he saw the fire burn behind those eyes. "It doesn't matter." He sank onto a nearby stone bench. "As long as I stay here in Philippi, I won't die."

"No one lives forever, my friend." Luke sat beside him. "Death comes for us all."

"Not me." His voice was calm, but haunted. "I'm safe as long as I don't get on any boats."

"What are you talking about?"

Epaphroditus rubbed his mouth, hesitating. He wanted to share the secret he'd kept buried, but wondered what the learned physician would think of a priestess' oracle.

His thoughts drifted to Luke's brother and the accident that had taken him. With a deep sigh, Epaphroditus finally spoke, "When I was a little older than Calli, my mother took me to Paphos. It was to be the first of many pilgrimages, offerings to Aphrodite's Sanctuary."

He dared a peek at Luke, who sat silently, waiting.

"While there, I spent time with my mother's parents and joined a grand festival honoring our goddess. But in the Temple, as I gave my offering, a priestess confronted us. Mother said she was the most respected among them. And well..." He rubbed the back of his neck, the memory tightening his throat. "She spoke a warning over me."

"What kind of warning?"

"More like a prophecy." He touched under his eyes. "Her eyes went blank while she spoke. It frightened me."

"What did she say?"

Epaphroditus drew a deep breath, closing his eyes to summon the words that had haunted him ever since. "'Death waits for you across the Great Sea; your life will be Aphrodite's fee.'" He opened his eyes slowly and met Luke's firm gaze. "I've had nightmares almost every night since. Drowning, gasping. I wake up soaked in sweat."

"I see." Luke's face was unreadable. "You think if you cross the Great Sea, you'll die?"

Epaphroditus nodded, voice tight. "So, you see, I won't die in this famine. Death isn't coming for me here, it's waiting for me out there." He waved his hand dismissively. "As long as I don't leave, I'll be safe."

Luke's expression shifted, more curious than accusatory. "All these years, you stayed in Philippi, worked in your family's grove, turned down every trade ship and opportunity... not because you lacked ambition, but because of a single moment in a temple?" A slight crease formed between Luke's brows, barely noticeable, but lingering just long enough to unsettle. "Fear carves deep grooves, my friend. But sometimes, what we call fate is only fear left unchallenged."

He bowed his head. "Better no boat than risk the wrong one."

"Is that why you never joined your father's trade?"

"If I had, I'd be on boats half my life. I couldn't risk it."

"That's... understandable."

The words tasted bitter as he forced them out, half hoping Luke would deny what he already feared. "Do you think I'm mad for believing it?"

"That's a whole other question." He crossed his arms. "Belief is powerful. I've seen people healed just because they believed. And others who should have lived... didn't, because they convinced themselves otherwise."

"You're saying if I don't believe it, I can sail without dying?"

"That's not for me to say. If the priestess had a

vision, it means something. They don't speak such terrible things lightly, especially over children."

"So, you're saying it could be true?"

"Perhaps."

"Epaphroditus!" Calliope's screech echoed through the house.

"Out here," he answered.

She came running into the courtyard, her hands grabbing Luke's arm. "Oh, Luke! Thank Aphrodite, you're still here." She tugged urgently. "It's Uncle Tarquin. He needs you."

Luke rose immediately and followed her inside. Epaphroditus trailed behind them.

Inside the dim room, Neda knelt by the low bed, wiping Tarquin's damp forehead. Zena stood on the other side, her expression tight with worry. Calliope pulled Luke toward the bedside. "Luke's here, Maia."

Neda spoke softly, "It's his breathing. I gave him some of the medicine, but it's so slow now."

Luke bent, pressing his ear near Tarquin's lips, then his chest.

Epaphroditus touched Calliope's shoulder. "Why don't you go find Father?"

She looked up with wide eyes. "What's wrong with Uncle Tarquin?"

"Luke's going to help him." He squeezed her shoulder gently. "Go get Father and Rufus."

She hurried out as Epaphroditus stepped closer to the bed.

Luke met his eyes, dread darkening his features. Rising, he spread his hands. "It won't be much longer."

Epaphroditus leaned in, voice barely a whisper. "What did you give him?"

Luke's gaze hardened. "Herbs to ease the cough and pain." He gestured to Tarquin. "His cough has eased."

"He's barely breathing," Epaphroditus said through clenched teeth, standing taller to hold his ground.

"I told you it wouldn't be long." Luke matched his intensity. "I can't stop death from coming, for anyone."

The fire in his friend's eyes stirred something in Epaphroditus. "You're right." He placed a hand on Luke's shoulder. "Forgive me. None of this is your fault. I know you're only trying to help."

"Forgiven." Luke's voice softened. "I know this isn't easy."

Epaphroditus shook his head. "I imagine it must be harder for you physicians. Seeing this all the time."

Kastas stormed in, followed by Rufus. "What's happened?"

Luke stepped forward to meet Kastas. "I gave Neda an herbal mixture to ease your brother's suffering. His breaths grow short, but he's comfortable. Your family should spend these last moments with him."

"Last moments?" Kastas's voice cracked. "He simply has a cough."

"I'm afraid it's much worse." Luke looked at Tarquin. "Your brother is breathing his last."

Kastas collapsed onto the bed. "He can't die."

Epaphroditus laid a hand on his father's trembling back as Rufus knelt beside Neda. In the sobbing silence, he listened to his uncle's breath—shallow, distant, growing ever fainter—until finally, his last breath slipped out.

The room held its breath. When no more came from Tarquin's lips, sobs erupted into wails of grief.

Epaphroditus added his voice, broken but fierce, to his family's mourning.

Oh that my vexation were weighed,
and all my calamity laid in the
balances!
Job 6:2

Epaphroditus stepped back, the soles of his sandals scraping softly against the worn tile. His chest constricted as if wrapped in iron bands.

Tarquin lay still; the life drained from him, and the house had become hollow, echoing with sorrow.

Zena reached into her tunic and produced her money pouch. From it, she withdrew an obol and pushed it past Tarquin's lips. She leaned forward and pressed her trembling lips gently to Tarquin's, a tradition to ensure the soul's safe passage. Her fingers brushed his eyes closed, but the moment shattered as a scream burst from her throat. Raw and guttural, it ripped through the air like fabric torn down the middle. She clutched her cheeks, tearing her nails down the soft skin. Blood rose in thin trails.

Kastas pounded his chest, the sound dull and desperate. Beside him, Rufus cried out, the grief tearing his voice ragged.

"Tarquin!" Zena's voice cracked open, splintering on his name. Her cry carried a wild edge, as though naming him might bring him back.

Neda collapsed beside the bed, her sobs sharp, gasping. Her hands clutched at the linen around Tarquin's still body. She rocked slightly, murmuring his name like a chant.

Epaphroditus stood frozen, his throat burning. No sound came. His chest heaved with breath he could hardly catch, his body swaying with the weight of grief he couldn't shape into words.

Luke's hand landed on his shoulder, warm, firm. "Come," he whispered. "We must let the women prepare him."

Epaphroditus blinked, his vision blurred. He tore his eyes from Tarquin and let Luke lead him into the corridor, where the light pressed heavy, too dim, too gold, too alive for what had just passed. He cast a wide gaze at Aphrodite, falling at her feet. Half desiring to plead for her to awaken from her frozen form and half yearning to thrust her across the room.

Rufus and Kastas emerged from the hallway, their work tunics replaced with dark togas of mourning.

The change was too jarring, as though his father

and uncle had aged years in mere moments.

Kastas's voice cracked as he reached for his son. "You must herald the news. His daughters need to be told."

Epaphroditus swallowed hard, but he nodded. There was no refusing the dead. Tradition called him.

"I'll go with you," Luke offered.

Epaphroditus met his eyes and nodded again. He didn't trust his voice yet.

Kastas held out a dark fabric. "Change first."

The mourning toga itched against his skin as he stepped into the street, Luke close behind. The weight of the garment was more than fabric, it was the weight of loss, of lineage, of duty.

Outside the villa, the city had not paused for their sorrow. Merchants still called out their wares. A mother shouted at her son. The clang of iron rang clear down the alley. And yet, a hush seemed to follow them, subtle but certain, as if the toga pulla wrapped the street in mourning as well.

Epaphroditus kept his eyes low, avoiding the faces around him. Every expression was an intrusion, every glance a reminder that grief made him visible in a way he didn't want. He hated the way they looked at him, not with cruelty, but with pity. Grief had made him porous.

Mourning walked beside him, wrapped around his shoulders. The world kept turning, but different now.

He walked these same streets with his uncle not days ago, speaking of the recent trade voyage and the price of olive oil. The memory struck him with fresh cruelty. How could Tarquin be both gone and still so present?

Epaphroditus and Luke reached his cousin Sophia's home first. Her husband answered, but she appeared behind him, eyes already wide.

"Epaphroditus…" Seeing his clothes, she crumpled. "No! No, no…" She folded to her knees, hands covering her mouth. "When?"

"Moments ago," Epaphroditus answered. "I came to gather you and Elena."

Sophia surged upright. "She doesn't know?"

"Not yet. I came here first."

She disappeared briefly, returning cloaked in haste and sorrow. "Let's go. The others will come soon."

They hurried, the three of them a line of mourning, heading east through the narrow streets until they reached Elena's home. Her face broke the moment she opened the door. Her grief echoed her sister's.

After sharing the news with the rest of the household, both women gathered their belongings and returned to the family villa with Epaphroditus and Luke.

Sophia and Elena disappeared into the rear of

the house, already preparing for the sacred task ahead.

Epaphroditus stood outside his uncle's room, listening to the murmurs of water, the rustle of linen, and the low voices of remembrance.

Luke stood beside him. "I should go. There's little more I can do now."

"You've done enough," Epaphroditus said, voice rough.

Luke gave a final, quiet nod. "You know where to find me."

Epaphroditus saw him out and shut the door, a signal to all that their mourning had officially begun. The weight of the silence was deafening, driving Epaphroditus back to the feet of his goddess.

He adjusted the freshly prepared offering, straightened a pile of flowers, but couldn't meet Aphrodite's set glare.

What else could he do to get her attention? Or did she care that little for his devotion?

Finally, the women appeared from the back. Tarquin's body, washed and oiled, lay draped in a dark robe. They arranged him on the funeral couch, his head propped on his hand, the way he often reclined during long evening meals.

They turned the couch toward the door, inviting the spirit to depart, unhindered.

Seven days passed. Seven days of lamentation and ritual. Epaphroditus stayed close to the couch, pressing a cloth of steeped herbs to his face to counter the growing sourness of decay that even the most fragrant oils could not wholly mask.

He grew numb to the sounds of weeping.

On the last morning, he woke before the others to prepare new offerings. He stood near Aphrodite, whispering a prayer. Not for Tarquin, his soul had already begun its journey. For those left behind.

That afternoon, the pompa began. Musicians arrived and waited outside, their instruments lacquered and somber.

Kastas approached Epaphroditus with something wrapped in cloth. When he revealed it, Epaphroditus's breath caught.

A funerary mask painted in the likeness of Pelagios, his grandfather. The stern features stared back at him, Roman and resolute. Epaphroditus held it reverently, the past pressing into his hands.

Pelagios, who fought in the battle of Philippi, was a valiant soldier. He carved a future from the soil Antony rewarded him with for his faithful service. Olive groves had matured and flourished in that earth. Three strong sons followed in his path. Now, a famine threatened to swallow the grove after consuming one of those sons.

How would his warrior grandfather have fought this kind of battle?

Epaphroditus placed the mask over his face, the world dimming behind its painted gaze.

Beside him, Rufus and Tarquin's sons-in-law donned their own masks, a procession of ancestors made flesh once more. They raised the lectus; Tarquin remained positioned as if mid-sentence in a story he would never complete. Epaphroditus's shoulder burned under the weight, but he did not shift.

They stepped into the street while the music started.

Behind them came the mourners, Sophia, Elena, their children, and others who had known Tarquin. Wails mingled with the low hum of flutes.

They displayed Tarquin's body in the Forum. Citizens came forward to pay respects, laying sprigs of myrtle and coins at his feet. Epaphroditus stood vigil, his eyes stinging, listening to their stories and praises. He chanted with the others, words ancient and rhythmic, carried through time.

After the public farewell, they crossed the city gate and followed the quiet road to the burial grounds beyond. The countryside held its breath, still and silent, as if mourning with them.

They laid Tarquin upon the wooden pyre at the edge of the open field. Flames licked the dry wood, and smoke curled upward, carrying the last of him toward the sky.

When the fire had burned low and the ashes cooled, they gathered them carefully and carried the urn among the carved stones where their ancestors rested.

Epaphroditus stepped inside the tomb, and a chill seeped into his skin. He remembered the others who had perished in distant lands and those who had fallen on foreign battlefields, denied a proper burial. At least Tarquin was home.

Nearby, other funerals gathered. The famine left no family untouched. Wailing echoed around them.

Epaphroditus stood outside long after the others turned back.

At least I will be laid to rest here. When my time comes.

Not in foreign soil.

Not across the Great Sea.

The prayers in his mouth were silent, but they carried weight as tears raced down his dusty cheeks.

Please, Aphrodite. No more death.

I shall ransom them from the power of
Sheol;
I shall redeem them from Death.
O Death, where are your plagues?
O Sheol, where is your sting?
Compassion is hidden from my eyes.
Hosea 13:14

Epaphroditus brushed aside delicate leaves and caught a glint of sunlight on the smooth green and purple olives, heavy with promise.

After the drought that nearly strangled the life from his grandfather's grove, the trees were bearing fruit once more. Their branches sagged under the weight, not just of food, but of life itself. Of hope.

Aphrodite, you've heard me.

He leaned into the sturdy trunk, scanning the grove underneath him. Even in abundance, death lingered.

Death wasn't a friend. Friends brought comfort and laughter. Death was none of that. But he was constant; always nearby. Death shared the world with life like a twin. Balance. But never a balance Epaphroditus would have chosen. Never a weight he would have carried willingly.

He'd witnessed Death's work, known its silence. In the hollowed-out beds. In the bloated animal carcasses. In the shriveled branches.

He had heard Death whisper. *I'm here. I have a place.*

Death had walked beside him for years. Quiet. Patient.

Still waiting.

Painful as it was, Death carved out a space for something new to grow. The grove had taught him that. So had life. But what would take root in the soil of his own loss, he didn't yet know.

Reaching up, he shook each branch. Olives dropped into the reed baskets below. Some with gentle plops, others bouncing across the soil.

Before shaking the next branch, he plucked an olive and slipped it between his lips. Bitterness flared instantly. As a boy, he'd spat them out. Now, though, the raw flavor tasted like a reward.

He remembered his grandfather spitting olive pits further than most men can throw a spear. The old man had taught him to respect the trees, to listen. "The grove speaks," he used to say, "but she's patient. Not silent." Epaphroditus had thought that nonsense. Trees didn't talk. Yet, standing among them now, the truth of that silence settled deep within him. The creak of trunks, the hum of bees, the breeze flicking through the branches, it was a language after all.

"Try not to eat all our profits!" Uncle Rufus called from below.

Epaphroditus shook away his memories and spat the pit into the dirt. "If the gods didn't want us to taste the fruit, they wouldn't have made it so good."

Rufus let out a short, amused bark of laughter, shaking his head as he stooped to gather the rogue olives.

By late in the day, the baskets brimmed. Some for pressing, others for preservation.

Emerging from the last tree, Epaphroditus stretched, his muscles aching but satisfied. He turned to take in the grove, now heavy with filled baskets and the scent of olives.

Kastas clasped him on the shoulder. "Tonight, we feast."

Rufus let out a cheer, raising both arms.

"But first, we bathe."

Epaphroditus lingered a moment longer in the grove, hands on his hips as his father and uncle started down the worn path toward the city. The baskets overflowed, proof of recovery, but part of him still waited for it to vanish, as if drought or disease might steal it all back.

He let the wind ruffle his tunic, eyes tracing the fading rows of trees. How many times had he stood here, praying for rain? For answers? For strength?

Aphrodite had answered, in her own time.

He took the lower trail through the trees, letting the others walk ahead. The slope curved gently down toward the city's western edge. Along the way, goats bleated on a distant ridge, and a farmer's song floated across the hills.

Within the city walls, children played, their chalk marks striping the stones with stick-figured gods and monsters.

"Epaphroditus!" Kastas called from up ahead. "We'll soak without you!"

He waved in answer and jogged the last stretch to join them.

The Thermae of Philippi rose ahead, domes glowing in the late sun, colonnades casting long shadows. Steam coiled skyward from vents as laughter mingled with the splash of water from within.

At the entrance, Epaphroditus handed over a modest fee to the stern-faced keeper. Inside, marble walls glowed in the sunlight, bouncing light across the mosaic floors where dolphins chased ships through a sea of blue tesserae. Familiar warmth seeped into his body the moment he crossed the threshold, muscles sighing in anticipation. His bones held the ingrained rhythm of undressing, sweating, and cooling. His body knew the sequence and craved it.

In the Apodyterium, he peeled off his dusty toga. Kastas slipped coins to a watching slave. Wise, in a place where untended things often vanished.

Wrapped at the waist, Epaphroditus stepped into the Palaestra, where men grappled, boxed, and tossed discuses beneath high-arched ceilings. After a bountiful harvest, his shoulders had their fill of strenuous activities. He opted for a massage while his father and uncle wrestled away their tensions.

Fragrant oil, myrtle and cinnamon, warmed in bronze bowls. Skilled hands pressed it into his back, unknotting tension thread by thread.

Then immersion. He gasped as the icy Frigidarium water hit his skin, shocking his senses wide open.

The dome above rippled with the reflection of the pool. His breath slowed. He would not delay here, not while the heat called to him.

He found his father and uncle Rufus in the Tepidarium, warmth already seeping into his limbs, coaxing tension from muscle and bone. They lingered there for a time, letting it soften them further before facing the true heat.

The Caldarium waited ahead, its air dense with steam, laced with the bite of burning cedar from the fires below. Heat bled up from the floors, soaked into the stone benches, curled around him like a heavy cloak.

He let the water lap his shoulders, half-listening to voices nearby as the last weariness from harvesting washed away.

"I heard Emperor Claudius kicked the lot of them out of Rome," someone rasped.

"Why?" another asked.

"Riots. Jews again. Stirring things up over that man... what's his name?"

"Chrestus?"

Epaphroditus opened one eye. That name, he'd heard it before. In Luke's stories, maybe.

He'd never met a Jew. His father had described them as devout, peculiar in custom, always wary of mixing with others. Quiet people, mostly. But this... this talk hinted at something else. Something more disruptive.

"Mark my words," the man muttered. "They'll come here next. Nothing but trouble."

A smirk touched Epaphroditus's lips as he leaned back into the water. For once, he might be the one bringing Luke a story.

His stomach grumbled. The massage, the baths... it had all stirred up a deep hunger.

He looked toward his father. "I'm heading to the food stalls." He swam to the edge of the pool and pulled himself up onto the side.

"We'll join you," Kastas said, hauling his bulk from the water.

"I was just about to suggest the same," Rufus added, following their lead.

Water streamed from Epaphroditus's skin as they left the pool behind, weaving through the crowd toward the stalls.

Market sounds crashed over them, shouts, clanging pans, meat sizzling on hot stones. The air swelled with cumin, pepper, and coriander.

The scent of sausage drew Epaphroditus. He took a fat lucanian link, drenched it in garum, and bit down. Crisp skin gave way to rich meat and the crunch of pine nuts.

Rufus devoured mussels with leeks and sweet wine. Kastas grinned over a roasted glis-glis.

Epaphroditus remembered his father's stories of visiting the bathhouse with his own father; the two of them enjoyed the delicacy together. He'd tried it on his first trip to the Thermae but could not stomach the traditional dish. Pork, pine nuts, and other flavorings all stuffed inside the gutted remains of an unfortunate dormouse was not his ideal meal. Not when there were so many other things a man could eat to satisfy his hunger.

Epaphroditus passed on his father's offer of a serving, once had been enough, choosing instead a patina, pears and honey, one of his favorites.

With a satisfied stomach and the sweetness of pears still lingering on his tongue, Epaphroditus surrendered to a servant's practiced hands. The strigil scraped sweat and oil from his back in smooth, efficient strokes, leaving behind a sense of lightness he hadn't realized he needed. One final plunge into the cold pool stole his breath and tightened his skin, leaving it gleaming under the flickering torchlight.

Togas on, coins exchanged, and a quick check confirmed his satchel was untouched. He stepped into the deepening dusk with the others, warmth still radiating from the bathhouse walls.

The sun sank behind the rooftops, casting long shadows across the stone streets. Laughter spilled from his chest at a joke his father shared. The sound rose to meet the breeze that carried the scent of baking bread and distant olive trees. Streets twisted gently toward home, where light spilled from the doorway and voices hummed within.

A feast waited.

What profit is an idol when its maker
has shaped it, a metal image, a teacher
of lies? For its maker trusts in his own
creation when he makes speechless idols!
Habakkuk 2:18

The scent of roasted pork and honeyed wine greeted Epaphroditus as he stepped into his family's villa. Female voices buzzed above the clatter of bronze dishes. Steam curled from the crowded table, where platters gleamed beneath the oil lamps: eggs soaked in garum, olives glistening with brine, spiced lentils dusted with cumin, and meats piled high and coated in herbs. His stomach growled again. The food at the bathhouse had only briefly appeased the beast in his belly.

"Everything is ready," Neda announced, trying to wedge a last bowl between the overfilled platters.

Rufus reclined at the head of the low table with solemn ease, the new family patriarch since Tarquin's passing. Kastas claimed the place to his right, while Epaphroditus took his seat at his father's side. The women, Zena, Neda, and Calliope, settled on brightly embroidered cushions across from the men.

Epaphroditus surveyed the spread. His mouth watered. The green olives, plump and firm, sat beside a small mound of dormice arranged like a temple offering. His gaze lingered there. Had Father requested them, nostalgic for the past, or had Mother chosen them as a subtle tribute to the dead? Whatever the reason for their appearance, he'd allow the elders to take his share.

Seafood courses followed, the curled tentacles of octopus, flaky river fish, and bronze-banded shrimp. The conversation skimmed over current affairs, of droughts endured, loved ones lost, and the quiet optimism of an ample harvest.

Neda leaned toward Kastas, her fingers brushing the rim of his plate. Epaphroditus paused mid-bite.

"Kastas, my love, I've been thinking," she coaxed, her voice like the silk folds of her stola.

"Oh?" Kastas plucked another octopus leg from the platter.

She sipped from a cup of wine, drawing out the moment. "Since Tarquin's death, Zena, Calliope, and I have strived to preserve the estate... despite everything we've lost."

The name sliced the air like a blade.

Epaphroditus's grip tightened around his spoon. A flash of pain crossed his father's features, yet fled just as quickly.

"With this year's harvest," Neda continued with soft urgency, "perhaps we can finally afford extra hands."

"You have two able bodies." Kastas gestured toward the other women beside his wife. "How many more hands does one house require?"

"Well..." Her tone wavered.

Epaphroditus shifted his gaze to the polished bones of the dormice. The strategy was obvious. His mother had made Kastas's favorites to ease him into agreement. Cunning, yes, but with no malice, only the desperation of a woman trying to steady a household.

"Zena and Calliope work tirelessly," Neda conceded. "But Calliope is coming of age. She'll marry soon."

Kastas turned sharply to his daughter.

"She's ready," Neda said, smoothing Calliope's dark hair. "Before long, we'll have only Zena and me to tend this grand home."

Epaphroditus watched his father's unreadable expression, a soldier's mask forged over the years.

"And what of Zena?" Kastas asked at last. "Rufus now governs this household. Her counsel matters most."

Neda's eyes turned to her sister-in-law in a quiet

plea.

A small gesture, but heavy with meaning. Epaphroditus didn't need to hear the unspoken words to know the two women had talked about this between themselves. Tarquin was gone, and his absence left space unsteady, shifting, like sand underfoot. No one had quite found their new footing yet.

"I'll yield that decision to Rufus." Zena nodded toward her husband. "He is the master of this house now."

"True enough," Rufus said, adjusting his position. "Yet, Father always trusted Kastas with finances. I still do." He raised an open palm toward his younger brother. "What say you? Father despised the idea of hired help, but that was when this table overflowed with life. Now we are three men and three women, one soon departing. It may be a necessary expense."

Kastas stroked his chin, recently shaved smooth. "At the Thermae, I heard talk of an influx of Roman exiles heading east."

Epaphroditus recalled the heated murmurings in the Caldarium.

"Some will surely arrive burdened with debts," Kastas continued. "We might find suitable hands among them."

The word, bondservant, pressed on Epaphroditus like a stone. "I have a thought."

Every face turned to him. His skin flushed hot.

"Speak," Kastas said, his tone even.

"I've been thinking," Epaphroditus began, heart pounding. "The famine... it made things clear. I'm not growing any younger." He forced his gaze from his father to his mother. "I've been considering marriage."

Neda's hands flew to her chest. "Truly?"

He gave a single nod.

"To whom?" Kastas asked, voice clipped and firm.

Epaphroditus swallowed the dryness from his throat. "Melody."

"The physician's sister?" Kastas straightened.

Epaphroditus nodded again, cautiously. "She's skilled."

"And beautiful," Neda added eagerly. "She'll give us fine grandchildren."

He shot his mother a look, equal parts disbelief and irritation. "I haven't even spoken with her family, and already you want grandchildren."

"You're not the only one battling time," she said, brushing silver strands from her face. "I'd like to hold a grandchild before I'm laid in the tomb."

"Well," Kastas raised his voice just above his wife's, "that settles it. Tomorrow we will visit her family. We'll strike a fair bargain."

Epaphroditus exhaled, long and slow. The decision came swiftly, carrying with it an unexpected relief. Marriage might delay the matter of servants. Perhaps even eliminate it, if Melody agreed.

Still, the thought nagged. Was he seeking a wife or a solution? Melody's face came to him not with warmth, but with a sense of calm competence. He admired her—her gentleness, her mind—but did admiration breed affection? Could love truly grow from respect alone, or was it merely a shield against loneliness and uncertainty? And what sort of husband would he make with half his heart caught between duty and doubt?

Melody could tend their home and add more than hired hands ever could. The corner of his mouth twitched, betraying a flicker of hope beneath the surface. Life, new life, returning to the villa.

"And after that, you and I will go to the market," Kastas added, slicing through Epaphroditus's thoughts. "We'll see what bondservants are available."

A weight settled squarely on his chest. "But Father—"

"Don't worry." Kastas placed a heavy hand on his son's shoulder. "I'll handle the terms."

"No, I mean…" Epaphroditus sat straighter, his thoughts twisting. "I want to speak about the servants."

The table quieted, but the silence was not receptive; it was wary. Rufus lowered his cup. Neda's fingers stilled over a linen fold. Only the oil lamp hissed in reply. Epaphroditus met his father's eyes and saw, not curiosity, but resistance, thinly veiled, already closing like a gate.

Kastas's grip tightened briefly, then dropped. "Enough business for tonight." He plucked a plum and bit into it, the juice spilling down his chin.

Epaphroditus studied the fruits—plump grapes, bright apricots, dark figs—all glimmering beneath the dancing flames. Even the libum, twin honeyed cheesecakes, sat untouched at the table's end. The family would eat one and offer the other to Aphrodite.

Across the table, Zena poured more wine into Neda's cup with practiced grace. The motion was small, almost invisible amid the flickering lamplight, but Epaphroditus noticed. He had noticed the food, the clean floors, the filled lamps, but never who kept them so. These women, Zena, Neda, even Calliope, had become the quiet builders of the household, binding its frayed edges with threadbare patience. No one sang songs for them, and no one offered them laurels. Yet the house stood because of their unseen labor.

Calliope, once all laughter and mischief, now wore her silence like armor. Her gaze, sharp and measured, flicked between speakers, missing nothing. She bore her mother's poise, but with it a harder edge, less innocence, more resolve.

Hunger vanished beneath the weight of his meditations. The libum caught his eye again, golden beneath the flame. His gaze shifted to the marble statue of his family's goddess, her expression unreadable in the flickering light.

What twist of fate would Aphrodite deal him next?

He who finds a wife finds a good thing
and obtains favor from the Lord.
Proverbs 18:22

Morning dawned bright and clear, as if the sky rejoiced. Epaphroditus found it irritating. Joy had no place on a day like this. He hadn't even spoken to Luke, and already he was walking into a negotiation that might win Melody's hand and possibly lose his best friend's trust.

After changing into a fresh toga, Epaphroditus hurried through breaking his fast, simple bread dipped in olive oil and a cup of watered wine. The villa stirred awake around him: distant footsteps, the soft clatter of women preparing meals, and the faint scent of fresh herbs carried on the morning breeze.

Kneeling before the marble likeness of Aphrodite, he traced the goddess's cheek with a trembling finger, the marble cold and unforgiving beneath his touch. His prayers poured out easily, but beneath their rhythm, a shadow of doubt lingered.

Did the gods truly hear the pleas of mortals, or were these petitions whispered into silence? Still, he repeated them, clinging to the fragile hope they might matter.

His mother often warned that the gods were too busy or too fickle to hear their prayers unless properly bribed. That's why so many worshippers offered blood or bodies.

At least Aphrodite forbade blood sacrifices. For that, he was grateful.

He whispered the words one last time, but they echoed hollow. What he really needed wasn't rote. He longed to unburden himself and his conflicted desires. But what god had time for that or a desire to listen?

Taking his place beside his father, they set off toward Luke's home.

Each step pressed heavy with betrayal. He wanted to marry Melody; he was sure of that. But she was also the treasured daughter of a household that had treated him like family. Would they deem him worthy enough to give her up?

Luke's modest family home stood on a narrow cobblestone street, the worn stones smooth beneath passing feet. The sun warmed the roof and the faded painted shutters, hinting at the home's age and quiet endurance. Nearby, the chatter of early morning vendors spilled into the air, mingling with the scent of fresh bread from the nearby baker.

"Alexander!" Kastas called out as they entered the courtyard. He extended his arm to Luke's father.

Alexander returned the gesture with a firm clasp of Kastas's forearm. "A pleasure to see you, friend. It's rare for you to visit."

"Trade keeps me busy."

"And yet, you're here at sunrise. What's the occasion?"

"I've come to speak to you about your daughter."

"Melody?" Alexander cast his eyes around the room, as if certain she was about to appear at any moment. "Is something wrong?"

"No, not at all." Kastas chuckled, brushing aside the concern. "I come on behalf of my son. He wishes to seek her hand in marriage."

Alexander let his gaze settle on Epaphroditus, eyes narrowing as he took in the young man's stance and bearing. He said nothing, holding the silence like a blade.

Epaphroditus straightened, locking his stance like a soldier before his general. Though he'd known Alexander most of his life, he was now a stranger, an outsider standing under sharp scrutiny.

"Let's go inside," Alexander finally said, gesturing behind himself. "This will take more than a moment."

They followed him in, where woven tapestries and a low table scattered with scrolls and medical instruments furnished the main room.

The two older men took their places at the table, shifting into the careful tones of business.

Epaphroditus hovered near but remained standing, the air thick with expectation.

Luke's entrance cut through the tense air like a sudden breeze scattering leaves. His familiar stride echoed softly on the stone floor, but Epaphroditus's heart pounded so loudly he feared it would give him away.

His friend's dark eyes locked onto him immediately, sharp and searching. "Another break from the grove?" His voice was calm, but there was an edge of suspicion beneath the casual tone.

Epaphroditus swallowed hard, trying to steady himself. The weight of the moment pressed down on him like a heavy cloak. His throat tightened; words dangled on the edge of escape.

Behind Luke's unwavering gaze, Alexander's voice rang out, cutting through the quiet room with practiced authority, "My daughter is worth far more than that."

Luke's expression flickered, uncertainty blooming before his features softened. He stepped closer to Epaphroditus, the warmth of their long friendship mixing with sudden awkwardness. "What are they talking about?"

"Melody," he rasped.

For a breathless moment, Luke didn't respond. Just stared.

Silence wedged between them like a blade. Epaphroditus' stomach twisted. This was the moment, the one he'd dreaded. The look in Luke's eyes wasn't anger, not yet. But confusion had cracked the surface of trust.

They'd grown up together, trading stories in the olive groves, daring each other to climb higher, run farther. He still remembered the summer Melody broke her arm and Luke didn't leave her side until it mended, sleeping by her pallet like a watchdog. Epaphroditus had teased him about it then. Now the memory turned sharp in his chest.

What if this ruined everything?

He hadn't just risked Luke's pride; he might've shattered something dear. A friendship forged over years. A trust Luke had never once withheld from him.

He wanted to speak, to soften the blow, to explain that it hadn't been a betrayal, only fear that had held his tongue. But fear was flimsy armor now.

Epaphroditus was the one to break the silent stare and hung his head.

"You want to marry my sister?"

He nodded once, without meeting his friend's eyes.

Luke punched his arm, hard. "And you didn't think to mention this earlier?"

"I meant to." He rubbed the spot. "I've thought about it since the famine. She's... she's a remarkable woman. I would be honored to make her my wife."

Luke snorted. "When I said we should marry sisters, I didn't mean my own."

"I wanted to talk to you first. Truly. But..." He rubbed the back of his neck.

"But?"

He exhaled. "Father plans to purchase a bondservant. Mother will lose Calli to marriage soon, and she and Zena are struggling to keep up the estate alone. I thought if they saw how capable Melody is, they might not feel the need to purchase..." The words strangled his throat from the inside.

Luke gave a small nod. "That's... honorable."

"It didn't work. We're heading to the market after this."

Luke's gaze turned sober. "You know, not buying one of them doesn't stop the trade."

The truth sat like a stone in his chest. "I know."

"But better a soul end up in your household than one of lesser mercy."

Epaphroditus hadn't thought of it that way. "That's... true."

"And in your house, there's hope. A respectable master might grant freedom."

"I hadn't considered that either."

"One day, you'll have full rights over the estate. Their fate could be yours to shape."

He looked down at his hands, hands that had

harvested olives and hauled sacks of grain, not accustomed to wielding power. Could they really carry another's life? "Thank you, Luke."

"For what?"

"For perspective."

"I've got plenty of it to share."

Movement near the table drew their attention. Alexander stood, followed by Kastas. They clasped forearms again.

Luke nudged him. "Looks like you have a bride."

Epaphroditus's relief knotted with fear, clawing at his throat. Melody. His.

"I look forward to your return," Alexander said, clapping Kastas on the back. "May the gods bless this union."

"As do I," Kastas replied. With a brief nod to Luke, he motioned to Epaphroditus.

"Take courage." Luke held out his arm to Epaphroditus.

He squeezed his arm in return.

"Things are rarely as bad as we imagine them."

Epaphroditus held his friend's forearm, praying he could remain instead of walking the path toward the market. Any other day, a few hours among the stalls would be a welcome reprieve from the hard work in the grove. Today's journey there held only the possibility of a dreadful end to his family's long-standing tradition of relying solely upon kin and Aphrodite for their survival.

Releasing Luke's arm, Epaphroditus followed his father out of the house and toward the Forum.

As they passed the city ovens, the warm aroma of freshly baked bread wrapped around Epaphroditus like a comforting cloak. For a moment, the simple rhythm of the city was a balm to his frayed nerves.

Clement, a broad-shouldered young baker with flour-dusted hands, arranged golden loaves on his wooden counter, greeting early customers with a booming laugh. The scent mingled with the freshness of herbs from a nearby stall and the faint briny air drifting from the river.

A pang struck Epaphroditus as life surged forward around him, his own future shrouded in uncertainty.

He waited until they neared the market before asking, "Are you pleased with the terms, Father?"

A smug smile tugged at Kastas's mouth as he lifted his chin. "I never leave a deal until I'm satisfied."

That was as much of an answer as he'd get, for now.

Still, a fragile peace stirred beneath his lingering anxiety. Even if the day ended with the purchase of servants, it had begun with something wonderful: the promise of Melody becoming his bride.

Is Israel a slave? Is he a homeborn
servant? Why then has he become a
prey?
Jeremiah 2:14

Bustling sounds reached them before the market came into view. Sellers barked prices like soldiers; buyers returned fire with counteroffers, beggars cried out for mercy in coin, and children dashed around with laughter and teasing that clashed with the serious work of the day. The tang of vinegar and sweat clung to the heat, mingling with the sweet drift of fig cakes. A donkey brayed nearby, hooves clattering on the uneven stones. Somewhere to the left, a woman shouted about fresh fish, her voice swallowed by the clang of a blacksmith's hammer striking iron.

A cluster of people stood near the broad stone steps. One by one, they were paraded up the steps and displayed like livestock, examined by impersonal eyes. It was here that Kastas stopped, searching for new servants.

Epaphroditus's stomach twisted. Humans, bound by rope, stood silent as strangers appraised their able bodies. It took little to end up here: drought, a failed wager, one poor decision. Rome made no allowances for misfortune. Only the favor of the gods had kept his family from falling this far during the famine. Others had not been so fortunate.

He still remembered the gaunt eyes of neighbors turned thin and hollow. His family had survived, trading everything short of dignity. He learned that hunger had a sound, like wood splintering under a weight, and he'd heard it often in his prayers.

The famine had taught him something else essential: how fragile freedom truly was.

He scanned the faces of the bound. Some were likely debtors who'd become servi publici, state-owned slaves condemned to work the mines or maintain the aqueducts. Public officials might receive others for errands and menial labor. Then there were the domestic ones, those bought by private households, living at the mercy of their master's whim. A drop in status, in rights, in hope. Even so, some might manage to save enough to purchase help of their own. A cruel irony: slaves owning slaves.

His gaze fell to their feet. Worn sandals and dirt-crusted soles. Simple tunics torn at the edges.

An old woman with clouded eyes clutched a strip of faded linen to her chest, her lips moving in silent prayer while the crowd surged around her. Another man stared at the sky, as if searching for an answer before someone took his name.

They were not hardened criminals. Likely exiles, cast out for offending a senator's sensibilities. If the bathhouse rumors were true, the wind scattered some of this group like seeds, and fate brought the unlucky ones here, under the watchful eye of the genius of the market.

Two aediles prowled the area, Roman magistrates with the authority to inspect goods and enforce order. Their red capes glinted with gold geometric embroidery, each thread a reminder of their power. They moved like herding hounds, quick to punish any disruption. With the increased activity of the slave auction, the two appeared on high alert, their eyes moving to and fro as they passed in front of the steps.

Epaphroditus took in the group's tension, slumped shoulders, averted eyes, feet that barely left the earth as they shuffled forward. All were silent.

Except for one.

He nearly missed her. A woman, a little older than Calliope, with tangled dark hair and a mud-smeared tunic ripped at the hem. Something about her reminded him of his sister. He saw the same defiant spirit beneath the grime.

She mirrored the others until an aedile passed, then she leaned toward her neighbor and whispered. As if sensing the magistrate's mind, she froze before his gaze could land on her. Each time he turned, she leaned to another. Whisper. Return. Whisper. Return.

Epaphroditus moved closer, straining to catch her desperate words, but the sounds of the market swallowed them.

Then she misjudged the rhythm. She turned to the man behind her, a breath too late.

The guard saw her.

"Quiet!" the aedile barked and brought his staff down hard on her.

She cried out, clutching her arm.

As the magistrate raised his weapon to strike her again, Epaphroditus stepped forward and caught it mid-air.

Gasps rippled through the crowd.

The guard whirled on him. "How dare you."

Epaphroditus didn't flinch. The man stood taller than him, but not by much.

"Release my weapon," the aedile growled.

"She's had her punishment." Epaphroditus shoved the staff aside and stepped closer, narrowing the space between them. "You'd damage merchandise? That won't sit well with the seller."

They locked eyes.

For a heartbeat, the tension stretched taut. Then

the magistrate snorted, like a mule denied its kick, raised his weapon toward Epaphroditus's face in a warning, and walked away.

Epaphroditus turned just in time to see the injured woman swallowed by the others.

"Order!" the other aedile barked.

The woman cradled her arm and slid between two others. She lifted her gaze to Epaphroditus just for a heartbeat. Confusion flickered there before she looked away.

He returned to his father's side, grateful Kastas withheld any opinion of his actions.

His father placed bids for two muscular men. "They'll do well in the grove," he said with satisfaction. "Just the strong backs I was hoping for."

Epaphroditus said nothing. His attention never left the injured woman.

When her turn came to stand on the stage, the crowd shifted with disinterest. Her insolence had already branded her undesirable. She stepped forward, chin high, a gesture of pride, or maybe defiance. It was hard to tell.

Epaphroditus shot a look at the aedile who had struck her. Their eyes met again. Epaphroditus held the stare, unyielding. Then, without looking away, he called out a fair bid. Part of him screamed that the action was foolish. But the rest stood rooted, unwilling to watch her vanish into someone else's cruelty.

A smirk curled at the aedile's mouth.

Embarrassment prickled his skin, but he shoved it aside. Let the dog laugh.

There was no counteroffer. The crowd didn't want trouble.

With a curt nod, the seller sealed the deal.

As Epaphroditus paid for her, Kastas appeared beside him.

"You think it wise to bring a rebellious woman into our home?" He lifted his silver brow. "Zena and Neda may not welcome your choice."

Epaphroditus thought quickly. "Isn't it tradition to give one's betrothed a gift to seal the agreement?"

"You intend to give her to Melody?"

Epaphroditus hesitated for the briefest moment. The lie had come too easily. Would Melody understand? "After we're married." He handed over the last coins. "She'll be Melody's handmaid. Another pair of hands for the women."

Kastas clapped him on the shoulder, pride glinting in his eyes. "So, the cunning of a merchant runs in your blood after all." He gave Epaphroditus a hearty shake. "A house servant for your mother and aunt, a wedding gift for your bride, all in one deal. I'm impressed."

A strained curve touched his mouth while his insides twisted tight and sour. This wasn't cunning. It was instinct. Compassion. She reminded him too much of Calliope. He couldn't allow them to beat her and force her into the mines or sell her to something worse.

The seller signed the parchment, then shoved the woman toward him. "She's all yours."

She stumbled, and Epaphroditus caught her by the arms as she sucked in a sharp breath.

"Your arm—" He let go at once. "Forgive me."

She shielded the injury with her other hand.

He glimpsed blood blooming through her tunic before she hid it. Her eyes dropped. But not before he saw the flash of pain.

"Father?"

Kastas turned to him.

"I'll take this one with me to Luke's. I didn't get a chance to speak with Melody. You can take the men and gather the family for the betrothal ceremony."

"An excellent idea." Kastas turned toward the newly gained laborers. "What are you called?"

"Isaiah," said one.

"Enoch," mumbled the other.

"You may call me Kastas. This is my son, Epaphroditus. I'll take you to our villa."

Epaphroditus watched them go before he turned to the woman now in his care. "And what are you called?"

She met his eyes with the same bewildered expression as before. "Shira."

"Shira." Her name tasted strange on his tongue.

Unfamiliar. A name with edges, belonging to someone who wouldn't vanish quietly. He wondered what it would cost to carry her defiance under his roof, and whether he'd already started paying for it. "You may address me as Epaphroditus."

"I heard."

Her quick wit caught him off guard. He swallowed a laugh. "This way."

I will be like the dew to Israel;
he shall blossom like the lily;
he shall take root like the trees of
Lebanon; his shoots shall spread out;
his beauty shall be like the olive,
and his fragrance like Lebanon.
Hosea 14:5-6

As Epaphroditus stepped inside, the smaller villa of Luke's family stirred with activity, the air warm with voices and bustling preparations.

"There he is." Bernice, Luke's mother, pressed kisses on both his cheeks and cradled his face in her hands. "Alexander told me the good news. We are so pleased!"

"Give the man some air," Luke's voice cut in before Epaphroditus could respond. "You'll have plenty of time to dote on him later."

Epaphroditus offered his friend a fleeting look of gratitude, gently deflecting the familiar swell of affection. It wasn't unwelcome but with his thoughts churning like storm-tossed seas, even kindness pressed too close.

Luke's tone turned teasing. "Come to snatch my sister away before the ink has dried on the parchment?"

"Actually, I've come to speak with Melody." Epaphroditus stepped deeper into the atrium, the stone cool beneath his sandals as he caught Shira's eye, a silent cue for her to stay close. "This betrothal is moving quickly. We haven't had a proper conversation."

Luke leaned against an archway, eyes drifting to Shira. "Melody," he called, voice raised just enough to carry.

Melody appeared almost instantly, as though she'd heard more than just her name. "Yes?"

Epaphroditus inclined his head in greeting. "I was hoping we might speak before my family arrives for the ceremony."

Melody crossed her arms. "I think that would be best."

"But first." He lifted his hand, cutting the moment short with a look at his friend. "Luke, would you look at an injury?"

Luke was already moving toward Shira. He studied her with quiet attentiveness before speaking, this time with the ease of recognition. "Your name, it means 'music,' doesn't it?"

Shira gave a small nod, a faint color rising in her

cheeks.

Of course Luke would know. Epaphroditus had always admired the way his friend pulled knowledge from seemingly nowhere. "Do you know every language?" he asked, half in jest, half in awe.

"Not hardly." Luke chuckled, his eyes glinting with mischief. "But I've tended to Jews. Their language isn't so difficult once you get the hang of it."

So, she is a Jew.

The thought pressed itself against his mind, already heavy with implications. He kept it to himself, unwilling to let her see that he knew part of her story, how she was likely one of those exiled for misdeeds. It seemed cruel, knowing what he knew, but he would not let her bear the weight of his pity.

Luke gestured to Shira's arm. "Let's have a look."

Shira hesitated, then lifted her sleeve. The wound was shallow but inflamed.

Luke extended his hand, palm open. "May I?"

She nodded again, her eyes darting between Luke and Epaphroditus.

Luke pressed along her skin with gentle fingers. "How did this happen?"

Shira looked at Epaphroditus, seeking some unspoken approval.

Luke's expression tightened, a flicker of question in his eyes.

Epaphroditus answered, "She found herself on

the wrong end of an aedile's stick."

"I see." Luke's voice softened as he bent her arm at the elbow. "Does this hurt?"

She answered with the barest shake of her head, her lips pressed into a thin line.

"Well, Shira, your injury isn't severe." He released his hold on her. "The skin is only slightly broken. My sister can make a salve and bandage it for you. Would that make you more comfortable?"

Her cheeks flushed brighter, but she nodded once.

"Melody?" Luke's voice carried across the room.

Already reaching for tools, Melody motioned toward the table. "This way."

Epaphroditus stepped beside Luke, keeping his voice low. "I brought her so you could tend to her wound and give me a moment to speak with Melody. Alone."

Luke turned to him fully, something sharp in his eyes. Not judgment, but the flicker of it. "If you want to own a Jew, you'll need to learn more about them."

The words hit harder than Epaphroditus expected, a slow burn beneath the skin. He opened his mouth, then closed it. Luke hadn't said it with malice, but the weight of it hung between them just the same. Not a reprimand, an invitation. And perhaps a warning. "How did you know what she was?"

"I hear more than you think." Luke's lips curved with a trace of quiet amusement. "When you mentioned the aedile and seeing her appearance, it made sense she was one of those exiles brought into the market."

Epaphroditus ran his hand through his hair, a nervous energy coursing through him. "I must be a fool for buying her. She's so..."

"Prideful."

"Yes!" Epaphroditus exhaled sharply, the admission sitting bitter on his tongue.

"It's the way of their people." Luke leaned against the wall and folded his arms. "They've survived this long by not bowing to others. You can't fault her for that."

"You know a lot about them."

"I listen." Luke glanced back toward Shira. "I spend half my time on ships. People talk, Epaphroditus."

"What else do I need to know about her?"

"You're sharp. You'll catch the rest." Luke's voice became more somber. "Be careful, my friend. Just because she's a woman doesn't mean you should let your guard down. She's frightened. Alone. Likely desperate. It's not a good state to be in."

Epaphroditus stared at him. "You got all that from a few moments with her?"

"I've treated all kinds of people in all kinds of circumstances. Trust me." Luke gave his shoulder a brief squeeze before walking off toward the kitchen.

Back at the table, Melody was wrapping Shira's arm with practiced precision, her expression cool.

Epaphroditus approached slowly, the weight of unspoken things tightening in his chest. "Melody," he began, keeping his voice low, "I know this betrothal is sudden—"

"Sudden?" Melody slammed down the bowl of salve, her hands planted firmly on her hips as she faced him. "It's come by complete surprise."

"I wanted to speak with you first, but things happened faster than I intended."

She folded her arms tightly over her chest. "Luke said you never even spoke to him about this. Your best friend."

Guilt twisted in his gut.

"What is my brother to do without me? I can't leave him to mend people on his own. He needs me."

"Luke will be fine." Epaphroditus's voice took on a quiet but firm edge.

Melody huffed, turning back to the task at hand, her motions swift and impatient.

"He travels the world, tending to people without you. It's not like I'd be taking you away from Philippi."

Still no answer from her.

The silence stretched between them before Epaphroditus added, "If you don't agree with the arrangement, you have every right to decline."

Melody paused mid-wrap, her gaze shifting to meet his. A flicker of resignation, maybe. Or something softer. Surrender? "I didn't say I don't agree with the arrangement." She resumed her work. "I simply wish you'd considered others before rushing into all of this."

Relief washed through him, tempered by the realization that what was done couldn't be undone. He studied her face, the tension still present but no longer brittle. He looked at Shira, her eyes downcast, and then back at Melody. "I've cared for you all these years as my best friend's sister," Epaphroditus said, finding the courage to speak the words he had avoided for so long. "Please allow me to care for you for the rest of my life, as your bridegroom."

Her cheeks flushed, a rare thing.

She pressed her fingers to her lips, gaze softening. "I'd be honored."

He turned to Shira and motioned gently. "As your first gift, may I present to you, Shira, your future handmaid."

Shira's gaze lifted, uncertain.

A quiet gasp escaped Melody's lips. "I didn't realize she was yours."

"Newly acquired," Epaphroditus admitted, his voice tight. "But she will be yours after our wedding feast."

Melody tilted her head, considering the woman before her. "I've never had a handmaid before."

"May she serve you well." He dipped his head in a formal gesture.

That evening, after agreeing on the dowry and exchanging gifts, they signed the betrothal scroll. The villa buzzed with celebration, and wine flowed freely.

Epaphroditus found Melody near the brazier. The green palla he'd gifted her shimmered in the lamplight, drawing out the depth in her eyes.

He stepped close, hesitant, heart drumming beneath his tunic. He bent toward her, lips brushing hers, just enough to say what words never could.

Desire tugged at him, but he held back. There would be time to explore the untraveled roads of his bride soon enough.

Two are better than one, because they
have a good reward for their toil.
Ecclesiastes 4:9

The heat of the June day settled in with the first rays of sun, the air thick and heavy, as if the gods themselves were watching. Both families insisted on the carefully selected date for the wedding feast, hoping to appease every god they could think of.

Epaphroditus fumbled with his clean toga, his fingers trembling. Sweat beaded on his forehead and collected at the back of his neck. He couldn't tell if it was the heat or the nerves clawing at him. He had prepared for this moment for months, yet now, with the ceremony finally here, his hands trembled, too unsteady to manage even the simplest tasks.

His mother and aunt had spent countless hours making sure everything was perfect. They scrubbed every crevice of the villa and carefully tended the courtyard garden. With Luke's help, they planted herbs with medicinal uses, hoping to make Melody feel more at home.

The day had finally arrived, and Epaphroditus was exhausted. A part of him was already looking forward to a week alone with his bride, starting the life they would build together.

Neda cleared her throat, causing him to look up. Her gaze softened as she crossed the room, her toga flowing like a river of light. "Are you in need of aid?"

"Please," he muttered, dropping his hands in defeat.

She moved toward him with grace, unwinding his toga and adjusting it until it sat just right. "It seems like only yesterday that I showed you how to wear this," she mused softly. "Yet here you stand, ready to welcome a bride into our home." A tear slipped down her cheek, glistening in the lamplight.

"Maia," his voice cracked as he brushed the tear away. "Don't cry."

Her lips trembled, a fragile warmth breaking through the tears as she dabbed at her cheeks. "It's been a while since you called me that."

A sharp stab twisted inside him. The last time was in Paphos, when he was still a child. After that trip, he'd outgrown such childish terms.

"There," she said, patting his chest with a finality that, for a moment, took him back to the boy he once was. "That's better. Now, we need to get you to your waiting bride."

Epaphroditus lifted his chin, setting his posture

tall and proud as he led his family toward Luke's home. The distant sounds of music and laughter greeted him as he stepped inside. A wash of peace swept through him. Today would be a joyful day. He had to remember that, he had to enjoy it, no matter the turmoil brewing inside him.

As he entered the home, his eyes immediately searched for Melody. His heart skipped when he found her standing among a group of female relatives. Time seemed to slow as he watched her. The buzz of the guests faded around him, leaving only the image of Melody in his vision.

Her saffron-colored veil shielded her from everyone, draping over her like a cloak of mystery. Childhood wedding memories flashed through his mind, his older cousins dressed in similar attire. It was the mother's task to prepare the bride. He knew Bernice had arranged each piece with care, ensuring it was perfect.

Melody wore a woolen tunica recta as the foundation of her outfit, overlaid with a simple white stola. But it was the leather belt, secured with a Hercules knot around her waist, that caught his eye. A quiet laugh threatened to break loose at the thought of undoing that knot with his own hands.

Her hair was arranged with meticulous care, crowned with flowers and herbs meant to bring fortune to the union. Though he couldn't see them entirely beneath the veil, he noticed the matching shoes peeking out.

For a heartbeat, he was certain her eyes met his beneath the sheer fabric, a spark of warmth that eased the tightness in his chest.

The hum of voices brought him back to the present. Between the two families, they easily fulfilled the legal requirement of ten witnesses. Kastas had brought along his two male servants to assist with any tasks so the family could enjoy the festivities. Shira, ever silent, stood by Epaphroditus' side, her face as expressionless as always. He couldn't help but wonder what she thought of the entire arrangement. Was the world she lived in before much different from his?

The priest began his prayers to Janus, Juno, Jupiter, Tellus, and Hymen, the gods and goddesses of thresholds, life, and marriage. Epaphroditus added his own quiet prayer to Aphrodite, hoping that the goddess of love would look kindly on the union and grant them her blessing.

Women gathered around Melody, offering whispered advice and encouragement, each of them taking turns speaking to her as they moved her closer to Epaphroditus. Finally, after their teasing, Melody stepped toward him.

Her warmth reached him as she approached, a glow that seemed to radiate toward him, drawing him in. He extended his right hand to her, and she mirrored the motion. Their hands met, and the priest tied a cloth around their joined hands as they vowed their promises to each other.

"Quando tu Gaius, ego Gaia," Melody chanted, her voice trembling.

"Ubi tu Gaia, ego Gaius," Epaphroditus recited, his voice steady despite the rapid beating of his heart.

The priest untied their hands, and Epaphroditus slid a simple ring from his toga, placing it gently on Melody's finger. Her mother handed her a ring, which Melody placed on his finger in return.

With the last pieces in place, they moved to the altar, and Melody, at last, removed her veil. The priest offered a libum to Jupiter and shared slices of honeyed cheesecake with them both.

As they tasted the sweet cake, the guests erupted in cheers, their voices mingling in a chorus of congratulations.

"Time to sign the contract so we can feast!" Alexander's voice cut through the celebration, his enthusiasm clear.

Epaphroditus and Melody affirmed their vows in writing on the parchment brought before them, using swift strokes of their quills.

For all their planning, nothing had readied Epaphroditus for this, how fully he belonged to this moment, to her.

"Bring in the hog!" Alexander shouted, his voice rising over the clamor.

Luke and Rufus entered with an enormous pig, its bulk commanding attention. Alexander raised a dagger high, bringing it down with precision to slit the animal's throat.

The crowd's cheers rang in his ears, and Epaphroditus joined them, knowing the act ensured Melody's fertility. But as his eyes wandered to Shira, his joy shifted to concern. She'd gone pale, her face nearly ashen. Before he could react, she turned away, hands pressed firmly to her mouth.

He grabbed Luke's arm. "Will you check on Shira? I don't think the sight of blood agrees with her."

Luke offered a rueful smile. "It's not the blood, my friend." His gaze followed Shira's retreating form. "It's the pig. They're unclean to the Jews."

Epaphroditus winced at the reminder. "Is there anything clean in their culture?"

"Their deity," Luke replied with a shrug. "Their faith requires different rituals."

He turned back to the celebration, watching as they removed the pig. The feast was well underway, and he joined the revelers in savoring the meats, fruits, and breads prepared by Melody's family.

Once everyone had eaten their fill, the procession began. Epaphroditus walked toward Melody with the strength of a man ready to claim his bride.

When he reached her, Bernice made a show of

pulling her back. "I've come for my bride," he said, his voice firm.

"You can't have her," Bernice replied, holding fast to her daughter's arm.

Epaphroditus gripped Melody's other arm gently, but with purpose, pulling her toward him. With a quick tug, Bernice released her, and he pressed Melody close, stealing a kiss. The surrounding crowd erupted into playful giggles.

Reluctantly, he stepped away, leading Melody to Luke. Her brother handed her a distaff and spindle before lighting a whitethorn torch. Three men and her brother positioned themselves around her, ready to guard her from any evil spirits that might threaten her as she traveled to her new home.

They paraded through the city as evening fell. The crowd scattered nuts, a blessing of prosperity, their voices echoing as they moved along the Via Egnatia.

Nearing the villa, Epaphroditus hurried ahead, eager to welcome his bride. As Melody stepped closer, her voice rose with the marriage chant, stronger and clearer than before, weaving a deeper connection around Epaphroditus.

He scooped her into his arms to carry her over the threshold, careful not to stumble and undo all their hard work.

Inside, guests gathered for another feast, and Melody performed the final rituals. She anointed the door with oil, hung woolen fillets, and prayed for a blessing from the gods. Afterward, she handed Epaphroditus a coin, which he exchanged for the key to their new home.

The day ended in merriment, but their life together had just begun. A rush of fulfillment washed over Epaphroditus, knowing the road ahead would be theirs to travel together.

*And the foreigners who join themselves
to the Lord, to minister to him, to love
the name of the Lord, and to be his
servants, everyone who keeps the
Sabbath and does not profane it, and
holds fast my covenant—*
Isaiah 56:6

Clanging dishes and heavy footsteps shattered the hush at the back of the house. Epaphroditus looked up from the scroll he hadn't really been reading. The sounds weren't random. Frustration had its own rhythm, and he knew Shira's by heart. Only one day a week ever stirred that level of noise from her.

Morning sounds had changed; the joyful bustle of women in the kitchen was gone. It was a void in the house that echoed louder than the most distracting clamor.

In the months since marrying Melody, the house had hollowed. Aunt Zena first, then Rufus not long after. His father was only a week gone, and already the emptiness of losing all of them had settled like dust in the corners. Today was supposed to be a breath, one full day without mourning clothes or ritual meals.

Having ordered his mother to rest, he also told Melody and Calliope to stay in bed a little longer, allowing their bodies to recover from the strain of funeral rites and endless guests. Foolishly, he had forgotten that this day would press Shira into a mood nothing could sweeten.

Setting down the parchment, he moved toward the kitchen and leaned against the doorway, taking in the scene.

Shira worked in sharp, exaggerated motions, scrubbing harder than needed, shoulders stiff beneath her tunic.

His voice broke the charged silence. "My mother used to say, 'Food tastes far better when it's prepared with compliant hands.'"

She stilled. Her gaze slid to him over her shoulder. No words, just that look, the one that pinned him to the spot and dared him to make her angrier. A warning.

He held her stare for a beat longer.

She moved without a word to prepare a bowl and slammed it onto the low table with more force than necessary. Her jaw tightened, eyes fixed somewhere beyond the task.

Epaphroditus stepped away from the doorframe

and lowered himself to the cushions beside the table, murmuring a thanks.

She didn't reply. Only turned back to the hearth with set shoulders and hands clanking through pottery like weapons drawn for battle.

His sigh came unbidden. Rising again, he crossed the room and halted just outside her reach. "Shira."

A small flinch. Barely perceptible, but there. Tension lived in her spine, her neck, and the set of her mouth.

"I know you're unhappy about working today."

She didn't turn. Only tossed another log onto the fire. Sparks leapt and crackled.

"I'll tell you what. You finish the morning work without turning the kitchen upside down, and I'll take you to the market with me."

Her hand hovered over a bowl. A breath later, she nodded once and resumed her work, quieter now.

He returned to his seat with the ease of a man who had just bartered peace with a lioness.

A few moments later, Isaiah and Enoch appeared. Respectful bows met him as each collected a modest portion of bread and dates. They belonged to him now. Epaphroditus had not wanted these kinds of hands. But after everything... he saw the necessity. Still, the weight of it sat heavy on his chest.

Footsteps, softer than the others, padded down the corridor. Melody entered, hair unbound, rubbing sleep from her eyes with the back of her hand.

He stood without thinking, his lips already curving upward. "Sleep well, my love?"

"Well enough."

There was a drag in her voice. Something unspoken beneath the simplicity.

She waved off his concern with a lazy flick of her hand and moved toward the kitchen. "I'm going to help Shira."

"Be cautious. Her claws are out this morning."

Melody halted abruptly and raised her hand to her temple as realization dawned. "It's Saturday."

"Already handled." He couldn't hide the teasing tug at his mouth's corner

"I hope you weren't cruel."

"No cruelty. Just a bargain."

She studied him quietly, eyes narrowing just enough to ask the unspoken, but didn't press further.

He bent and kissed her, soft at first, then lingering just enough for her to melt into it. "She'll behave. I'm taking her to the market."

"Market?" The warmth in her eyes faded, just for a breath.

That flicker in her eyes, was it worry? Or just the weight they all still carried? "Since Father... It's time. I need to speak with Lydia and his other partners."

Her hand rose without hesitation, pressing flat against his chest. He placed his hand over hers, his fingers curling around hers with the quiet reverence she always seemed to deserve.

"Neda and I will manage here. Take your time."

"You are an incredible woman. Aphrodite smiled on me the day you agreed to be mine."

He pulled her close and kissed her fully now, not rushed. Not when the world had so recently taken too much.

"Go," she whispered, lips barely leaving his. "Before I change my mind and keep you all to myself."

He laughed quietly, brushing her temple with his mouth. Her affection steadied him more than anything else had in weeks. "I won't be long."

His hand slipped from hers at last. He turned back toward the kitchen, already searching for Shira.

The walk to the market carried the usual clamor, boots on paving stones, mule carts groaning, merchants calling out their wares with the same feigned urgency as always. Bronze coins clinked into open hands. Somewhere a child laughed, and a seller cursed a runaway goat. The city pulsed with its usual life, and yet Epaphroditus moved through it with a mind still too loud with grief.

Arriving at the market, he saw no signs of a new shipment of exiles. No frightened eyes watching from the edges of the steps, no auctioneer's cadence rising above the crowd.

He stepped between the columns, his eyes searching past linen merchants and spice dealers. Then he saw it, the unmistakable wash of deep purple, rich as wine and bold amid the browns and whites of lesser cloth. Lydia's stall stood like a banner, her dyed wool arranged with deliberate elegance.

She caught sight of him as he approached, offering a half-formed smile that didn't quite reach her eyes. "Epaphroditus, I didn't expect you today."

"I was hoping to catch you before you left for Thyatira again."

A soft laugh escaped her, and she shook off a stray lock of hair, smoothing the folds of cloth. "I had planned to. But I had a feeling someone might need me."

He hesitated, tugging slightly at the edge of his toga. "My father was deeply grateful for your friendship. And your partnership. I was hoping both might continue, with me in his place."

Her gaze softened. She held his eyes a moment longer than necessary before it shifted, curious, over his shoulder. "And who is this?"

"Shira." He stepped aside, gesturing to the young woman behind him.

Lydia looked her over with a familiarity that surprised him. A flicker of recognition passed across her face. "She's one of the ones from Rome."

"How can you tell?"

Lydia's lips twitched into something between amusement and sympathy. "I've never seen so many people look uncomfortable in a toga."

Shira's hands moved instinctively, tugging at the draped fabric.

Her discomfort was evident in every angle of her body, and yet he had missed it entirely. "She came with a tunic, but it was in tatters. Mother showed her how to wear the toga."

"The Jews prefer simpler dress," Lydia said with quiet certainty. "I have nothing suitable today… but, with your permission, I could make something for her. Something more fitting."

He looked at Shira. The hesitance in her posture still lingered, but he caught a flicker, just under the surface. Hope. The kind that didn't show itself often. "You have my permission."

Lydia lit up. "Wonderful. I already have the perfect design in mind."

"Nothing extravagant."

She waved him off. "I know their customs."

"You do?"

"I took their God as my own some years ago," she said, chin lifting with quiet conviction. Then she looked at Shira again before continuing. "In fact, I meet with a group of women by the river when the sun reaches its peak on this day."

"For what purpose?"

"Prayer." A softness filled her expression, the same warmth she'd turned toward Shira, as if the answer needed no further explanation. "It's been a comfort," she added, "especially with the influx of devotees we've had lately." Her gaze returned to Epaphroditus. "Shira would be welcome to join us. If you're willing."

Shira hadn't moved, but he noticed the shift in her stance, one foot angled forward, ready to step. She held herself back.

"I will consider it."

"We gather just beyond the Neapolis Gate." Lydia's voice remained gentle, even as her smile turned practical. "If you bring her there, I'll have a tunic ready for her."

He inclined his head, the gesture part gratitude, part retreat. "If you'll excuse us... I have more business to attend to."

They left the stall and moved through the crowded square together, the morning unfolding one slow conversation at a time. Merchants who had once dealt with his father greeted him with the weight of memory in their voices, some with firm clasps of forearms, others with subtle nods of mourning. Each offered condolences. Each swore loyalty.

By the time they wound their way back toward the heart of the market, the weight of the day had shifted, not lessened, but beginning to take on a shape he could carry. These choices would soon be his alone to make, whether or not he ever set foot on a ship again.

He glanced sideways at Shira. She hadn't spoken, but her face softened. Whatever passed between her and Lydia had soothed something in her. Her shoulders eased, no longer drawn so tight.

A small mercy. He'd take it.

Just ahead, a figure caught his eye. Tall. Broad-shouldered. A young man, not quite grown, but familiar.

He narrowed his gaze. The face tugged at his memory. But from where?

A friend loves at all times,
and a brother is born for adversity.
Proverbs 17:17

"Felix," the name slipped out while memories of the boy tumbled around Epaphroditus's mind.

He hadn't seen the boy since the day Felix's mother delivered payment to Luke the day after the accident. With careful strides to ensure Shira followed his pace, he approached him. "Felix?"

The boy's gaze shifted upward. "Yes?"

"You've grown," Epaphroditus remarked, taking in the changes in him.

Felix tilted his head to the side. "I'm sorry. Do we know each other?"

"Epaphroditus." He pointed to his chest. "The physician's friend who helped with your head wound."

"I remember now. I guess it's been a while."

"It's good to see you well," Epaphroditus noted, studying how Felix had filled out. "How's your mother?"

Felix's gaze dropped to the ground. "We lost her during the famine."

A sharp pang of sorrow struck Epaphroditus. "I'm sorry to hear that. She seemed like a kind woman."

"She sacrificed everything," Felix's voice wavered with a mixture of pride and sadness. "Gave me her portions so I could survive."

Epaphroditus nodded, understanding the sacrifice. "I lost family as well," he replied softly, the grief still lingering.

"I'm sorry," Felix murmured.

"Me too." Epaphroditus exhaled slowly, a weight pressing down on him. "How are you?"

"I started working with my uncle during the famine." Felix ran his hand through his hair, leaving a few locks askew.

Epaphroditus noticed the scar as Felix brushed his hair aside. He pointed to it. "That healed nicely."

Felix rubbed at the line. "Luke was right. My hair grew in to cover it."

"Luke is usually right about everything."

Felix chuckled lightly. "How's your sister?"

"Calliope? She's well."

"Good." Felix sighed. "I think about her sometimes. Does she still wear that veil?"

"Lydia's purple one?" Epaphroditus attempted to recall the last time he'd seen her wear it.

"Sometimes."

"She was quite striking in it."

"I think that's the reason she doesn't wear it often." He hesitated, lips pressing together as the reason came into focus. "She gets a lot of attention when she does."

"I'm sure she does." Felix's neck flushed.

The shift in Felix's demeanor said enough; it wasn't just friendly interest. "Why don't you join us tonight for the evening meal?"

Felix blinked, his shoulders drawing tight. "Truly?"

"We'd love the company," Epaphroditus said, trying to ease his nervousness. "I'll even invite Luke so he can see the fruit of his labor."

"Count me in."

Epaphroditus gave him careful directions to his villa and the time they would eat, then watched as Felix turned to leave.

Felix flicked his thumb over his shoulder. "I need to get back to my uncle."

"I look forward to seeing you tonight," he called after him.

With his business in the market complete, Epaphroditus stopped by Luke's house before returning home.

Bernice met them at the door, her grin radiant. "How is my favorite son-in-law?" She planted a kiss on each of his cheeks.

"I'm well," Epaphroditus responded, returning the gesture.

"And my daughter?"

"She's well, too."

Bernice's expression softened as she patted his forearm. "I've been praying for you. Losing so much family is hard. I'm glad Melody is there to aid you."

"She is a true blessing," he said proudly. "May I speak with Luke?"

"He's tending to a patient but should finish soon."

Luke appeared from deep within the house. A man followed him, clutching his bandaged hand to his chest.

"Come back in a few days," Luke said to the man as he saw him out the door. "I'll monitor that wound."

The man nodded and left, and Luke turned to Epaphroditus. "To what do I owe this visit?" he asked, flicking a brief look at Shira. "Pick another fight with an aedile?" He winked at her.

Shira ducked her gaze.

"Nothing like that," Epaphroditus answered quickly. "I've come to invite you to eat with us this evening."

"Any reason?"

"Does one need a reason to invite a friend to dine with them?"

"Sometimes."

"Actually, there is something."

Luke held up his finger. "I knew it."

"Guess who I ran into at the market today?"

"Lydia."

"Well, yes. But she's not who I'm talking about."

"Then who?"

"Felix."

Luke blinked several times, clearly surprised. "How is he?"

"Well. Though he lost his mother," Epaphroditus replied.

"Poor boy. It seems the only thing feasting during those years was the famine."

Epaphroditus hesitated before continuing, "The reason I'm here is that I've invited him to my home tonight, and I wanted you to join us."

"For what purpose?"

"I think he's interested in Calliope."

"Truly?"

Epaphroditus nodded. "He was just a boy when you stitched his head back together. Now... I see the look of a young man caught in a woman's pull."

Luke pulled his arms across his chest. "That would be something."

"I want you there tonight, to help put Felix at ease and to help me assess what kind of man he is. If he's interested in Calli, I want to be sure of him before I agree to anything. I trust your judgment."

Luke pinched his chin. "Don't you think it's too

soon for that kind of talk?"

Epaphroditus shook off the doubt. "Calli is nearly of marriageable age. I know Felix is a little older, but we both know how fleeting life is. Between famines, floods, and the gods' whims, it's a wonder any of us survive as long as we do."

"That's certainly true."

"He's been working with his uncle, learning a trade. If he's a good man who will work to provide for my sister, I want to move forward sooner rather than later."

Luke's nod came slowly, thoughtfully. "I would recommend you speak with Calli first. You don't want a repeat of your impulsiveness with Melody."

"That's excellent advice," Epaphroditus agreed.

"Then I'll be there tonight."

Epaphroditus bid farewell and returned home to seek Calliope.

In the kitchen, he found Neda and Calliope preparing for the evening meal. "Mother, we're expecting two guests tonight."

"Who?" Neda asked, looking up from her work.

"Luke and Felix," Epaphroditus replied, keeping his eyes on his sister.

Neda tilted her head, a flicker of confusion crossing her face. "Who's Felix?"

"You remember the boy Luke treated at the market, the one with the head wound?"

Calliope's hands faltered in their task, her

attention fully caught.

"I ran into him at the market today and invited him over." Epaphroditus paused. "I invited Luke as well, so he can see how the boy is doing."

"Then I'm glad you've returned with Shira." Neda placed a bowl down. "We'll need her help to prepare for guests."

Epaphroditus heard Shira's soft huff under her breath. "I'm sure she'll be happy to help," he said, casting a pointed glance at her.

Shira lowered her head, yielding.

"Calliope," Epaphroditus continued, his voice softening, "may I speak with you privately?"

"Not too long," Neda cautioned. "Shira, you can take over her tasks until she returns."

Shira approached and reached for the knife in Calliope's hand, but she held firm.

"Calliope," Epaphroditus called her.

"Coming." She relinquished the knife to Shira.

"I'll return her soon," he promised, leading his sister out of the kitchen.

In the open courtyard, he let his eyes drift upward toward the sky. "I think it will be a clear evening. We'll leave the doors open to enjoy the fresh air."

"Did you bring me out here to speak about the weather?" Calliope asked, arching her eyebrow.

"I did not," Epaphroditus chuckled, appreciating her directness. His honesty would flow more easily, given her blunt nature. "I brought you out here to talk about Felix."

She straightened. "What about him?"

"Do you remember him?"

"The boy whose blood soiled my veil?" She gazed toward the open doors. "Of course."

Epaphroditus heard a chill in her words but pressed on, "Do you find him disagreeable?"

"Disagreeable?" she echoed. "I hardly know him."

"Would you like to know him better?"

She shrugged.

"Well, he remembers you fondly." He let the words linger in the air, watching her closely. "I want to know if you'd ever consider a match."

"With someone I hardly know?"

"Calli." He placed his hand on her arm. "That's why I want him to visit. Give us all a chance to know him."

She pulled away and continued walking.

"Calliope." Epaphroditus caught up to her. "He said you were striking in your veil."

She fixed him with a sidelong look, eyes narrowing slightly.

"Wear it tonight," he said, stopping her. "Let him see you as you learn to see him. If you don't agree to the match, we won't move forward."

She sighed, exasperated. "I suppose one meal won't do any harm."

*And he found a Jew named Aquila, a
native of Pontus, recently come from
Italy with his wife Priscilla, because
Claudius had commanded all the Jews to
leave Rome.*
Acts 18:2

Epaphroditus greeted Luke and Felix as they
arrived, welcoming them into his home as Neda
placed the last vessels on the table. As requested, the
doors to the courtyard stood open, letting the crisp
evening air refresh the room.

"Please, make yourselves comfortable."
Epaphroditus gestured toward the table.

Felix, clearly pleased, reclined onto the
embroidered pillows. "Thank you for having me.
Everything looks amazing."

"Some family favorites," Epaphroditus said, a
gentle warmth softening his expression.

Luke scanned the offerings. "Minus the glis-glis,
I see."

Epaphroditus stifled a shudder. "Not tonight."

The stuffed field mouse had once been a regular on their table, especially during the mourning week after his father's death. Since then, he had banished the traditional dish. If he never saw another glis-glis, it would be too soon.

A soft, yet deliberate cough broke the moment.

Epaphroditus turned to see Calliope entering the room. Their mother had pleated her hair and pinned the purple veil in a way that not only complemented her face, but also highlighted her natural beauty.

Felix gasped and jumped to his feet, jostling the table in his haste. The clatter of dishes echoed through the room.

Epaphroditus shared a knowing glance with Luke before he turned back to take in the sight of his sister.

Calliope stood just inside the archway, framed by the flickering lamplight. The golden embroidery on her stola shimmered faintly in the glow. She looked every bit the daughter of their house, elegant, poised, and far too aware of the attention she commanded.

"You look... incredible," Felix managed, pulling at his toga as if to ease the tightness around his throat. "Will you be joining us?"

Epaphroditus did not show amusement, though inwardly, he approved. Good. Let the boy sweat a little.

"I invited her along with my wife and mother," Epaphroditus explained. Tonight, he wanted all eyes on the potential match. It was one of his most important arrangements, and he needed the counsel of those he trusted the most. "Join us, Calli."

She stepped onto the mosaic floor without hesitation, selecting a crimson cushion across from the men. Her movements were smooth and practiced, though her eyes flicked once toward Felix before she settled beside her mother.

Felix returned to his reclining position, but his attention never strayed far from her.

Neda took her seat next to Calliope. "Melody will join us shortly. I asked her to bring the pitcher of honeyed wine from the kitchen."

Almost as if summoned by name, Melody entered, raising the pitcher in greeting. She set it down on the table and made herself comfortable beside Calliope.

Epaphroditus offered a prayer to Aphrodite for health and prosperity, then gave thanks for the company at his table. As he made the first selection of olives, he invited the others to feast.

The conversation began lightly, with recent news and events flowing easily between them. It was the perfect setting for Epaphroditus to learn more about Felix. "So, my boy, you mentioned you work with your uncle. What does he do?"

"Works with wood, mostly," Felix replied with an eager brightness in his eyes. "He's been teaching me a lot. Says I'm getting pretty good at it."

"Do you come from a large family?" Neda asked.

"Oh, yes." Felix's head bobbed enthusiastically. "My father has many brothers. They all look out for me."

They moved on to dishes of oysters and saltfish, passing flatbread and jars of pickled herbs between them.

Neda shifted her attention to Luke. "How was your recent voyage?"

"Wonderful." Luke reached for a leg of boiled octopus, breaking it off with a sharp crack. "I received a summons to aid a friend's son. The boy had a raging fever that no one else could treat."

"Oh my." Neda's hand flew to her chest. "Were you able to help?"

Luke nodded. "I'm pleased to say he made a full recovery."

"He's lucky you were there," Neda remarked.

"I do what I can." Luke chewed thoughtfully, savoring the tough meat.

Shira emerged from the shadows beyond the dining circle to gather dishes. Her face was calm, but tension pulled at her shoulders.

Luke's gaze tracked her movements. "While I was away, I met a fascinating couple."

"Oh?" Neda leaned forward, intrigued.

"Yes," Luke said, his voice becoming more vibrant. "They were part of those exiled from Rome."

Shira froze at her task.

"It seems several of them follow a man from Nazareth," Luke continued, his tone loud enough to carry across the table.

Epaphroditus noted the subtle shift, like the change in air before a storm. He picked up an egg, turning it over in his fingers. "I've heard he's caused trouble for Rome, and his followers have been driven from the city."

Shira grabbed his cup and filled it, setting it down harder than necessary.

Epaphroditus caught her tense reaction, offering a quick, questioning look, but she moved away without acknowledging his silent inquiry.

Luke softened. "That's what some are saying. But this couple shared with me that the Nazarene's message is one of peace, not violence."

"Then why did he die a criminal's death?" Epaphroditus asked, his voice sharper than intended, as he wagged a piece of fish in his friend's direction. "And why did authorities exile his followers for their violent actions?"

"The couple explained to me that some have fought against Rome, even when others tried to guide them away from violence."

"And you believe them?" Epaphroditus leaned

back slightly, letting the words hang between them in silence.

"I've seen what people do when they're oppressed." Luke ran a hand through his hair. "People can only take so much before they break."

"It's still no excuse for violence," Epaphroditus retorted.

Luke met his gaze with a challenge in his eyes. "Have you forgotten that Rome was built on violence? Your own bloodline was forged on the battlefield in the name of Rome?"

Epaphroditus thought of his father, his uncles, his cousins, and his grandfathers, men who had bled for Rome's empire. "They were brave men who fought for freedom."

"Freedom often comes at someone else's expense," Luke mumbled.

The heat of the conversation burned in Epaphroditus's chest, and his face flushed. He didn't want this topic to continue, not here, not now. The discussion needed to shift, and he took control of the room. He turned his attention to Felix. "I invited you here tonight for a reason, Felix."

The young man swallowed hard.

"I know of your interest in my sister." Epaphroditus inclined his head toward Calliope. "I wanted her to see the man you've become and decide for herself if she would agree to a match with you."

Felix's eyes widened. "Me?" He touched his

chest. "I'd be honored." His gaze flicked to Calliope. "Truly, I would."

Calliope raised her chin slightly but remained silent, her gaze distant.

Epaphroditus made sure the rest of the evening passed without incident. The conversations remained light, though he continued to ask questions about Felix and his family. By the time they had finished the honeyed cakes, Epaphroditus was certain Felix would make a good match for his sister.

When the time came to bid Felix good night, he arranged plans to meet with the boy's family and secure the documents necessary for a betrothal. Felix and Calliope both needed a few more years to prepare for a life together, but this would set the plans in motion for when the time was right.

After seeing the young man out the door, Epaphroditus turned to find Luke waiting for him in a quieter corner of the room.

"Something you'd like to discuss?" Epaphroditus asked, folding his arms across his chest.

"There is," Luke replied.

"It's not about those Nazarene followers, is it?"

"No." Luke raised a hand in defense. "I wanted you to know I think Felix would make a good bridegroom for Calli."

Epaphroditus relaxed, a small sigh escaping his lips. "I agree."

Luke stepped closer, his gaze shifting. "I'd also like to extend an invitation."

"To what?"

"To sail with me to Troas."

"You've just returned from a voyage." A tightness gripped his chest before he even registered the thought, something wasn't right. Concern surged up, sharp and instinctive.

"And there was word waiting for me of another friend in need of aid in Troas. I'd like you to join me."

The image of a sinking boat flashed through Epaphroditus's mind. His heart raced in response. "I can't."

"Come now." He squeezed his shoulder. "It's barely a voyage."

Epaphroditus stepped away slightly, distancing himself from the offer. "You know I can't."

"The nightmare still haunts you?"

"Almost nightly." An icy shiver ran through him. "But it's not just a nightmare. A prophecy doesn't fade with the sun like a mere dream. It stays until it's fulfilled."

Luke's expression darkened with concern. "And this one will only be fulfilled with your death on a boat?"

"Across the Great Sea," Epaphroditus murmured, the vision of Arianna's wild eyes and blood-red lips flashing in his mind once more.

"Troas isn't across the Great Sea. It's barely across the Aegean," Luke argued, frustration creeping into his tone. "How are you going to keep your father's trade going if you never get on a boat?"

Epaphroditus wrestled with the question, the weight of it pressing down on him. Inheriting his father's connections, he kept the business running, but knew it wouldn't be enough. At some point, taking to the seas would become necessary.

Dropping his head, he muttered, "When do we sail?"

There shall come forth a shoot from the
stump of Jesse, and a branch from his
roots shall bear fruit...
In that day the root of Jesse, who shall
stand as a signal for the peoples—of him
shall the nations inquire, and his resting
place shall be glorious.
Isaiah 11:1, 10

Epaphroditus shifted the pack on his shoulder. Though it carried only a few days' supplies, its weight pressed down like a millstone. He spent the previous night tossing in his bed, each turn leading him deeper into one nightmare after another. His steps dragged, his energy sapped not just by lack of sleep, but by dread over what lay ahead.

Luke had instructed him to meet near the gate leading to Neapolis at dawn for their journey. Epaphroditus spent the hours before sunrise trying to concoct an excuse that would convince his friend to release him from his promise of accompanying him on this trip. But each excuse, no matter how elaborate, seemed to dissolve the moment he tried to speak it.

Luke waited at the gate, his eyes bright with anticipation. "Ready?"

"No," Epaphroditus muttered, his voice thick with reluctance.

Luke passed through the gate. "What better traveling companion than a physician?" He clapped Epaphroditus on the shoulder. "And you've got one who's been on more boats than I can count."

Epaphroditus noticed Luke was carrying two packs. He assumed one was for traveling supplies, and the other was his worn leather satchel that often held medical items. "You know, we could reach Troas by land."

"True," Luke said, walking ahead with a spring in his step. "But there's something about the sea. Plus, it's faster and less worry about thieves."

Epaphroditus snorted. "Sure, less worrying about thieves. But plenty of other things to worry about, shipwrecks, disease, starvation, getting lost at sea."

Luke chuckled. "Says the man who's sailed twice in his whole life."

"You don't need to feel the lion's teeth to know they're sharp."

The walk to Neapolis did little to revive Epaphroditus's waning energy. He tried to make conversation. "Why are you going to Troas?"

"There's a family there," Luke replied, his gaze fixed ahead. "One of their little girls has been very ill, and they can't figure out why."

"So, this is what you do when you're not in Philippi? Rescue the world?"

Luke lifted a shoulder in a half-shrug. "I try."

When the port at Neapolis finally came into view, Epaphroditus wasn't sure what prevailed, relief that his journey on foot had ended or anxiety that the one by boat was about to begin.

His stomach tightened seeing the vessel that would carry them. It was unimpressive, a plain ship built for transport, not for splendor. The waves rocked it gently. Only a few ropes tied to the dock and the anchor somewhere below kept it from drifting back into the sea.

Luke moved with confidence, his steps light as he made his way toward the ship.

Epaphroditus moved slowly, burdened not just by his pack but by memories of his last voyage. He hadn't set foot on a ship since he was ten, and that trip had been a struggle, leaving him with little desire to repeat the experience.

Luke held out his arm.

Epaphroditus took it, steadying himself.

"We won't be aboard long enough for you to get your sea legs," Luke explained, leading him onto the ship. "But it's a start."

Epaphroditus groaned inwardly. His steps were heavy, like a lamb led to slaughter.

"Have you eaten anything?" Luke asked suddenly, his tone shifting from friend to physician.

Epaphroditus shot him a glance. "Do I look that bad already?"

"Your color has faded," Luke observed.

Epaphroditus turned away, hiding his face from his friend's concerned gaze. "I didn't want to see the return of my meal while aboard this cursed vessel."

Luke exhaled. "Not wise, but I understand."

The crew shouted orders as they prepared the ship to sail, their voices a cacophony against the rhythm of the waves.

As the ship eased from port, Epaphroditus's empty stomach churned. He motioned toward one of Luke's bags. "Got anything in there to put me to sleep, so I don't have to endure this torture?"

"I've got everything I need in here to heal the sick or kill the body," Luke replied, patting his medical satchel. "The difference lies in the hands that wield it. But I'm afraid I only administer aid to those in genuine need." His gaze turned serious as he looked at Epaphroditus. "I think this trip will be good for you. It'll show you there's nothing to fear. Prophecy or not."

Epaphroditus shifted, a breath slipped out sharp and low. Discomfort prickled beneath his skin, unmistakable and impossible to hide.

"Besides," Luke added, "smooth seas don't make for skillful sailors. If you want to be a traveling merchant, you've got to get used to sailing."

The ship lurched, and Epaphroditus stumbled forward.

Luke caught him with surprising ease. "Let's find you somewhere to rest." He guided Epaphroditus to the side of the ship, where a stack of cargo provided a makeshift seat. "Here." He reached into his bag and pulled out a small sack. "Eat these."

Epaphroditus eyed the sack. "Medicinal berries for this storm in my gut?"

"Just plain almonds," Luke said with a laugh. "I don't recommend sailing on an empty stomach."

"Aphrodite recommended I not sail at all." He took a few almonds. "By the end of this trip, we'll see if you're a match for her."

Luke settled next to him, his eyes focused on the horizon. "Speaking of deities, there's something I want to talk to you about."

Epaphroditus popped an almond into his mouth, trying to quiet the war between hunger and nausea. He gestured for Luke to continue, focusing on each nut as he chewed slowly.

"The other night at your house," Luke began, his voice quieter now, "I was trying to share something about the couple I met on my recent trip."

"Not the Chrestus followers again,"

Epaphroditus muttered, his stomach twisting anew. "Is this the real reason you wanted me on a boat? So you could speak about them without me escaping? Or was it that I'd fling myself overboard and let Aphrodite finally have her way?" He rose and pushed himself toward the side, swaying worse than the boat.

Luke's eyes narrowed. "Sit down before you hurt yourself."

Epaphroditus managed to regain his seat. "I don't want to hear about them."

"You've made yourself clear," Luke said, his tone now sharp with frustration. "But I have more to say."

Epaphroditus rolled his eyes but relented, unwilling to repeat his threat to jump overboard. "Fine. If it matters that much, I owe you my ears."

Luke let out a heavy sigh, as if he'd been carrying the words he was about to say for months. "The couple I met,"—he glanced at the sea—"they have followed the man from Nazareth for several years. They shared his teachings, and I don't believe he would agree with the acts of violence some of his followers have committed in Rome."

Epaphroditus let curiosity take hold, his eyes fixed on his friend while he nibbled almonds and drank in every word.

"They spoke of prophecies concerning this man from Nazareth," Luke went on.

Epaphroditus's interest piqued despite himself.

"What kind of prophecies?"

"Where he would be born, what he would do for his people, and specific details about his life that they say he fulfilled." Luke gestured vaguely toward the sea. "The kind that spoke of him bringing peace, fulfilling ancient writings."

"And yet, they act violently?"

"Frustration," Luke answered, shaking his head. "He didn't come the way they expected. He didn't come to make war or establish a military kingdom. They say his kingdom is of another world, and his message was one of peace."

Epaphroditus frowned. "What does any of this have to do with you?"

"Everything." Luke's gaze locked onto his, and for a long moment, they both simply stared at each other. "The more they spoke, the more something burned inside me." He placed his hand to his chest. "I've worshipped every god known to Greece and Rome. It's always been cold, empty. But when they shared about Adonai and His Messiah... It was different. Something I can't explain with my education. For the first time, I felt a connection to something beyond myself."

Epaphroditus gave a low snort. "So, add this god to your family's collection."

"I don't think it's that simple."

Epaphroditus's mouth twitched with cynicism. "Sure it is. All deities want is sacrifices and entertainment, playing with our lives like children in the market."

Luke turned his gaze back to the waves, his voice soft but resolute. "I think this Adonai is different."

Epaphroditus stared at him, his mind spinning. "How different can any god really be?"

And when they had come up to Mysia,
they attempted to go into Bithynia, but
the Spirit of Jesus did not allow them. So,
passing by Mysia, they went down to
Troas.
Acts 16:7-8

After three days at sea, Epaphroditus nearly leapt for joy at the sight of Troas's port. His legs, unaccustomed to the ship's sway, threatened to buckle, and his stomach mirrored the sea's unrest. Only Luke's insistence had coaxed him to eat, an effort that led to several unfortunate returns.

When the ship finally docked, Epaphroditus rushed ashore, nearly tripping down the platform in his haste.

"Slow down," Luke called from behind. "I don't want to set a broken bone while we're here."

"The sooner I get my feet on solid ground, the better," Epaphroditus muttered, pushing through the crowd of disembarking passengers.

When his sandaled feet met dry earth, he paused, inhaling deeply.

Luke caught up, glancing sideways at him. "Feel better?"

He briefly considered kissing the ground until he imagined the countless sandals and hooves that had trampled it. "Much," he said instead, keeping his feet firmly planted.

"Let's keep moving." Luke lifted one of his packs to his shoulder. "I need to see my patient."

Epaphroditus fell into step beside him, his mind still wrestling with the memory of the ship's relentless sway.

As they wove through Troas' bustling streets, the city reminded him of Philippi, people of all shapes and sizes weaving in and out of the crowds, merchants shouting their wares, children darting through the throngs. Some walked with purpose, their steps sure; others drifted like boats without anchor or aim.

Luke, as always, walked with purpose, his determination clear in every step.

Epaphroditus followed, still unsure why his friend had insisted on bringing him.

They turned down several narrow streets before reaching a small stone dwelling. Luke called into an open archway, "Greetings to the owner of this house."

A little old woman appeared in the doorway,

her face lighting up at the sight of Luke, her wrinkles creasing with delight. "Luke!" she exclaimed and reached to pull his face close for her to kiss each of his cheeks.

"I'm here now, Judith." Luke straightened, brushing off her affectionate grasp. "Where's Shiloh?"

"Inside." She moved aside, gesturing for them to enter.

Luke stepped through the threshold first, then turned to Epaphroditus. "Judith, this is my friend, Epaphroditus."

"Greetings," Epaphroditus said, offering a dip of his head.

"Any friend of Luke's is welcome here," she said warmly, ushering him inside.

Epaphroditus stepped carefully into the dimly lit room, staying close to Luke.

In the corner lay a small girl, her tiny frame swathed in blankets of animal skins.

Luke moved quietly toward her and knelt at her side. "Greetings, Shiloh."

Epaphroditus lingered near the wall, careful not to intrude, though he caught every labored breath.

The girl stirred but did not speak.

Luke placed the back of his hand gently on her forehead. "Can you tell me how you're feeling?"

Epaphroditus caught the ragged pull of her breath, thin and uneven, but she stayed silent.

Luke lifted the edge of her blanket and pressed gently on her stomach. "Judith?"

The older woman came closer, her face lined with concern.

"Tell me what you know."

"The poor little thing's been suffering so." Judith clicked her tongue, her gaze sorrowful. "It all started with a headache. She said the room was moving when she stood still. She refused food sometimes, saying it burned her chest."

Luke hummed thoughtfully. "How are her bowel movements?"

"Loose."

"Vomiting?"

"Sometimes."

"Is it red?"

Judith nodded slowly.

Epaphroditus kept his eyes on the girl, noting the slight quiver in her limbs beneath the blankets.

Luke returned the blanket to its place and continued his examination, moving his hand slowly over the girl's face, studying her eyes.

Judith wrung a rag between her hands. "Do you know what's wrong with her?"

"Not yet," Luke answered, rising to his feet. "Where are her sisters?"

"Playing in the back."

Luke marched toward the back of the house, and Epaphroditus followed, unsure what else he could contribute.

Outside, three other girls of varying ages played together in the yard.

The resemblance was clear in the curve of their brows and the shape of their eyes. These girls shared blood with Shiloh.

"Luke?" called the oldest girl, noticing their approach.

The physician raised his hand. "Greetings."

"Luke!" the three girls chorused, rushing toward him, speaking all at once.

"Did you bring us anything?"

"Who's that man?"

"Are you here to fix Shiloh?"

"Enough." Luke lifted his hands to quiet them.

The girls fell silent, their eager faces expectant.

"This is my friend, Epaphroditus," Luke said, gesturing to him. "These are Shiloh's sisters, Esther, Naomi, and Meira." He pointed to each of them. "Girls, Shiloh is very sick. I need your help to make her better."

Esther spoke up, "What can we do?"

"Have any of you experienced any of the same sickness as Shiloh?" Luke asked.

Three heads of thick, dark hair shook in unison.

Luke held their gaze for a long moment. "Be honest now. Anything?"

The girls gave another quick refusal.

"Have you been playing anywhere new?" Luke

asked.

Esther and Naomi shook their heads.

Luke turned to the youngest, Meira, who stood frozen, her eyes downcast.

Epaphroditus watched as Luke crouched beside the child, who couldn't have seen more than four harvests.

"Meira,"—Luke placed his hands on his thighs and brought his face close to hers—"I need to know if you and Shiloh have been playing anywhere new."

Fear flared in Meira's eyes, her body stiffening as if bracing for something unseen.

"Can you show me?"

The little girl peered up through a veil of her dark hair and nodded, her small hand reaching for Luke's. She took hold of his fingers and led him toward the southern city gate, her tiny form pulling the physician behind her.

Epaphroditus moved in step with the other girls, their silent procession trailing just behind Luke.

Out of the city, Meira led them through patches of trees until they came to a small clearing.

Meria stopped. "Here."

"Good, Meira." Luke turned to Epaphroditus. "Spread out. Look for anything that might be dangerous."

"There are dozens of plants here." Epaphroditus gestured to the lush vegetation surrounding them.

"How are we supposed to figure out what's making her sick?"

"We'll have to try," Luke said, moving toward a cluster of flowers.

The three girls scattered through the meadow, each searching the thick foliage.

Epaphroditus ventured further from the center, scanning the trees and bushes. The variety of plant life overwhelmed him. How could he know which, if any, might be deadly in an area he'd never explored?

Dry grass crunched beneath their feet as they searched. The girls occasionally returned with plants, showing them to Luke, who examined each one but sent them back to seek more.

Then, further from the group, Epaphroditus spotted a familiar bush. Long, dark leaves framed white blooms, with ruby berries gleaming among them. He knew the plant instantly.

With a rush of urgency, he gathered a handful of fruit, flowers, and leaves and hurried back to Luke.

"Luke." He approached quickly. "Look at this."

Luke reached for the plant, but Epaphroditus pulled it back.

"Don't," he warned. "It's already burning my skin." He held up his hand, where a patch of red bloomed beneath the foliage.

Luke drew back. "What is it?"

"Daphne," Epaphroditus said, inspecting the plant. "At least, I think so. It's very toxic. Every part of it can harm."

"It can also be used to heal," Luke muttered, leaning in to look again. "But if you're right, we need to get back to Shiloh. This plant should have stolen her life days ago." He whistled sharply, calling the three girls back to him. "Meira."

The youngest girl approached him.

Luke pointed at Epaphroditus's hand. "Did Shiloh eat any of this?"

Epaphroditus angled it downward so she could see clearly, careful to keep it just beyond her grasp.

Meira's eyes darted between Luke and her feet.

"Meira." Luke crouched. "This is very important. Did Shiloh eat this?"

She nodded, eyes dropping to the dirt. "I put some in her tea," she admitted quietly. "She said she liked it."

"How much did you give her?"

"Only a little, Luke. I promise."

Luke glanced at Epaphroditus, concern etched across his face. He turned back to Meira. "How many times did you make your special tea for Shiloh?"

Meira hesitated, then whispered, "When she started getting the headaches, I made her more to help her feel better."

Luke exhaled slowly. "Thank you for being honest." He rose to his feet. "Let's get back."

They hurried back through the trees and into the city.

Once inside the house, Luke immediately gathered his medical supplies.

Judith rushed into the room from the back. "Any news?"

"We think we might know what's causing the illness." Luke continued rummaging through his medical bag. "Could you boil some fresh water?"

Judith nodded and hurried to obey.

Epaphroditus returned to his position beside Shiloh, his gaze never leaving Luke as he worked with careful precision. "Do you think you can save her?"

Luke set a few items down near Shiloh. "She's had too much of it. I pray we're not too late."

Judith returned with a bowl of hot water.

Luke took it from her, adding a few drops of oil. "Snowdrop," he explained. "I hope it'll counteract the Daphne."

"Daphne!" Judith gasped. "Where did she get that?"

"She and Meira found it outside the city," Luke replied, stirring the mixture. "Meira's been giving it to her. That's why she's gotten worse."

Judith set her fists on her hips. "Oh, that girl."

"She didn't know," Luke defended. "But you might want to speak with all of them about eating things they don't recognize."

Judith stormed out, muttering under her breath.

Epaphroditus kept his eyes fixed on Luke's careful movements as he raised Shiloh's head and brought the bowl to her lips.

"Shiloh," he whispered, his tone soft yet insistent. "I need you to drink this."

The girl groaned, a weak sound that barely escaped her throat, and then, with an almost imperceptible shift, she parted her lips just enough for Luke to coax the liquid inside.

Epaphroditus held his breath, his chest tightening with every passing second. His heart pounded in his ears, every beat an echo of the tension that twisted inside him, watching the fragile exchange between them. All he could do was plead with every god he knew, including Luke's strange new deity.

*And a vision appeared to Paul in the
night: a man of Macedonia was
standing there, urging him and saying,
"Come over to Macedonia and help us."*
Acts 16:9

Luke poured the mixture into Shiloh's mouth, a little at a time, until the bowl was empty.

Epaphroditus knelt beside them, his gaze fixed on the frail girl. "What else can you do?"

Luke set the empty bowl aside and returned several items to his bag. "Now, we wait. All we can do is see how she responds."

Epaphroditus watched her closely. Her face was as pale as a sheer veil. Sweat clung to her brow, and she still trembled, as if caught in a winter chill only she could sense.

"Let me see your hand," Luke ordered suddenly.

Epaphroditus blinked. He'd completely forgotten about the toxic plant burning his hand.

Luke held out a rag. "Here."

"Are you mad?" Epaphroditus glared at his friend. "You want to keep it?"

"It holds as much medicinal purpose as it does poison." Luke lifted the linen.

"If you say so." Epaphroditus wiped the crushed plant onto the cloth.

Luke carefully folded the rag and tucked it into his bag.

Epaphroditus held out his open hand, inspecting the damage caused by mere moments of contact with the plant.

Reaching for his hand, he inspected the burn and muttered, "Not bad. I'll mix up a salve."

Epaphroditus kept his focus on Shiloh, surrendering to Luke's ministrations, though the sting in his hand gnawed at him.

After slathering the paste across his palm, Luke wrapped a fresh linen around Epaphroditus's hand. "That should do it."

Epaphroditus cradled his freshly bandaged hand close to his chest. "When will we know if she makes it?"

"Soon," Luke said, settling himself on the floor with a sigh. "If the Snowdrop works, it'll counteract the poison. But if we're too late…"

The room fell silent, save for the soft breathing of the girl.

A little while later, Judith returned, her face lined with worry. "I reminded the others to stay away from plants they don't recognize. Poor Meira is beside herself. Any change?"

Luke placed a hand on Shiloh's forehead. "At least she doesn't seem to be worse."

"Her color's a little better," Epaphroditus offered.

Luke's expression brightened, his tone teasing. "Well now, look who's caring for our patient."

Epaphroditus grinned, though his heart was still heavy with concern.

Judith sank to Shiloh's feet. "I should've asked that new teacher to come pray over her."

Luke's interest piqued. "Teacher?"

"A man from Tarsus," Judith replied, leaning back on her heels. "He spoke in the synagogue the other day. Shared about the Nazarene."

Epaphroditus's mouth twitched with surprise. "You're Jewish?"

Judith arched one silver brow at him. "Is that a problem?"

"No." Epaphroditus raised his hands in surrender. "I just haven't met many."

"He doesn't get out much," Luke added with a smirk.

"I see," she said, eyeing Epaphroditus with amusement. "The teacher is still in the city. They're letting him speak again."

"Savta," Shiloh groaned, her voice barely a whisper.

"Shiloh!" Judith rushed to her granddaughter's side, crawling toward her head. "I'm here."

"Savta," Shiloh repeated, her voice cracking.

"I'm here, child." Judith kissed her forehead, her voice a soothing murmur. "I'm here."

Luke's expression softened with quiet satisfaction.

"Praise Adonai," Judith said softly, lifting her face toward the ceiling as she held Shiloh tightly to her chest.

Luke rose to his feet and motioned for Epaphroditus to follow him.

They stepped to the far side of the room, away from the pair.

"I think she'll recover," Luke said, keeping a watchful eye on the girl. "I'd like to stay a day or two longer, just to be sure."

"Of course you're staying," Judith called from her place. "We're holding a feast in your honor."

Luke waved his hands dismissively. "That's not necessary."

"It most certainly is." Judith gently brushed Shiloh's damp hair away from her face. "You gave us our girl back." She smothered her with kisses, her eyes brimming with gratitude.

For the next several hours, the small home was alive with activity. The three girls helped their mother and grandmother prepare a lavish meal, while Epaphroditus and Luke shared stories from their travels and recounted the tale of the toxic plant with their father, Ichabod.

"I can't thank you enough," Ichabod said, his voice thick with emotion as he looked at Shiloh, now propped up against the wall. "I don't know what I would have done if we'd lost her." His gaze softened as he watched his daughter. "She brings so much joy to our family."

"I'm glad I made it in time." Luke lowered his head, humbled. "I came as soon as I received your message, but I had been away. If I'd stayed longer, it might have been too late."

"And you"—Ichabod pointed a large finger at Epaphroditus—"you discovered the plant."

"I'm no physician." Epaphroditus clapped Luke on the back. "This man is the true healer."

"I might not have recognized the plant on my own," Luke admitted, pushing a large platter of fish toward Epaphroditus. "I'm glad you came along."

"I am as well." Epaphroditus piled pieces of fish into his bowl, his appetite stirring as relief washed through him.

Luke turned back to Ichabod. "Judith mentioned a new teacher at your synagogue. What do you know about him?"

"Not much." Ichabod stuffed an egg into his mouth, chewing thoroughly before continuing. "He mostly spoke of the Nazarene and told us about his travels. He claimed to be traveling from Phrygia and

Galatia, explaining that he wanted to go east but was prevented from doing so. Then, he went to Mysia, attempted entry into Bithynia, but was again prevented from entering."

"Did he say what prevented him?" Luke asked, leaning forward.

Ichabod's shoulders dipped in a slight shrug. "Nothing that I understood. Whatever it was, it led him here to Troas." He reached for another egg. "He's supposed to be speaking again, if you want to hear him for yourself."

Luke fixed his eyes on Epaphroditus, curiosity flickering in his gaze.

"We really should get back to Philippi," Epaphroditus countered. "I can't be away too long."

Luke's countenance fell, disappointment flickering across his face.

Epaphroditus glanced toward Shiloh. Her health had improved over the past few hours, though she still looked weak. "But if the man speaks while you're tending to Shiloh, it wouldn't hurt to attend."

A grin spread across Luke's face at the suggestion.

Ichabod leaned over, digging into the platter of fish. "I'm sure he will."

That night, Epaphroditus tossed on a borrowed reed mat, haunted by images of sea and wreckage. He woke with a start, clutching his chest. His heart hammered in his ribcage, and sweat dampened his hair.

"Another nightmare?" Luke's voice came softly from the dark.

"Luke?" Epaphroditus whispered, his voice hoarse.

"I got up to check on Shiloh," Luke replied, moving closer so Epaphroditus could see him in the dim light of a single oil lamp.

Epaphroditus ran a shaking hand through his damp hair. "How is she?"

"Better." Luke settled next to him, his voice calm. "What did you dream about?"

Flashes of gray waves and jagged pieces of wood filled Epaphroditus's mind. He winced at the familiar nightmare. "Same thing I always dream about. My death aboard a boat."

"Do you take stock in dreams?"

Epaphroditus grimaced.

"I guess you're not the right person to ask," Luke said, glancing at Shiloh's peaceful form across the room. "I had a dream, too."

Epaphroditus fought a yawn. "What was yours?"

"I dreamt I found the teacher. The one they told us about. I begged him to come to Philippi."

"Why would you do that?"

"So he could share about the Nazarene," Luke said, his voice quiet.

"If he came, do you think they'd listen?"

Luke shrugged, his expression thoughtful. "Don't know." He picked at his tunic. "Do you think he'd come?"

"The teacher?" Epaphroditus hesitated before answering. "By Ichabod's account, he seems to travel a lot. He might."

Luke's gaze held a spark of hope. "That's my prayer tonight." His voice dropped, almost a whisper. "I pray he comes to Philippi, and they listen to his message about the Nazarene."

Epaphroditus lay back down, his thoughts drifting. The family had shared their faith in Adonai during the meager feast, and Luke had asked many questions. Epaphroditus listened, but to him, the god of the Jews didn't seem much different from Aphrodite or any other Roman deity.

He stretched and yawned, settling back onto the woven reed mat. He'd indulge Luke's wish to hear the teacher and ensure Shiloh was well enough, and then, perhaps, he could return home and leave the sea behind him once more.

And when Paul had seen the vision,
immediately we sought to go on into
Macedonia, concluding that God had
called us to preach the gospel to them.
Acts 16:10

Sunlight broke over the horizon, heralding a new day Epaphroditus was not yet ready to face. The familiar nightmare, dark waves swallowing the ship whole, the cold saltwater filling his lungs as he struggled to stay afloat, the endless sky blurring into a void, fractured his sleep. Each time, the terror of drowning pressed down with unbearable weight, a shadow clinging to him long after waking. He awoke to the sounds of Luke tending to Shiloh.

The faint scent of crushed herbs lingered in the air, mingling with the damp earthiness that rose beneath the soft morning light filtering through the small window. Outside, the distant clatter of carts echoed through the narrow streets. Inside, the soft sounds of footsteps.

Epaphroditus scanned the room, his eyes falling on the young girl. She sat propped against the wall, sipping from a bowl that quivered in her hands. Her color was returning, though every movement still carried fragility. He rolled up his mat and leaned it against the wall.

Luke stood and crossed to him. "All is well," he said, voice calm but certain. "With a few more days' rest, Shiloh will be back to her games and chores."

"Both would be a blessing." Judith's eyes lingered on Shiloh as she swept stray reed pieces from where he'd slept. "Don't know what troubles you, young man, but it looks like you wrestled a pig in here."

"Forgive me," Epaphroditus muttered, hearing his grandmother's rebukes echo in her tone. "I didn't mean to add to your chores."

"Don't fret over me." Judith swept with practiced ease. "I'd sweep every house in this city if it meant Shiloh's return to health."

Luke chuckled. "Fortunately for you, that is not my fee."

Judith brushed dirt out of the front door, then moved on to another task.

Luke turned back to him, humor gone. "Ready to meet the teacher?"

He lingered a moment longer, the weight of responsibility pressing heavily against his chest. What if she faltered while they were gone?

"She'll be fine," Luke assured him, his voice calm. "I wouldn't leave her if I thought otherwise."

He nodded, reluctant, and followed Luke through the bustling streets toward the synagogue.

The building was nothing like the grand temples Epaphroditus had seen in Greece and Rome. It was small and unremarkable. Stone walls gave the place sturdiness, but there was nothing magnificent about it. The central room was bare except for a tall wooden cabinet behind a raised platform, and stone seating arranged in steps along three of the four walls. No altars, no statues, no priests, nothing to mark it as holy.

Epaphroditus frowned. Had Luke brought them to the wrong place? Surely no god would choose to visit this humble dwelling.

The gathering was small, a mix of Jews and God-fearing Greeks, their warm greetings creating an air of comfort. They moved to find seats, and Luke lifted his chin. "Let's sit at the top. Give the lower seats to those in need."

Epaphroditus agreed and followed Luke up the steps.

As they settled onto the stone, Epaphroditus continued his assessment of the synagogue. More theater than temple, it held no signs of divine presence. The center platform resembled a stage more than an altar. The only furniture aside from the cabinet was a stone chair with a high back and a small table.

A man stepped forward to lead the assembly in a simple song. Epaphroditus struggled to match the tune. The melody was joyous, though he did not understand the words. Yet, the emotional response was unmistakable. Some people wept openly, others raised their hands in praise, while others clapped in rhythm. Despite not recognizing the tune, he recognized worship when he saw it.

When the song ended, the man offered a modest prayer and introduced the traveling teacher, whom he called Paul.

Epaphroditus watched as a short, stocky man wearing a simple tunic shuffled toward the stage. In stark contrast to the speakers he'd seen in the Forum at Philippi, whose proud demeanor and imposing stature shouted authority before they even spoke, this man was quiet and humble. He appeared less a teacher and more a merchant, out of place on such a platform.

Another man retrieved a large scroll from the wooden cabinet and placed it on the table beside the stage.

Paul unrolled the scroll and began reading aloud.

Epaphroditus was relieved to hear the reading was in Greek, though it may as well have been Aramaic for how little he grasped. The words blurred together, and he struggled to keep up.

Once the scroll was returned to its place, Paul sat in the high-back chair and began his teaching.

Epaphroditus leaned forward, straining to grasp the meaning of the man's words. Paul's words piled deliberately and sharply, each idea building on the last. When someone from the crowd asked a question, the teacher answered swiftly, with a clarity that cut through the confusion. Epaphroditus prided himself on being able to keep up with the brilliant thinkers of his city, but he believed this little Jew could talk circles around even those academic giants.

As Paul spoke, something stirred inside Epaphroditus, unfamiliar and unsettling, as if the words were reaching into a dormant part of his soul. He glanced sideways at Luke to gauge his reaction. Luke, ever the patient listener, seemed to absorb every word.

Returning his attention to Paul, Epaphroditus found the teacher had paused, his eyes locking onto Epaphroditus's. For a fleeting moment, Epaphroditus wondered if he had missed something in the lecture, but the sharp intensity in Paul's gaze unsettled him, as if the man perceived something beyond the walls.

Shaking off whatever troubled him, Paul continued speaking, his words once again flowing like a rushing river. Epaphroditus, overwhelmed, stopped trying to follow the logic and instead let the words wash over him. Something still stirred within him, as if attempting to rise from a deep slumber.

When Paul finished, the man who had led the song came forward to offer another prayer, dismissing the assembly.

As the meeting broke, Epaphroditus's mind churned with fragments of the lesson.

Luke rose at once, hurrying to speak with Paul.

Epaphroditus rose more slowly, caught in the tide of people moving toward the exit. Some were eager to leave, while others swarmed around the stage, seeking to speak with the teacher. He lingered, watching Luke wait among the crowd.

By the time Luke reached Paul, the collection had thinned enough for Epaphroditus to move closer.

"That was a wonderful speech," Luke exclaimed, wide-eyed, as if greeting royalty.

Epaphroditus noticed Paul's confused expression.

"What's your name?" Paul asked.

"I'm called Luke," he replied, gesturing toward Epaphroditus. "My friend and I traveled from Philippi."

"Macedonia," Paul said, not as a question, but as a fact.

Luke hesitated. Even Epaphroditus noticed the peculiar certainty in Paul's voice.

"I had a dream last night," Paul continued, taking a step closer, his voice taking on a strange tone. "You came to me. I wasn't sure if it was a dream or a vision, but you came to me and pleaded, 'Come over to Macedonia and help us.' As clear as you are standing here now."

A chill settled in his chest, heavy and immovable. He saw Luke's face pale at the words.

"How did you know that's what I was going to ask?" Luke murmured.

"I didn't," Paul answered, spreading his hands in explanation. "I recognized you while I was teaching."

"What does this mean?" Luke asked, his voice barely above a whisper.

"It means I must gather my companions." Paul stepped off the platform. "We must go to Macedonia."

Luke stepped back, confusion and excitement battling in his expression. "You're coming to Philippi?"

"This is a sign from Adonai." Paul's calm resolve filled the room. "I must walk through the door He opens."

Epaphroditus closed the space between himself and Luke, his mind swirling.

Luke turned to him. "Did you hear that? Paul's coming to Philippi."

Epaphroditus stared after him, his heart still pounding. "What about Shiloh?"

"She will make a full recovery," Luke assured him. "But we don't know how long Paul will stay in

Philippi. We should go ahead and prepare for them."

Epaphroditus weighed the words for a moment before nodding. "If you're sure Shiloh will return to full health in our absence, I'm ready to go home. As soon as we can find a boat."

*So, setting sail from Troas, we made a
direct voyage to Samothrace, and the
following day to Neapolis,*
Acts 16:11

As Epaphroditus followed Luke into Ichabod's
home, the three girls swarmed them with eager
questions: "Did you meet Paul?" "What song did you
sing?"

Luke lifted his palms. "One at a time."

The girls quieted, their wide eyes fixed on him.

"Where's your father?" Luke asked.

"He's at the market," Esther said. "He'll be back
soon."

"And your savta?"

"I'll get her." Naomi scampered off.

"Are you leaving us?" Meira asked, her voice
barely above a whisper.

Luke knelt beside her. "What makes you think
that?"

She raised her finger. "Your eyes are all sparkly.

Other people had eyes like that after hearing the teacher. Then they left."

Epaphroditus blinked. She was right. There was a brightness in Luke that he hadn't seen before.

"Yes, Meira. We're leaving," Luke said, glancing at Shiloh. "The teacher wants to visit our home."

"Will he talk there too?"

"I hope so."

"He talks a lot," Meira said, seriousness edging her tone.

Epaphroditus hid a chuckle.

Luke tousled her hair. "He sure does."

"But his words are nice. I like them."

"So do I," Luke replied. "Have you been taking care of your sister?" He moved toward Shiloh.

"Yes." Meira trailed behind him.

"No more special teas, though, right?"

She stopped, head bowed. "Right."

Epaphroditus followed them, watching as Luke checked on his patient.

Warmth returned to her skin, and her breath steadied. Mere days before, she had hovered near death. Now, she seemed nearly well again.

He studied Luke, not just a healer, but something more. No wonder he traveled so often. His gift needed to be shared. People needed him.

After their farewells and a few last instructions, they left for the port.

Luke hurried ahead to confirm their vessel.

Epaphroditus scanned the harbor, his gaze drifting over the organized chaos that pulsed along the waterfront. Salt encrusted the ropes coiled neatly beside weathered posts, and the planks beneath his sandals were slick with seaweed and the greasy remains of gutted fish. The inaudible murmur of voices mingled with the creak of rigging and the distant clang of hammers. Children darted between barrels and crates, their laughter brief and bright, cutting through the briny air like gull cries.

The sun pressed warm against the back of his neck, yet a chill threaded through his bones, a warning, perhaps, or just the sea's breath. He set his jaw, trying to ignore the familiar knot tightening in his stomach.

As they approached the ships, his unease deepened. With every step, old memories rose like storm swells: the violent heave of waves, the helpless lurch of a deck beneath his feet. The air reeked of salt and tar, sharp with fish and sweat and fear. Sailors shouted over the groan of timber and the slap of ropes. Seagulls wheeled overhead, their cries cutting through the noise and setting his teeth on edge.

He reached out, fingers brushing the coarse rope stretched along the dock. Sunlight glinted off the water's restless surface. A cold spray caught his cheek.

Epaphroditus scratched his palm, where the

wound still itched.

"I wouldn't do that," Luke said, gentle but firm.

Epaphroditus froze mid-scratch.

"You don't want that reopening at sea." Luke lifted the bandage to check. "Boats are filthy."

"If the voyage kills me, it won't matter."

"Then I'll refuse to treat you for not listening." Luke lowered the bandage, shooting him a pointed look.

They boarded a simple ship and found a spot to settle while the crew prepared to depart. Even in the calm port, the ship rocked, and Epaphroditus's stomach churned.

"I'll give you something for your stomach once we get out to sea," Luke promised.

"Now I'm worthy?"

"You were worthy before." Luke gave him a sideways glance. "But I didn't know what I'd be facing with Shiloh. I knew you'd survive an upset stomach. I didn't know she'd survive whatever was making her sick."

"That's fair." Epaphroditus propped an arm on the railing. "You were inspiring. The way you handled her situation, and the whole family..."

"Lots of practice," Luke said, eyes on the sea. "With illnesses and emotions."

Epaphroditus hesitated. "I don't think I've ever told you this, but I'm amazed by what you do."

Luke's eyes glinted with a touch of humor. "I

was beginning to think you never would."

"Well, I should." Epaphroditus exhaled. "People like Felix and Shiloh, they wouldn't be here if not for you."

"I'm happy to help." Luke's gaze softened as he turned to Epaphroditus. "I feel led to."

He nodded. The same pull, whatever had gripped him when Paul spoke, rose again.

With preparations complete, the ship sailed out of port, heading into the waters of the Aegean Sea. True to his word, Luke provided a remedy for Epaphroditus's stomach troubles.

The day passed more peacefully than Epaphroditus had dared hope. Luke's remedy kept the worst of the seasickness at bay, allowing him to eat, move, and even hold a conversation without gripping the rail for dear life. Freed from the grip of nausea, he and Luke often returned to Paul's words, turning them over, puzzling through them like stones pulled from the depths. To Epaphroditus's relief, Luke had found the message as cryptic as he had.

The ship rocked gently beneath them, its rhythm steady and almost lulling. Golden light spilled across the waves, painting the sea in molten blue and silver. They sat shoulder to shoulder, speaking in quiet tones as wind and water wrapped around them. The air carried the scent of salt and sun-warmed wood, touched faintly by the sharp, earthy trace of herbs from Luke's bag. For a while, the ocean no longer loomed like a threat, it became something vast but knowable.

On the second day, the sea changed.

As they neared the island of Samothrace, the sky dimmed, pale blue bleeding into sullen gray. Clouds gathered in thick, coiling layers, and the wind sharpened into something mean and alive. It tore at loose tunics, snapped ropes taut, and shrieked through the rigging like a curse. Thunder rumbled low, distant at first, then closer, deeper, shaking the air before crashing waves slammed against the hull with growing force.

Salt spray struck Epaphroditus's face, sharp as glass. He tasted it on his lips. His breath turned shallow, chest tight, as the world tilted and groaned around him. The crew's shouts rose above the wind, barked commands swallowed by the storm's fury. The sails flailed, ropes snapped, and the sea raged.

Epaphroditus gripped the railing with both hands, knuckles white. The ship pitched violently beneath his feet, and with it came the old fear, cold, breathless, consuming. A lifetime of nightmares closed in around him, suffocating, inescapable, like shadows that had always been there, just waiting to attack.

"Stay here!" Luke shouted over the wind. "I'm going to find the captain."

Epaphroditus obeyed. Not even Luke's remedies

could calm the tempest within him.

The ship lurched in the other direction, its hull groaning as waves crashed over the sides in relentless succession. Sailors darted across the slick deck, slipping and shouting, their movements urgent and chaotic. They tugged at sodden ropes, reefed the sails, and lashed down loose cargo as seawater drenched them from all sides.

What began as shouted orders soon dissolved into something more primal. Barked commands gave way to panicked cries, some to each other, others cast skyward in desperate appeal to whatever god might hear above the wind.

The storm showed no mercy. Despite every effort, the vessel was being driven toward the shore, helpless against the combined force of sea and wind.

Salt water sprayed over Epaphroditus, soaking his hand and stinging his wound. He braced himself against the side of the ship as another wave surged over him.

He heard a voice, strange above the din, shout, "Hold steady!"

It was the last thing he heard before a wave engulfed him. The force of it hurled him from the deck, and the world went silent.

Cold darkness swallowed him whole, the crushing pressure coming from every side as sounds turned muted and distant. Salt burned his eyes and filled his mouth, choking him. Limbs grew heavy, numb as if weighted with lead. A choking silence pulled him deeper into the abyss.

Panic set in as unseen hands seemed to drag him deeper. Pieces of the ship sliced around him in the dark blue. No matter how hard he flailed, he made no progress toward the light that seemed to come from the wrong direction.

Every instinct screamed for him to open his mouth and gulp in air, but he held onto what little breath he had left.

Bubbles escaped his lips, and he fought to keep his body moving, but the water seemed to hold him captive, pulling him farther from life.

As the blackness crept in, the voice of Arianna echoed in his thoughts. *Your life will be Aphrodite's fee.*

He fought to hold his breath. Then the darkness claimed him.

*The Lord once called you 'a green olive
tree, beautiful with good fruit.' But with
the roar of a great tempest he will set
fire to it, and its branches will be
consumed.*
Jeremiah 11:16

Fingers clamped around Epaphroditus's arm,
wrenching him from the brink. Light pierced the
blur as his lids snapped apart. Above him, Luke's
face, eyes stretched wide with terror.

Then the pull, upward, relentless. Luke dragged
him toward the light.

He kicked, every limb seizing with panic, his
chest cinched tight, throat raw.

Then they broke the surface. Air hit him like
fire. He coughed, choked, and sucked in another
breath.

"Swim!" Luke's voice cracked through the chaos
as he turned and struck out toward land.

Each flailing stroke dragged him forward, a

clumsy echo of Luke's sure pace. He had never learned to navigate the water, he'd never had to. Now he cursed the oversight.

The sea clawed at him, each pull a promise to drag him under. Luke cut through the water ahead, fluid and fast, as if Poseidon himself had granted him favor. Stroke by stroke, Luke surged toward shore. But for Epaphroditus, every motion was a struggle, his arms heavy, his legs slow, each breath a desperate fight against the drag of the deep. The water clawed at him, relentless, trying to claim him for good. Would Aphrodite finally have her fee?

Luke stood waiting in the shallows, arm outstretched, refusing to let him go under.

Epaphroditus clawed through the last stretch, limbs screaming, vision tunneling. Luke's grip found him again and hauled him the last few steps to solid ground.

He hit the shore face-first, hacking seawater from his lungs, the sand biting his lips. Each gasp scraped like broken glass down his throat. Air. Too sharp, too bright, too much. His chest burned, his body wracked with coughs, but he was alive. Just barely.

"On your knees," Luke ordered.

He didn't know if he had anything left. Every muscle cried and twitched with exhaustion. Even lifting his head was impossible. The sand shifted beneath him, pulling him sideways with every breath.

Luke slammed his palm between Epaphroditus's shoulders. He jolted forward, a raw, animal sound tearing from his throat as more seawater erupted from his lungs. The coughing came from somewhere deeper than his body, somewhere panicked and desperate. Luke struck again. And again. Each blow wrenched the air from him, left him gasping and shuddering, the world spinning at the edges.

When the convulsions subsided, his limbs sagged. He dropped face-first, too weak to lift his head.

Warmth licked his skin, jarring after the frigid grip of the sea. But the ache inside him ran too deep for comfort.

"Rest," Luke said from above, his voice thinner now, as if pulled into the wind. "I'm going to check on the other survivors."

Epaphroditus's eyes fluttered shut, the weight of his body sinking deeper into the warm sand cradling him. Sound and light dissolved together, leaving only the pull of darkness.

The world blurred at the edges, slipping away in fragments. The rough press of sand against his cheek was the last thing he could hold on to. Somewhere beyond the haze, Luke's footsteps faded, distant and hollow. Then even that was gone.

When he woke, the sun had fled, and the

shadows fell in new directions. Time had slipped without him. The sun no longer hung where it had been, and the world around him had shifted. The crash of waves was gone, replaced by the murmur of voices nearby, soft, careful, as if spoken in reverence or fear.

He was no longer on the shore.

The gritty sting of sand was gone, his clothes no longer wet or clinging to his skin. Something soft cradled his body now, and the air was still. He lay cocooned in unfamiliar calm, only a thin veil separating him from the quiet conversation in the next room.

A cough tore through him, deep and raw, shaking his ribs. Before he could draw another breath, Luke appeared suddenly beside him.

His eyes softened, but the hollows beneath them told the rest. Still, his voice came light, almost teasing. "He lives," Luke declared, kneeling next to him.

Epaphroditus managed only a glare, his voice absent.

Luke, unperturbed, placed an ear to his chest, listening intently. "It was lucky for you I left you on deck," he said, voice low. "Some others below... they weren't so lucky."

The words landed hard. Epaphroditus turned his face away, bile rising at the thought of the crew and other passengers below deck. A cold shiver crept down his spine, as though death itself had brushed past him. The warmth of Luke's hand on his shoulder was the only thing that grounded him.

"Some people at the port saw our plight," Luke continued, but there was an effort in it, a careful strain to keep the words light. "They rushed to help the ones who could make it to shore. We're staying with the family of one of the men until you're well."

Epaphroditus opened his mouth, but words wouldn't come. Instead, a strangled croak escaped his throat, a sound so foreign to him that it seemed to belong to someone or something else.

"Rest." Luke's hand was firm on his shoulder, urging him back down. "I'll be right back."

Luke's absence left a quiet in its wake, and Epaphroditus's mind raced. He could hear murmured voices outside, but none of them were familiar. What had happened to the others? How many survived? How many had... not made it?

Epaphroditus tried to focus, but the tightness in his throat made it impossible to concentrate. His mind drifted to Philippi, the olive groves, the rhythm of soil and sun. A world too far now. He longed for the calm of that life, the stability of the familiar. Instead, he was here, in a foreign place, with his life hanging by a thread.

Luke returned with a stone cup. "Drink this," he said simply, handing it to him.

Epaphroditus hesitated, the heat from the cup

seeping into his skin as he accepted it. Steam curled from the surface, the liquid inside glinting dark gold. A syrupy sweetness hung in the air, unnatural, almost sticky. He raised it to his lips, but the aroma alone made his stomach lurch. Still, he managed a small sip, and the taste nearly made him retch, like honey left in the sun.

"It's a tea made from the Daphne leaves," Luke explained.

Epaphroditus coughed and spat the liquid back into the cup. "You trying to kill me?"

Luke pushed the cup toward him. "It's just the leaves. Unlike Meira, I know what I'm doing." He sighed and sat down beside him. "I told you, the plant has as many medicinal uses as it does poison. If the leaves are boiled properly, the tea they produce can soothe sore throats. It's fortunate for you I saved it with me in my bag."

Epaphroditus grimaced. The memory of the plant was not a pleasant one. Its burn still lingered in his palm. He clenched his fist at the thought.

Luke gestured to his hand. "Let me look at that."

He extended his hand. The skin was darkening, the smell faint but foul.

"I need to make a pack for that," Luke muttered, barely glancing at the wound. "I warned you it could get infected."

Epaphroditus nodded, but his thoughts were elsewhere. The weight of Luke's words pressed on him, the urgency in his tone unmistakable.

"Unfortunately, the seawater damaged some of my supplies." Luke stood, rubbing the back of his neck. "I'll ask the family for herbs. The market may offer others."

With that, Luke stepped out, leaving Epaphroditus alone once more. The silence was almost oppressive, and Epaphroditus couldn't shake the sense that he had inconvenienced the strangers on the other side of the veil. This wasn't his bed, his home. He was a guest in their lives, an unwanted one at that.

He eyed the cup in his hand again. The cloying sweetness still hung in the room like perfume left too long on the skin. But if Luke said it would help, he would have to believe it.

With a deep breath, Epaphroditus brought the cup to his lips and drank it in one motion. He set the cup down with more force than needed. The sound rang sharp in the quiet room.

To his surprise, the tea soothed his throat, easing the tightness that had made it difficult to speak. A warmth spread through him, leaving a strange sense of relief.

His muscles melted into the mat, but his mind clung to Melody, her fingers brushing his cheek, the press of her head against his chest.

A tear slid down his cheek. He longed to be back with her, wrapped in her embrace, returning to the life they were building together. But he was here, without her, and he wasn't sure when he would see her again.

He stared at his wound, teeth clenched. If he ever reached Philippi again, nothing would drag him away.

The Lord is near to the brokenhearted
and saves the crushed in spirit.
Psalm 34:18

"Epaphroditus."

Luke's voice pulled Epaphroditus from the thin edge of sleep. He stirred, muscles aching. "Luke?"

His hand braced his back, lifting him upright. "You sound better."

Epaphroditus blinked against the flickering lamplight. "I feel better," he rasped, throat raw.

Luke set another cup in his hand. "This is the last of it."

The small bundle of Daphne had yielded only a few cups. He didn't know whether to mourn or be grateful for the shortage. He drank it in one gulp, the sickly sweetness clinging to his tongue.

Luke took the empty cup and set it aside, then placed his palm lightly on his forehead. "Your fever's broken."

He glanced around the room. "What hour is it?"

"Early." Luke settled beside him. "I've acquired passage on a ship. If you're well enough to travel."

The thought of the sea violently tossing him churned his stomach. "So soon?"

"If we don't leave now, we may miss Paul entirely."

Epaphroditus took a deep breath, forcing calm into his chest. "No chance for land travel?"

"We're on the island of Samothrace." Luke rose and snatched up the cup. "Unless you've got Poseidon tucked away in your toga, we'll have to take a boat."

"Perhaps one of the other gods could part the sea for us and let us walk on dry land back to Philippi."

Luke tapped the cup. "I've heard the Jew's God once did that, but only for His own."

"Truly?" The thought of a god parting the sea was absurd and yet oddly compelling.

Luke shook his head with a soft laugh. "I doubt Adonai will split the sea for you today, my friend, but the boat will be ready soon."

"If we must." Just the thought of the sea made his stomach pitch again.

"Gather your strength," Luke suggested, moving to the veil that separated the small space from the rest of the house. "I'll inform our host."

Epaphroditus pushed aside the goatskin blankets. His limbs ached, as if the sea had bruised him down to the bone. His palm throbbed, but when he lifted the bandage, he saw that Luke's care had worked. The wound was healing, the discoloration retreating.

Taking a moment to gather his strength, Epaphroditus rose on unsteady legs. With quiet care, he rolled up the reed mat, determined not to be a burden or leave his hosts with a mess. Once he neatly laid it in a corner, he picked up the lamp and stepped through the veil.

Several women were busy with their tasks around the larger room, their voices soft and familiar. Luke was deep in conversation with one of them, and the exchange seemed to hold some importance.

A small sniffle drew Epaphroditus's attention down.

Beside him stood a young boy, dark hair sticking out in every direction, his wide eyes fixed on him. "Maia said you swam in the sea."

Epaphroditus struggled to keep a straight face, managing a quick, crooked smile at the boy.

"Maia said your boat went for a swim, too." The boy wiped his nose with the sleeve of his tunic. "Maia said—"

"That's enough, Jason." One woman shooed him away with a playful swat. "Stop bothering our guest and get to your chores." She flashed Epaphroditus a shy, apologetic smile.

He returned her smile with a raspy, grateful

nod.

Luke ended his conversation, accepting a satchel from the woman. He waved, beckoning Epaphroditus to follow him toward the door.

With a brief bow of gratitude, Epaphroditus turned and followed his friend outside.

Outside, he pointed to the bag Luke was holding. "I'll carry that."

Luke passed it to him. "Sorry, it ended up in the sea." He adjusted his medical supply bag on his other shoulder.

"Nothing irreplaceable." Epaphroditus hefted the bag to his shoulder. "I'm just glad I didn't join it."

The rising sun painted the world in gold and orange as they made their way to the dock.

As promised, a ship was waiting for them. Crew members were busy preparing the ship for departure, their movements efficient and rhythmic.

Epaphroditus's midsection twisted as he approached the boat. "Does it ever get easier?" he asked, his voice tinged with reluctance.

"When you face it long enough, everything gets easier," Luke answered, something in his voice hinted at a memory.

The first steps onto the boat were as rocky as they had been before, and Epaphroditus swallowed hard, trying to keep his footing as the boat lurched with the gentle swell of the water.

"We only have to go a short distance to reach

Neapolis," Luke reminded him, his voice calm. "You'll soon be back in your villa."

Epaphroditus found a small space to settle as the rocking of the boat filled the air with memories of the storm. He closed his eyes, grateful for the brief respite, even if the journey wasn't over.

Luke settled in front of him.

"Tell me the story," Epaphroditus murmured, his voice barely above the sound of the water lapping against the boat.

Luke tilted his head. "What story?"

"The one about Adonai parting the sea for his people," Epaphroditus replied, his throat still sore, but curiosity consuming him.

Luke set his medical bag at his feet. "I don't know if I remember all of it."

"Make up the details if you have to," Epaphroditus urged, the spray of sea air mixing with the coolness of the morning on his face. He fought the rising discomfort in his chest.

Luke looked at the sky. "As I recall, Adonai's people were slaves in Egypt when He sent a deliverer to free them. Egypt pursued them until they came to the sea. Their leader prayed to Adonai, and the waters parted, leaving a dry path for them to cross."

Epaphroditus frowned, his mind grappling with the tale. "But didn't that leave a path for the Egyptians to follow?"

"It would have." Luke's expression shifted, a

glimmer of understanding in his gaze. "But Adonai released the waters on the Egyptians, and they all drowned."

"That's it?" He leaned back, exhaustion dulling his senses. "You need to work on your storytelling, physician."

"I'm foremost concerned with facts," Luke replied, lifting his chin, a faint tension tightening his jaw. "But yes, that's the gist. Years later, Adonai parted the sea again to lead his people into the land of Canaan."

"A god who splits the sea." Epaphroditus hummed, his thoughts wandering. "I wonder what Poseidon thinks of that."

Luke's gaze met his, sharp and searching. "I think the better question is, what do you think of that?"

The weight of the question settled on him. "I think, if a god could do that, he'd be a god worth fearing."

The brief journey from Samothrace to Neapolis was uneventful. When they finally docked, Epaphroditus rushed off the boat, legs grateful for the solid earth. Luke struggled to match his pace as they made their way to Philippi on foot.

Entering the large gate was like a warm embrace; the familiar sights and sounds of home filled Epaphroditus with relief. Without a word, he hurried toward his villa, not waiting for Luke to follow.

He burst through the door and searched. His heart was pounding, his mind racing until he finally found her. Melody.

She greeted him with a radiant expression and outstretched arms.

He buried his face in her plaited hair, inhaling her sweet scent. A wonderful mix of olive oil and cinnamon enveloped him. "I've missed you."

She giggled. "Then why did you stay away so long?"

Epaphroditus glanced over his shoulder at Luke. "Blame your brother."

Luke leaned against the archway, his expression one of mild amusement. "It's not my fault you wanted to swim in the Aegean Sea."

Melody looked up at Epaphroditus, concern flickering across her face. "What?"

"We're safe now," Epaphroditus said quickly, his cheeks warm at the thought of their unexpected adventure.

She turned to Luke, her eyes narrowing slightly. "What happened?"

"Just a little shipwreck."

"Shipwreck!" Melody's voice spiked.

Epaphroditus pulled her close, pressing her into him as she sobbed against his chest. "We are well," he whispered, trying to soothe her.

Luke stepped forward, placing a hand on

Melody's shoulder. "Everything is well."

"Everything most certainly is not well." Melody pulled back, her eyes locking with Luke's. "I almost lost the father of my child because you forced him onto a boat when he said he didn't want to—" She crushed her hands against her mouth, choking on the rest of her words.

Epaphroditus's heart lurched in his chest, a sudden, sharp jolt that left him breathless for a moment. "The what?"

Her eyes widened, and she stared at him, unblinking. "The father of my child." Her hands dropped to her midsection, her gaze never leaving his.

"Melody, that's wonderful news." Luke's voice softened as he ran his fingers through her hair.

She glanced at him before returning her gaze to Epaphroditus. "I was going to wait a while longer to tell you. Neda and I aren't fully certain yet."

While she and Luke discussed her symptoms, Epaphroditus's joy and relief were tempered by a deep, gnawing fear. Many Roman children didn't survive their first breaths, and far too many often stole their mother's last. Losing children was so common that parents often waited until their child saw their first harvest before legally registering them. He prayed all the rituals and protections they'd performed would hold, that the life growing inside her would see many harvests.

One who heard us was a woman named
Lydia, from the city of Thyatira, a seller
of purple goods, who was a worshiper of
God. The Lord opened her heart to pay
attention to what was said by Paul.
Acts 16:14

Epaphroditus rose early, slipping quietly away from Melody. Her rhythmic breathing told him she was still deep in sleep. His own sleep had been restless, and he worried he'd kept his wife awake most of the night.

As he neared the kitchen, the sounds of preparations filled the air. He approached quietly, not wanting to startle anyone.

A sorrowful hum, laced with a foreign tongue, drifted from the room.

Epaphroditus dipped his head past the archway, glimpsing Shira alone, busy with her chores. She was singing.

In all her time in his service, he'd never heard

her sing. Her song echoed the tune he'd heard in Troas. But this one was different, soaked in sadness and grief. He hesitated, as though drawn to the mournful tune.

Only when Shira turned and caught his gaze did she stop.

They stood for several heartbeats, staring at one another in silence.

Epaphroditus was the first to break it. "What were you singing?"

"I wasn't singing." She turned her back and continued her work.

"I heard you." He stepped fully into the room.

She ignored him, moving briskly about the space.

"Is it a song of your people?" he asked, his voice softer.

She spun around, her eyes flashing with sharpness. "You know nothing of my people."

Anger flared in Epaphroditus, hot and sudden, but the instant his gaze met the sorrow in her eyes, it melted away, leaving only a dull ache where the fury had been. "You're right."

Shira blinked, her expression softening for an instant.

"I know nothing about your people," he continued. "Or about you. Forgive me for not asking sooner."

Shira fumbled with the cloth in her hands, her

defense slipping. "What do you want to know?"

Epaphroditus's expression softened ever so slightly, pleased by the minor breach in her defenses. "Let's start with my original question. What were you singing?"

She sighed, her shoulders slumped. "A song that brings back memories of someone I miss very much."

"Who?"

"A friend."

"In Rome?"

"How did you..." Shira's voice faltered as she fixed him with a searching gaze.

"Rumors," he answered with a small shrug. "People talk."

"I am from Rome." She returned to her task. "Lived there all my life."

"And your family?"

She froze, her gaze shifting to a distant place beyond the room. "I don't have a family anymore."

Epaphroditus's heart plummeted, a heavy weight dragging him down, as if the ground beneath him had vanished entirely. "I'm sorry to hear that," he said sincerely, more moved than he'd expected. "And your friend?"

"I don't know if she's alive or dead." She shook away the stillness. "Probably dead. Or exiled. I sing that song when I think of her. It helps me remember the lesson she taught me."

He leaned nearer. "Lesson?"

"That even in sorrow, one can still find Adonai's hand."

"Adonai?" Epaphroditus paused, his forehead creasing slightly. "I thought you followed Chrestus."

"Chrestus." She clicked her tongue and rolled her eyes. "Not Chrestus. Christ. It's a title from our word for 'Messiah,' the Anointed One. The man's name is Jesus."

"Was."

"Pardon?"

"You said 'is,' but I thought he died."

"He did," she confirmed, "but Adonai raised Him from the dead. He's alive."

"You've seen Him?"

"No." She exhaled softly. "But there were many who did. And He's coming back."

"So, you worship both Adonai and this man from Nazareth?"

"Jesus is Adonai's son."

"Like a demi-god?"

She hesitated. "Not exactly."

At that moment, Isaiah and Enoch entered the kitchen, engaged in a lively conversation with each other.

Epaphroditus waited, allowing Shira to prepare their morning portions. When the two men retreated to the low table in the main room, Epaphroditus and Shira had the kitchen to themselves again.

Shira broke the silence. "Today is Shabbat. I was hoping you remembered our arrangement."

"Arrangement?" he echoed, frowning.

"Lydia invited me to the river." Shira gestured around the room. "That's why I rose early, to ensure I completed my tasks before we left."

"Of course. Finish up. I'll walk you there."

After leaving instructions with Isaiah and Enoch, Epaphroditus walked Shira to the Neapolis Gate, then to the small stream that lay just outside the city. A group of women had already gathered under the shade of a cypress tree.

Lydia lifted her hand in a quick, graceful wave before slipping away from the group. She moved toward them with an eager glint in her eyes. "I was hoping to see you today."

"I know Shira appreciates the inclusion," Epaphroditus answered for her.

"Here." Lydia produced a folded garment from the pack across her body and handed it to Shira. "I finished the tunic, as promised."

Shira gave a quick glance at Epaphroditus before accepting the garment and holding it close to her chest.

Epaphroditus produced a few coins, placing them in Lydia's hand. "There's enough here to cover this one and another." He noticed the quick, almost imperceptible shift in Shira's expression as he looked her way. "She'll need something to wear when this one's being cleaned."

"A practical thought," Lydia teased.

"I'll speak to our two menservants as well," Epaphroditus continued. "Their garments were less damaged, and they seem fine with the Roman style, but I'd like to extend the offer to them as well." He turned to Shira. "Let Lydia know what color you'd like the other garment to be, and I'll return later to escort you back to the villa."

"We can escort her back," Lydia offered. "I'll be heading to the market after we're done here."

"You're sure it won't be out of your way?"

"Not at all." Lydia intertwined her arm with Shira's. "It'll give us a chance to talk."

"If you're sure." Epaphroditus hesitated. "That will be..." His words trailed off as his attention shifted to three men approaching up the path from Neapolis. "I don't believe it."

Lydia turned to follow his gaze. "What?"

He squinted, lifting his hand against the glare of sunlight. "It's Paul, from Troas."

"Who?"

"A man Luke and I met. Luke invited him to Philippi. I thought we'd missed him."

"Shalom," Paul called out when they drew close. He extended his arm to Epaphroditus. "I'm pleased to see you again."

"Greetings." Epaphroditus grasped the man's

forearm. "Luke thought we'd missed you. He'll be glad to see you made it."

Paul glanced around. "Where is the good physician?"

"My best guess would be tending to an ill person." Epaphroditus flicked his thumb toward the city gate. "I can take you to his home."

"Wonderful." Paul's gaze shifted to the gathering of women. "Have we interrupted something?"

"May I present Lydia from Thyatira." Epaphroditus waved toward the women. "And her collection of women. They've come here to pray."

"And to whom do you pray, Lydia from Thyatira?" Paul asked, his eyes twinkling with curiosity.

"To the One true God, Adonai," Lydia answered proudly.

"Splendid." Paul clapped his hands. "Would it trouble you if we joined in your prayers?"

Epaphroditus's lips parted slightly in surprise. "You want to join a group of women for prayer?"

Paul's gaze turned back to him. "I'd like to share with them what Adonai has entrusted to me, yes."

Epaphroditus's brief encounter with Paul in Troas had been enough for him to recognize the man's oddities. His eagerness to sit among a group of women and pray to their god only solidified Epaphroditus' suspicions.

"This is Silas," Paul said, nodding to the man at his side, "and Timothy," he gestured to the younger man on his other side. "We've just arrived from Samothrace."

The name sent a shudder through Epaphroditus. "We, unfortunately, came through there as well."

"Unfortunately?" Paul echoed. "We found it a lovely island with welcoming people."

"It's not so lovely when a shipwreck lands you there."

"Shipwreck?" Shira's voice faltered as she repeated the word.

Epaphroditus turned to see her hand pressed against her lips as if trying to shove the word back inside.

"I know a little about those." Paul's gaze drifted to a distant place, his tone softening. "If you'll have us, Lydia, I'd be honored to speak."

"It would be we who receive the honor." Lydia motioned toward the shade of the trees.

The three men followed her.

Shira looked at Epaphroditus. Her eyes searched his, asking something unspoken.

Epaphroditus flicked his chin toward the group. "Go on."

Shira hesitated, but then joined the others.

As he watched the group, something stirred within, a faint, familiar tug, the very same that had drawn him in Troas.

In the cypress's shade, the women lifted their voices, and Epaphroditus sensed it once more, an invisible force, something beyond him, drawing him. Though his olive grove called to him, he remained. Perhaps Paul's words, meant for women, might be plain enough for him to grasp this time.

And after [Lydia] was baptized, and her
household as well, she urged us, saying,
"If you have judged me to be faithful to
the Lord, come to my house and stay."
And she prevailed upon us.
Acts 16:15

Recalling Luke's warning about the Jews' desire for space, Epaphroditus positioned himself near enough to hear Paul, but not close enough to intrude on the women. A nearby cypress offered shade and a place to lean. As he listened, Paul's voice seemed to echo the rhythm of the nearby stream, flowing calmly and clearly. Paul's message, still logical, was easier to grasp. More approachable, more human.

The teacher spoke of the Nazarene and his teachings, recounting miracles, and sharing ways to treat others. Much was a repetition of his speech in Troas, but some elements seemed clearer, more precise.

A woman raised her hand. Euodia.

Epaphroditus had often seen her by the dye sellers in the marketplace. She always spoke with purpose and carried herself taller than those around her. "You say this Jesus fulfilled the words of Moses and the prophets," she said, lowering her hand. "But how can a crucified man be Messiah when the Law says, 'cursed is anyone who hangs on a tree'?"

Paul paused, brow furrowed in thought. "He became a curse for us," he said at last, "so that we might be freed from the curse of the Law. As Isaiah wrote, 'He was pierced for our transgressions, crushed for our iniquities.' Through His suffering, we are healed."

Euodia did not speak again, but her gaze stayed fixed on Paul.

When Paul finished speaking, Lydia rose to her feet, her presence commanding. "I have feared the God of the Jews since first hearing of Him years ago," she said, her voice filled with conviction. "Today, Jesus has opened my heart." She placed her hands on her chest. "What must we do?"

"Repent and be immersed," Paul answered simply.

Lydia glanced first toward the stream beside them, then her gaze traveled south, to the Gangites River where the brook emptied.

"There," Lydia pointed. "There is deeper water upstream."

Without a word, Paul began walking toward

the river. The women followed him, their pace quickening as they moved like a flock of sheep trailing after their shepherd. Curious, Epaphroditus stayed close to them.

Paul stepped straight into the river, wading in until the water reached his waist. Lydia lifted the hem of her toga without hesitation and moved with purpose toward the middle of the stream.

The women gathered as close to the edge of the water as they dared. On the bank, Epaphroditus stood watching, eyes fixed on the unfolding scene. Paul positioned Lydia's hands over her face, then gently lowered her into the water. When Lydia resurfaced, soaked and gasping, the women on the shore erupted in joyful shouts.

One by one, the women moved into the river, each coming up from the water with hair and clothing heavy from the weight of the stream.

Epaphroditus shifted his weight, strangely moved by the scene before him. He'd witnessed rites in temples across the city, but this was different, quiet, personal, almost tender. These women emerged from the water as if something within them had changed. He couldn't name the curl in his chest, only that it left him uneasy.

Silas and Timothy, Paul's companions, added their voices to the chorus of praise as they helped the women in and out of the water. Soaked and smiling, the women were speaking at once, their excitement palpable.

Shira moved toward Paul, her face lit with a rare smile. Her hands went over her face, and she closed her eyes. Paul assisted her into the water, and when she emerged, her joy mirrored that of the others. Shouts of praise rang out from the surrounding women.

Shira and Paul were the last to emerge from the river. Drenched, their clothes stuck to their skin as they chatted on the bank. Shira caught Epaphroditus's gaze and dipped her head.

Paul whispered something in her ear, and she nodded before moving to Lydia's side.

Epaphroditus passed Paul. "We Romans usually bathe at the Thermae."

"This was no bath," Paul answered with quiet authority. "This was a cleansing."

Epaphroditus gave a small shake of his head. "Those women were not dirty. And it is customary for slaves to worship the deities of their masters."

"True." Paul wrung out his beard, his tone thoughtful. "Immersion only symbolizes the inner cleansing Jesus brings. Every person should have the freedom to choose who they worship."

"Internal cleansing?" The phrase gnawed at him. "Like a physician's remedy for an internal condition?"

Paul laughed softly. "You're on the right path." He adjusted his tunic, trying to shake off some of the water from his sandals. "The soul, my boy. The soul. Jesus has cleansed the souls of these women today, and their choice to be lowered into the water is an outward display of the inward change."

Confusion twisted through him. None of the teacher's words made sense. "But how did they know their internal condition had changed?"

Paul's gaze held his. "You'll know."

Epaphroditus wanted to ask more, but Lydia's voice broke through his thoughts.

"Paul,"—she shook out her toga—"if you have judged me faithful to the Lord, come to my house and stay."

Recalling Luke's eagerness to hear the traveling teacher again, Epaphroditus spoke up, "I'm sure Luke would extend a similar offer."

"I must insist," Lydia countered, her tone warm but firm. "I have many rooms and much to offer you and your companions after such a long journey."

Paul shot Epaphroditus a pleading glance.

"The lady has insisted," Epaphroditus said with a bow of his head. "You must indulge her."

"Very well." Paul turned to Lydia. "Lead the way, dear one."

With that, Paul and his two companions followed Lydia and the group of women toward the Neapolis Gate.

Epaphroditus said nothing to Shira, but her silent decision to follow him brought quiet relief.

They walked back to the villa in silence, the weight of the day settled heavy between them. Epaphroditus turned over Paul's words and the scene by the river in his mind. The followers of Adonai were strange to him, their rituals foreign, their beliefs even more so. Yet something within him stirred, subtle, but undeniable.

As they reached the door of the villa, Calliope was sweeping dirt into the courtyard. "Shira, you're all wet." Her lips curved in mischief. "Did my brother push you into the stream?"

Shira's face flushed, and she quickly peeked at Epaphroditus.

"He did that to me once," Calliope added with a chuckle. "Tried to convince me I could see the smooth stones at the bottom better if I leaned closer... then splash! Next thing I knew, I was nose-to-nose with them. Mother was furious."

"You deserved it for hiding my sandals," Epaphroditus reminded her.

"Oh, yeah," Calliope grinned. "I forgot about that."

"And no," Epaphroditus corrected. "I didn't push Shira into the stream. She... well..."

"I went willingly," Shira interjected as she entered the house.

Calliope fixed Epaphroditus with a steady gaze, silently asking for more.

He simply shrugged, as unable to explain the

events of the river as he was to explain the sun's daily rise. With firm steps, he crossed the threshold.

"Melody's not here," Calliope remarked, her tone unexpectedly solemn.

Epaphroditus froze. "Oh?"

"She went to see her brother."

Something in Calliope's voice made Epaphroditus's heart drop. "Did something happen?"

"They wouldn't tell me anything," she replied, her gaze shifting downward. "But you'd better go see her."

Without another word, Epaphroditus rushed to his friend's house. One look at her confirmed his worst fear. He'd seen that hollow stare on a woman's face before too many times.

Melody sat at the low table, her face streaked with tears, her eyes swollen and red. "Epaphras," she whispered, her voice fragile.

He rushed to her side, pulling her into his arms, desperate to shield both her and himself from the pain that was sure to follow her next words.

"I'm sorry," she sobbed, clinging to him. "I'm so sorry."

Tears stung his eyes as he held her close, burying his face in her hair. Sorrow pressed down on him like a stone. No words came out, just numbing silence and raw grief clawing at his chest.

Is this your reward, Aphrodite, after all my

devotion? Denied my life, you claimed my child instead?

The only answer was silence, and Luke's firm hand on his shoulder.

As we were going to the place of prayer,
we were met by a slave girl who had a
spirit of divination and brought her
owners much gain by fortune-telling.
Acts 16:16

Weeks slipped by without notice. Epaphroditus took refuge in his olive grove, avoiding the restless thoughts pressing at the edges of his mind. Luke tended to Melody's physical needs, but Epaphroditus, unable to soothe her emotional wounds, left her care to her family.

Grief tore through him like a plow through soil. Nothing he did seemed to fill the deepening chasm within. The more he prayed and offered to Aphrodite, the wider the emptiness grew.

Shira rubbed oil across his forehead, trying to cool him as he prepared to return to his grove after the midday break. The oppressive heat was nothing compared to the cold absence in Melody's eyes. She'd healed physically, but emotionally, she remained distant. The bright woman he had once loved lay hidden behind the mask of indifference she wore each day. He wondered if he would ever see her smile again.

Oil dripped from his brow, where Shira rushed through the application. "In a hurry?"

"Sorry," she mumbled. "Lydia is waiting for me."

"Of course, prayer time." He'd lost track again.

"She'll understand." Shira smeared the excess oil across her own forehead and returned the jar to its place.

"I'll escort you."

"You don't have to," she countered too quickly.

Epaphroditus studied her closely. "Why not?"

"I meant... I could manage on my own," she said, her gaze softening. "I know you're eager to get back to your grove."

He wondered how transparent his actions had become if even Shira had noticed. "Still, you're my..." He hesitated, the word "property" almost slipping from his mouth, but he stopped himself. "You're under my protection. I won't see you harmed."

Shira gave him a measured look, standing still for a moment as if weighing his words.

"I could use the walk to clear my head," he admitted.

She nodded, apparently satisfied.

They walked toward the Neapolis Gate, and Epaphroditus found solace in Shira's quiet presence.

Unlike some women he knew, she was content with silence.

As they neared the gate, he noticed Paul, Silas, and a growing group of women standing with Lydia. Another woman seized his attention. He'd seen her countless times near the Forum. She twirled around the group like a dancer, shouting, "These men are servants of the Most High God, who proclaim to you the way of salvation!"

A crowd was forming around the commotion. Epaphroditus recognized the woman as Delphina, or at least, that was the name her owners had given her. A set of particularly foul brothers who profited from her so-called gift of divination. As a slave, Delphina had lost her true name, her true identity. The people of Philippi knew her simply as the slave girl who saw the future.

Her owners claimed that the spirit of Python, the serpent Apollo slew who once guarded the oracle at Delphi, possessed her. With her uncanny ability to predict the future, the brothers spread tales of her gift, charging desperate people a hefty fee to glimpse their fates while filling their own pockets with coins.

Epaphroditus didn't need Delphina's prophecies; he already bore the mark of fate on his soul.

"These men are servants of the Most High God!" Delphina's voice grew louder as Epaphroditus and

Shira drew nearer. "They proclaim to you the way of salvation!"

Shira murmured, "She's back."

Epaphroditus leaned in. "How long has this been happening?"

"She's been here every time we've come to pray. Shouting the same thing over and over again and disrupting our gatherings."

Epaphroditus watched as Paul attempted to speak with Lydia, gesturing in frustration as Delphina spun around them. Lydia spread her hands in defeat.

Then Epaphroditus saw the exact moment when Paul's patience reached its limit.

Paul stepped forward, blocking Delphina's spin. He fixed his gaze on her, his face resolute. "I command you, in the name of Jesus Christ, to come out of her."

For a heartbeat, everything stilled. Delphina's mouth hung open in silence, her limbs twitching as though caught between flight and collapse. A strange wind swept through the area, subtle but charged, like the moment before a thunderclap.

Then came the scream. It wasn't like the ones she used when prophesying. It was raw, guttural, torn from some hidden place. Her body convulsed, knees buckling beneath her. She clawed at her throat as if trying to rid herself of something lodged deep inside. The crowd recoiled, some gasped, others shouted in alarm.

Epaphroditus' stomach twisted. Whatever power Paul had invoked, it was real. But was it good?

Delphina thrashed on the ground, foam bubbling at the corners of her mouth. Several women from Lydia's group shouted prayers over the girl. The line between miracle and madness had never been so thin.

Paul didn't move. His gaze remained fixed on Delphina, not with anger, but with aching compassion.

Shira gripped Epaphroditus's arm. "Shouldn't we help her?"

He hesitated, unsure. He'd never witnessed anything like this and didn't even know how to help. Still, he stepped forward. "What are you doing to her?"

Paul's fiery eyes met his. "I'm freeing her."

"She's a slave!" Epaphroditus looked toward Delphina, who was writhing on the ground. "You're torturing her!"

"The spirit in her is the one torturing her," Paul said, his voice unwavering. "I am setting her free."

Delphina's shrieks intensified, and Epaphroditus instinctively covered his ears. "Stop this, or—"

"What is the meaning of this?" A booming voice interrupted.

Epaphroditus recognized Remus, one of Delphina's owners, storming toward them. Calvus, the younger of the two brothers, followed close behind, both clearly enraged.

Fearing for Paul, Epaphroditus placed himself between the brothers and the teacher. "The teacher means no harm."

Remus hesitated, his gaze flicking between Epaphroditus and Paul. "Get out of my way." He shoved Epaphroditus aside, stepping toward Paul. "What are you doing to my property?"

Though a head shorter, Paul stood firm in the face of the Roman's anger. "I commanded the spirit to come out of her."

Calvus arrived a few steps behind, his fury matching his brother's. "You did what?"

Delphina's cries broke into ragged sobs.

"In the name of Jesus of Nazareth," Paul said, turning toward Calvus. "I commanded the spirit to come out of her."

Remus grabbed a handful of Paul's tunic, lifting the man off his feet. "How dare you damage my property?"

Silas rushed forward, trying to intervene. "Release him at once!" He reached for Remus, trying to pull the man's hand off Paul's tunic.

But Calvus caught Silas's arm, twisting it behind his back. "I say we take both of them to the duumviri and let them right this injustice."

"Excellent idea, brother," Remus agreed, turning Paul toward town.

Shira caught Epaphroditus with a desperate look. "What does this mean?"

"Nothing good for them." Epaphroditus motioned toward Lydia with a tilt of his chin. "Stay here with the others. I'll see what I can do."

He followed the brothers as they dragged Paul and Silas through the bustling streets toward the Forum.

The rectangular plaza housed a stone bema seat at the northern end. Upon it sat one of the duumviri, while the other paced anxiously.

"Praetor!" Remus shouted, dragging Paul before the judgment seat. "These men are Jews, and they're disturbing our city." He threw Paul at the feet of the confused magistrates. "They advocate customs that are not lawful for us as Romans to accept or practice."

Calvus shoved Silas next to Paul.

Epaphroditus edged forward, straining to hear.

"They've damaged our personal property," Remus added, his voice growing louder. "They've cost us dearly."

A man from the crowd shouted, "I've seen them encourage women to gather by the stream!"

"They do not pay respect to our gods!" another voice cried.

The murmurs grew louder, accusations piled

on.

"They're troublemakers!"

"They'll bring more disruption to our city if they're not stopped!"

"Remove them!"

"Lock them up!"

"Enough!" The magistrate rose from his seat. He set a hard gaze on Paul. "Strip them and beat them."

Epaphroditus's heart sank as six lictors stepped forward, their rods in hand.

They tore the outer tunics from Paul and Silas and proceeded to thrash them. Epaphroditus watched, frozen, as rods split their flesh, unable to move as their flesh broke under the blows.

Only one thought pierced the horror.

Luke.

*And when they had inflicted many blows
upon them, they threw them into prison,
ordering the jailer to keep them safely.*
Acts 16:23

Epaphroditus rushed toward his friend's home, bursting through the open doors. "Luke!"

The physician was tending to a man at his low table but paused, his eyes lifting to meet Epaphroditus's. "What is it?"

"It's Paul." Epaphroditus's words tumbled out in a rush. "You've got to come, quickly."

Luke muttered an apology to the man, placed his tools aside, and followed Epaphroditus without question.

Epaphroditus led the way, footsteps heavy as they moved toward the Forum. He only stopped when they reached the scene.

The lictors' rods struck Paul and Silas, blood streaking their backs, their faces twisted in pain.

"What happened?" Luke demanded.

Before Epaphroditus could answer, the duumviri, who had returned to his seat, lifted a hand. "That's enough. Take them to the prison and order the jailer to keep them secure."

"This is illegal," Luke spat. "They don't know Paul is a Roman citizen. They have no right to beat him."

"There was no formal testimony," Epaphroditus said, his voice tight. "The entire city seems to be against them."

Luke's eyes landed on Remus. "Why does he smirk like a wolf feasting on its latest kill?"

"He and Calvus are the accusers," Epaphroditus explained. "Paul commanded the divining spirit from Delphina. The brothers sought retribution."

"He what?" Luke's eyes widened with disbelief. "The spirit listened to him?"

"Evidently," Epaphroditus said. He flicked his chin toward the brothers. "They believe her of little use now, so they brought Paul and Silas to the judgment seat."

Calvus returned, dragging Delphina by the wrist.

Luke's face darkened. "She will still be of use to them," he murmured, his voice filled with dread. He slowly lifted his eyes to meet Epaphroditus's gaze. "Just not in the same way as before."

A shudder crawled down Epaphroditus's spine as the full weight of the situation hit him. Delphina whimpered as Remus barked at her, spit landing on her face. Calvus's grip made her cry out.

"Come on," Luke muttered, already moving toward the lictors. "I want to see where they're taking them."

Epaphroditus forced himself to follow Luke toward the prison.

Inside, the stench of sweat and mildew clung to the stone, thick and oppressive. Epaphroditus scanned the dim chamber, unease curling low in his gut.

A guard stepped in front of them, arms crossed over his chest.

"I'm the physician of the two men who were just brought here," Luke said, his tone sharp with authority. "I need to examine their wounds."

The guard didn't flinch. "No visitors. Praetor's orders."

Epaphroditus shifted, his body coiled tight. This wasn't justice, it was theater. A display of power for power's sake.

"These men are being held illegally," Luke continued, unrelenting. "They are Roman citizens and yet placed in cells reserved for the most serious of crimes."

The guard's eyes narrowed. "A crime against a Roman citizen is a crime against Rome," he said, stepping in close enough to shove Luke back with his forearm. "They've been charged with stealing profit and reputation."

Epaphroditus's jaw clenched. So that was the story now; twisted truth into something sharp enough to cut.

"As should many Romans who hold others captive under the guise of grace and redemption," Luke snapped.

"I don't make the law," the guard growled, arm firm against Luke's chest. "I'm just here to make sure they carry out their punishments."

"You can't bar us," Luke said. "It's their right."

The guard looked Luke over, as if weighing consequences, then finally stepped aside with a grunt.

Epaphroditus followed Luke deeper into the prison, past cell after cell, until they reached the innermost rooms. There, they discovered Paul and Silas, their feet secured in stocks.

Luke strode to the cell, his voice rising. "Paul?"

Epaphroditus followed, a cold pressure building in his chest. He needed to see Paul for himself, to understand what kind of man could make spirits obey his commands and still end up behind bars.

"We are well, physician," Paul called from the shadows, calm despite the circumstances. "But we require a favor."

"Name it," Luke replied.

"I need you to find Timothy," Paul said. "He was supposed to meet us at the gate, but he must have gone to the market. If he arrived after we were taken away, he may have gone to Lydia's."

"Of course, right away." Luke turned to leave but paused. "Epaphroditus is here. He can stay with you until I return." With a simple motion toward the cell, Luke exited.

After Luke left, Epaphroditus stood in the cold, damp air of the chamber. The distant drip of water, the muffled coughs and grunts of other prisoners, broke the silence of the underground cells.

Moving closer to Paul and Silas's cell, he grabbed a torch from the wall and held it out, the flickering light casting shadows in the dark space. It revealed the extent of their injuries, torn tunics, their bodies caked with blood and dirt. He wondered, with a deep sense of helplessness, if Luke would be allowed to treat their wounds before infections took hold.

"Don't worry about us." A tired smile touched Paul's face. "This isn't the first time we've been on this side of bars."

"Probably won't be the last either," Silas added, his voice dry.

Epaphroditus couldn't speak. The words refused to come. After everything, they looked calm. Bruised, bound, locked away in filth... and still, a quiet strength clung to them like armor. Despite the brutality they'd suffered, Paul and Silas were making light of the situation, as though they were in no more pain than men at the baths. "How many times?" he finally asked, barely audible.

Paul blinked. "Pardon?"

"I saw your scars when they pulled off your tunics." Epaphroditus motioned to his own back. "How many times have you been beaten?"

Paul looked up at the ceiling, his mouth moving in thought. "This makes four."

"Five," Silas corrected, a hint of sadness flickering in his smile.

Paul nodded. "Five."

Epaphroditus' shoulders seemed to burn as though they, too, bore the lashes of a whip. "And you continue to teach?"

A faint chuckle escaped Paul. "Of course."

"Even after all you've endured?" Epaphroditus asked, his voice thick with disbelief.

"I've experienced attacks, persecution, beatings, imprisonment, and even a few shipwrecks." Paul's face lit with a quiet, triumphant smile. "Yet the Lord has been faithful to preserve me so I may continue to do His will."

"Shipwrecked?" The word tumbled from Epaphroditus's mouth.

"Oh yes." Paul nodded. "I was even adrift on the sea for a night and a day after one."

A cold, wet chill of memory flooded Epaphroditus' senses. The stormy waves of the Aegean Sea. The saltwater stung his eyes. His limbs ached from fighting the current. Melody's tear-streaked face flashed in his mind. His chest tightened, and he sank to his knees. "My goddess nearly drowned me, too."

A rattle of chains broke through the tidal wave of dreadful memories.

"Are you a soldier?" Paul asked.

Epaphroditus glanced away, refusing the label. "My father was, and his brothers, and their father before them." He met Paul's eyes. "But not me."

"I've known many soldiers." Paul leaned forward. "Many of them battled the longest and hardest against fear."

Epaphroditus's expression tightened. No one in his family had ever shown fear. They were warriors, unflinching in battle, resolute in their duty. But Epaphroditus himself, from childhood, had wrestled with fear.

"No matter how hard they tried," Paul continued, "spilling blood in foreign lands never conquered their fear."

"Is that why you're here? To conquer Rome with your weapon, your message?" Epaphroditus asked, skepticism edging his words.

"No, my boy," Paul's words softened as he eased back. "Rome is not my enemy. There is only one way to conquer fear, and it's not with a sword."

Epaphroditus's eyes narrowed, his mind racing. This short, battered man, chained and broken, could not possibly know anything about conquering fear. And yet... when he looked into Paul's eyes, he saw something he had never seen in his own reflection, the absence of fear. "What is this weapon?"

"Faith." Paul's eyes lit with conviction. "Fear is only conquered through faith."

"I have faith," Epaphroditus snapped. "I've worshipped my goddess faithfully for years, and so has my family before me. For some reason, Aphrodite thinks it best if my grave lies beneath the waves."

"And so you live in fear?"

Epaphroditus nodded slowly. "After everything you've endured, aren't you afraid?"

"Sometimes," Paul admitted, glancing at Silas. "When the nights get long, and the pain becomes nearly unbearable." He turned back to Epaphroditus. "But I simply do it afraid. Adonai will decide my fate. I'm called to follow Him."

Epaphroditus opened his mouth to speak, but footsteps echoed down the corridor. No doubt Luke had found Timothy and was returning. He shifted to let Timothy pass, holding the torch out to light the way.

The younger man surveyed the cell, his arms folding as he took it in. "What's the charge this time?"

"Theft, I think." Paul looked at Silas, who gave a subtle nod.

Timothy tilted his head, studying the grimy wall. "And how long do you think you'll be enjoying these"—he swept his hand on the stone and rubbed grime between his fingers—"accommodations?"

"We'll leave that decision to Adonai." Paul met Epaphroditus's eyes. "We were just telling our friend here that many of us are in cells, some of us just don't know it."

Timothy's gaze flicked toward Luke. "Like the young girl shackled by a demon?"

Paul sighed heavily. "How is she?"

"Her masters dragged her away from the Forum." Luke shivered. "I fear for what they'll do to her now."

Epaphroditus's thoughts darkened. The girl's tortured screams, Calvus's grip, Remus's smirk, they all pressed into his mind, crowding alongside the memory of Shira on the seller's stage, bound like an object.

"Pardon me." Epaphroditus passed the torch to Timothy. "There is something I must tend to."

And this she kept doing for many days.
Paul, having become greatly annoyed,
turned and said to the spirit, "I
command you in the name of Jesus
Christ to come out of her." And it came
out that very hour.
Acts 16:18

Men's voices faded behind Epaphroditus as he hurried down the corridor, past the guards, and stepped into the street. His attention shifted toward the market.

Aphrodite, guide my steps and grant me the strength to break another's chains.

It didn't take long to find Remus and Calvus. They stood outside a booth along the street outside the Forum, collecting coins while screams of pain echoed from behind the fabric flapping in the wind. Epaphroditus wove through the crowd, the screams guiding him toward the booth.

"Get back in line," Remus said, holding out his

hand. "Everyone who pays gets a turn."

"I'm not here for her services." Epaphroditus's voice was crisp, fury simmering just beneath the surface as another cry rang out from the tent. "I'm here to purchase her outright."

Remus's eyes widened, then narrowed into slits. "What's the matter? Wife not providing enough of her services?"

Calvus let out a loud, braying laugh.

Heat climbed Epaphroditus's neck. He reached inside his tunic and pulled out his money pouch, holding it out with deliberate calm. "A down payment," he said. "We can draw up a bill of sale for the rest."

"Why would I sell one of my most valuable resources?"

Epaphroditus knew the game well. The seller's pride was a thin veil in an attempt to inflate the price. His father had taught him well. "Because you know she's not worth as much to you now that the spirit of Python is gone from her."

"She still has other uses."

Another scream cut through the fabric behind them.

Epaphroditus tightened his grip on the pouch, then shoved it into Remus's chest. "Only for as long as her body holds up. And by the sounds of it, that won't be long."

Remus flicked a glance at Calvus.

The younger brother shrugged. "Better coins today than a promise of coins tomorrow."

"True enough," Remus muttered, his fingers closing around the pouch. "We'll write the bill while our current customer gets what he's paid for."

Epaphroditus pulled his hand free from Remus's grip and, with his father's zeal, bargained until they agreed on a price. Having settled the terms, he signed the parchment.

"If you would be so kind." He nodded toward the tent, tamping down the urge to rip away whoever had hold of the young girl.

A man emerged from the tent, hair unkempt, eyes flitting. He nodded to the brothers and slipped into the crowd.

Remus pulled back the tent flap, grabbed Delphina by the arm, and pushed her forward. "She's ready." He thrust her toward Epaphroditus.

She tumbled into Epaphroditus's hold. He drew her close and wrapped his cloak around her in one motion, hiding her from the eyes of the crowd. She looked up, her face ashen, eyes wide and unseeing. Tremors shot through her, and she appeared ready to bolt.

Steadying her with his arm, Epaphroditus whispered, "I won't hurt you."

Her frightened gaze flicked to Remus and Calvus.

"You don't have to worry about them anymore."

Epaphroditus kept his arms around her, partly to keep her from fleeing and partly to shield her from the brothers and the pressing crowd. "You're mine now." He patted his copy of the bill of sale sticking out of a fold in his toga. "Let's get you out of here."

Murmurs followed, but no one blocked their path as the crowd dissolved around them.

Delphina moved with faltering steps, her face wincing as she walked.

"I have a friend who's a physician." Epaphroditus steadied her. "I'll have him look at you."

She trembled against his hold.

"Don't worry," he added. "I trust him with my life."

When her knees gave out, he caught her and lifted her into his arms in one swift motion. She weighed less than he imagined, realizing her tunic hid her delicate frame. He fought against imagining what other tortures the woman had endured at the hands of the brothers.

"Apologies for the close contact," he muttered. "I'd rather carry you than see you collapse again."

She shivered against his chest.

For a moment, his thoughts drifted to Calliope as a young girl, nestled in his arms during a thunderstorm when both their parents were away at sea. She'd been safe and dry inside their home, yet fear still wrapped around her. Delphina's life had been nothing but subject to cruel masters. He wondered if the cloak of fear ever left her thin shoulders.

His mind raced. How would he justify this purchase? What would he say to his mother and wife?

At the door of his villa, Shira looked from him to the girl, saying nothing, a mercy he hadn't expected.

"Get Melody," he whispered.

She nodded and disappeared into the house.

Epaphroditus went in and laid Delphina on a cushion. He knelt beside her, attempting to meet her gaze. But she kept her eyes down, fear rolling off her like heat. He stayed quiet, waiting for Melody.

When Melody entered, her eyes widened in disbelief. "Epaphras?" she asked, her voice tight with concern. "Is that..."

"I know what this looks like." He gestured weakly toward Delphina. "But I can assure you, there's an explanation."

"I should hope so." Melody looked at the girl, then back at him. "She needs medical attention. Where's Luke?"

"In jail."

"What?" Melody's voice rose in alarm.

"I didn't mean Luke's in jail," he explained quickly. "Paul and Silas were arrested. It's a long story. Why don't you find your brother,"—he dipped his head to Delphina—"and I'll have Shira clean her up? I'll explain everything when you return."

Melody paused, glancing between him and the girl. "Do you think he's still at the jail?"

"I'm uncertain. And, while I know you've assisted Luke with countless patients..." He closed his eyes. "It would give me peace if Luke were able to be here while you both examined her for injuries."

"I'll find him." Melody left without another word.

Epaphroditus opened his eyes, his shoulders tight under the strain of what he'd done.

Shira drew closer, her gaze fixed intently on the girl. "Must be quite a story."

Epaphroditus hummed in agreement. "Partly your fault."

She narrowed her eyes at him.

"I had to pay a small fortune for her," he explained. "But it was necessary. I'll have to add part of her debt to your account."

Shira lowered her head, resigned.

Epaphroditus turned his gaze to the girl. "I'm giving her to you."

"What?"

"You'll need to name her." He met her wild expression. "I don't think she even remembers her true name, and I refuse to have that serpent's name spoken in this house."

Shira turned to the girl. "Talia."

"That doesn't sound Roman."

"It's from my people," she mused. "It means 'dew from Adonai.'"

Epaphroditus's heart tightened. "It's beautiful."

"It was my mother's," her voice faltered.

Epaphroditus winced at the sadness hidden within her words. "The day I bought you in the market... I saw you whispering to the others. What did you say that was worth risking punishment?"

Her cheeks flushed as she looked away. "I told them the truth."

"The truth?"

"That Jesus is the Messiah," she said, "and He would rescue them even though they were bound."

"He didn't come to rescue them... or you."

"People can be rescued in more than one way," she replied softly.

Her words echoed through his thoughts, reminding him of Paul's.

"My people had a tradition," she continued, her voice distant. "Every seven years, all servants were to be set free."

"Sounds like a good deal for the servants."

"And bad for the masters," she replied. "That's why it didn't happen as it should. If a master bought a servant in year six for a hefty price, what could he do? Forgive the debt a few months later? Most decided against it. They disobeyed." She glanced at

Talia. "Still, it's a blessing to rescue her from a worse fate, even if she never knows true freedom." She turned to Epaphroditus. "But I don't understand. Why are you putting part of her debt on mine?"

"She's Roman," Epaphroditus said. "If she's your bondservant, she can work for you, and you can work off part of her debt."

Shira's eyes lit up as realization dawned.

"At least she'll work Saturdays." He forced a smile, but the tension in his shoulders clung to him until Luke and Melody rejoined him.

Luke looked at the girl, then at Epaphroditus with a smirk. "Planning to rescue every woman in Philippi?"

"You know I couldn't leave her in the hands of those brutes," Epaphroditus said, the memory of Talia's cries still haunting him.

"I'm partially sorry I didn't think of it first." Luke moved to kneel beside the girl. "Greetings…"

"Talia." Shira bent near them.

Luke's eyes softened as he said, "That's a lovely name." He turned to the girl. "Talia, may I examine you so we can treat your wounds?"

Talia's eyes welled with tears as she hesitantly lifted her gaze to meet his.

"We won't hurt you," Epaphroditus promised. "You're under my protection now."

"He's not so bad." Shira leaned close to Talia's ear. "They're both good men."

Talia gave a small nod.

"Wonderful," Luke said, unpacking medical supplies from his pack, glancing up at Epaphroditus. "I've just come from Lydia's. The women have gathered to pray for Paul and Silas. I'm going back to the jail in the morning."

"I'll come with you," Epaphroditus said.

"I was hoping you would." Luke set to work, his hands gentle yet efficient.

Shira stood. "May I go to Lydia's?"

Epaphroditus looked down at Talia, who still trembled. "I think she needs you more than Lydia does."

"Talia's in the best hands in Philippi." Shira lifted her chin. "I think Paul and Silas need my prayers more."

Considering her petition, Epaphroditus weighed her words. "Granted, but I want you back here before it's time to prepare for the evening meal."

She gave a quick nod and darted off, feet barely touching the ground.

His gaze drifted toward Talia. Images of her wailing in agony at Paul's feet would not leave him. This Adonai, who heard the prayers of women while his servants sat bruised and chained, what kind of god was he?

*About midnight Paul and Silas were
praying and singing hymns to God, and
the prisoners were listening to them, and
suddenly there was a great earthquake,
so that the foundations of the prison
were shaken. And immediately all the
doors were opened, and everyone's bonds
were unfastened.*
Acts 16:25-26

Early the next morning, Epaphroditus eased his way through his villa. A nighttime quake had shaken him from his watery nightmare, but it was difficult to survey the full damage before sunrise. In the golden rays of sunlight, he discovered broken pottery, shifted furniture, startled women, and... Aphrodite lying on the ground.

Easing toward her, he lifted the statue and settled her back in her niche. Running his finger over her face, he discovered cracks and chips. Her once flawless marble was now marred with imperfections. His chest squeezed.

Shira swept broken bowls into a pile near his feet. "We'll take care of the mess." She flicked a sideways glance at the statue. "Please go check on Paul and Silas."

He gave her a nod without words and left the villa.

Outside, people were tending to their homes, sweeping up debris, rearranging altars, and securing their properties. The quake had been significant enough to disrupt the normal flow of morning life.

As Epaphroditus neared the jail, Luke stood waiting for him. "Did you feel that quake last night?"

"Woke my entire house." Luke let out a breath. "Mother was furious over several broken bowls. Meanwhile, I had to pull shards out of Father's foot. He'd been scurrying around the house thinking someone was attempting to knock down our walls."

"The girls had a mess to clean up, too." Epaphroditus rubbed his chin. "Strangest thing."

They entered the jail, only to be halted by the same guard who'd tried to prevent their visit the previous day. "If you're looking for those two troublemakers, they're not here."

"What have you done with them?" Epaphroditus demanded.

"Not me," the guard replied, shaking his head. "The keeper took them into his house."

Epaphroditus met Luke's eyes, tension coiling

in his chest. "What do you think has happened to them?"

"I don't know, but we're going to find out."

They made their way through the courtyard.

The sounds of light-hearted chatter grew louder as a servant appeared in the doorway. "May I help you?"

"We're friends of Paul and Silas," Epaphroditus explained, motioning between himself and Luke. "The guard told us we could find them here."

"Follow me." The servant bowed and gestured inside.

The voices in the room grew clearer as they entered. A group had gathered in the large living space. Epaphroditus searched the faces, then paused. In the corner sat a woman he almost didn't recognize. Syntyche, a woman he often saw at the baker's stall. She was next to Lydia, her eyes red-rimmed, her fingers clutching the hem of her tunic as if holding on to something invisible.

"The physician and his friend." Paul raised his cup in greeting. "Please, join us."

Epaphroditus hesitated for a moment, still taken aback by the sight of Paul and Silas. Just hours ago, guards had shackled them in a filthy jail cell, their tunics torn and backs bruised. Yet here they sat, clean, wearing fresh tunics, and smiling as though nothing had happened.

"Why are you not still in chains?" he asked,

glancing around the room.

"A marvelous story I'd love to share," Paul replied with a grin, motioning toward an empty place. "Join us, and we'll recount the tale of Adonai's rescue."

Luke stepped forward and claimed a spot beside Paul, but Epaphroditus hesitated.

Silas stood and gripped his shoulder. "He's going to insist until you agree," he said, squeezing gently before releasing him. "It's a great tale. I think you'd be particularly interested in it."

Reluctantly, Epaphroditus lowered himself to sit beside them.

Paul cleared his throat. "Last night, Silas and I were praying and singing to our God."

"It was hard enough to sleep," Silas added with a chuckle, settling on his cushion and taking a sip from his cup. "Praying and singing help."

"Yes, yes." Paul gave a brief wave, brushing off the comment. "But while we were singing, Adonai was moving. He shook that jail until the doors opened wide."

Epaphroditus turned to Luke. "The quake."

"But the doors were not the only things opened,"—Paul lifted his arms dramatically—"our chains, too. The locks gave way like loosened jaws, and our bonds fell off." He lowered his arms, glancing at the jailer. "Poor Salvus here woke up to the sounds and drew his sword on himself, thinking we'd all escaped."

"What else was I supposed to think when every door in my jail was open?" Salvus muttered, rubbing the back of his neck. "The magistrates would've had my head. Being sent here to Philippi is a dream for most retired soldiers, but for me, it was exile. I've spent my years rotting here alongside countless prisoners. Though I've never seen anything like last night. Truth be told, I was terrified."

Paul's eyes softened. "We shouted for him not to harm himself and assured him we were all accounted for. When he came into our cell, the man was trembling. We knew the Lord was shaking him up, too." He slapped Salvus on the back. "Then he brought us out of the cell and asked us the most important question a person can…"

"What must I do to be saved?" Salvus said, his gaze moved from person to person before resting on Epaphroditus. "They told me all I had to do was believe in the Lord Jesus, and I would be saved. I'd heard of him before, even had some of his followers help me when I was younger, but I didn't fully understand their words at the time." He scratched his chin. "I brought Paul and Silas here to tell my family about Jesus and to clean them up. It seemed the least I could do after all the trouble."

"And then we immersed them all!" Paul laughed, the joy in his voice contagious. "Adonai was shaking up the whole family." He turned to Epaphroditus, eyes sparkling. "We've been eating and sharing all night."

"Pardon me, sir." The servant who had greeted them at the gate entered the room. "Several lictors are asking for you."

Salvus stood, his face hardening. "I'll see what they want."

Epaphroditus leaned toward Luke. "What do you make of all this?"

Luke's gaze drifted toward the floor, his expression tightening. "Not sure, but I hope it means Paul will stay in Philippi for a while."

When Salvus returned, he knelt next to Paul. "Good news," he said with a sly grin. "The magistrates have sent word to let you go. You're free and can go in peace."

Paul leaned back. "No."

"No?" Salvus blinked in confusion, tilting his head. "What do you mean?"

"They have beaten us publicly, we who are Roman citizens, and thrown us into prison. Now they want to throw us out secretly?" Paul let out a short, incredulous huff. "Let them come themselves and take us out."

Salvus hesitated, then nodded slowly. "I'll pass along your message." He rose and left.

Silence crept into the room. Epaphroditus stared at the archway, pulse ticking faster.

It was Paul who broke the quiet. "What

happened to the young woman I cast the demon out of?"

"She's safe," Epaphroditus assured him, keeping his eyes on the entrance. "She's under my servant's charge now."

Salvus reentered, settling beside Paul again. "It's done." He grabbed his cup and emptied it in one gulp. "I don't think they're going to like the message."

"We'll see what Adonai wants to do," Paul replied calmly.

Salvus set his cup down with a decisive clink. "Abusing a Roman citizen could result in their expulsion from office and disqualify them from ever serving again. Possibly even worse punishment." He looked at Paul with genuine confusion. "I don't understand. You've gained your freedom. What's the point of this?"

"They are the governing authorities,"—Paul gripped Salvus's shoulder firmly—"they must be held accountable for their misdeeds, just as they hold others accountable for theirs." He released his grip and shared stories of his previous beatings and imprisonments, recounting how Adonai had rescued him each time in diverse ways.

Epaphroditus was just starting to relax when the servant appeared once more.

"The magistrates are here, sir," he said, bowing low. "They request you escort Paul and Silas to them."

Salvus turned to Paul. "Well?"

"Let's see what they have to say for themselves." Paul rose and waved for Salvus to lead the way.

Epaphroditus rose quickly and fell in step behind them.

Outside, the two magistrates stood surrounded by their lictors. Their fasces gleamed in the sunlight, axes wrapped in rods, a cold reminder of who held power in Philippi.

Salvus marched Paul and Silas toward them.

One magistrate stepped forward, extending his arm toward them.

Paul clasped his arm with a firm, unwavering hold.

"I want to apologize for your mistreatment," the magistrate said, releasing his grip. "We were unaware of your citizenship status and only acted in the best interest of our citizens."

"Of course," Paul said with a serene nod. "My companion and I intended no harm to your citizens or your city. We are simply travelers delivering an important message."

"Splendid." The magistrate beamed. "Then you'll have no problem continuing your journey."

Paul glanced at Silas, his lips curving upward. "I suppose our path is open now."

"We encourage you to leave as quickly as possible," the magistrate added, lifting his chin slightly. "Just so there are no more... misunderstandings."

"We understand," Paul said, his tone even.

"Then we shall take our leave." The magistrate turned and signaled for his guards to follow.

Epaphroditus approached as the guards withdrew, uncertainty tightening his chest. "I guess this means you'll be leaving Philippi."

Paul remained still, his gaze following the retreating figures. "Not yet."

"But the magistrate—"

"I understand their request," Paul said, his voice soft yet firm. He turned to face Epaphroditus. "But I want to visit Lydia before we leave the city. Luke tells me I have some women to thank for praying for us."

Epaphroditus couldn't stop the rush of faces, Shira, Lydia, the others who had knelt together in the purple seller's villa, their voices lifted in desperate prayer. Had the god of the Israelites truly heard them? Had he shaken the earth itself to free Paul and Silas? The thought was wild, impossible. And yet... Luke had claimed this same god split the sea in two. Was there anything he couldn't do?

*So they went out of the prison and
visited Lydia. And when they had seen
the brothers, they encouraged them and
departed.*
Acts 16:40

After Paul had bid blessings to Salvus and his family, Epaphroditus and Luke followed him and Silas to Lydia's home. The estate rivaled his own in grandeur. Purple sellers were rare and exceedingly profitable. Lydia was rarer still, a woman managing successful trades both in Philippi and her native Thyatira, where she'd learned the craft from her family. Epaphroditus recalled his father describing her Thyatiran house just as stately and formidable.

Shira opened the door, her eyes wide with relief. "Paul? Thank Adonai, they have freed you. Please, come show yourself. The others won't believe it until they see you."

As Epaphroditus passed her, she caught his eye. "I told you he needed my prayers."

He chuckled. "Wait until you hear the story."

Inside, familiar faces turned toward them, some from the riverside gathering, others new, their expressions hopeful and full of awe.

"We've been praying since sunrise," Lydia said, approaching. "Some of us haven't stopped since the quake."

Paul settled in the center of the room, the group gathering as if his presence alone steadied the walls. He spoke of chains falling away, of trembling foundations, of a jailer ready to end his life, then falling on his knees to ask how to be saved.

Epaphroditus listened, but part of him drifted, eyes moving across the room. The same flame he'd seen in Salvus and his family now burned in each face here. Even Luke, his closest friend, seemed changed, as though Paul's words had sparked something deep inside him.

For the first time, Epaphroditus was a stranger among familiar faces. And yet, something stirred in him, just as it had in Troas. That low burning in his chest when Paul spoke. As if something asleep inside him was rising.

After the story ended and murmurs of praise circled the room, he pulled Paul aside. "I'd like to add Adonai to my worship of Aphrodite."

Paul spread his hands in gentle refusal. "I'm afraid that won't work."

"Why not? Most Romans worship many gods. I

would give Adonai a place of honor in my home."

"I understand," Paul said, placing a firm hand on his arm. "But Adonai is not one god among many. He is the only true God, and He demands our whole allegiance. He's jealous for His creation. If you follow Him, it must be Him alone."

Epaphroditus hesitated. "You mean I'd have to give up Aphrodite?"

Paul nodded. "And every other chain that holds you back."

"But she's blessed my family for generations. Our crops, our prosperity..."

Paul's gaze sharpened. "You think a carved statue has done this for you? That clay figures on household shelves wield power over fate and weather?"

Epaphroditus's mind flashed to the altar in his home and the chipped face of Aphrodite.

"You've heard me speak of Adonai," Paul continued. "Of Jesus and the salvation He offers."

"There is a stirring inside me," he murmured. "Like fire beneath my ribs. Like something trying to awaken."

Paul's eyes lit up. "That's Adonai's Spirit calling you to life."

"To life?" Epaphroditus echoed. "I am alive."

"You are awake, yes. But your soul is sealed in a tomb."

A tremor passed through Epaphroditus.

Priestess Arianna's blood-red lips. Her prophecy echoed like thunder. *Tomb.* The press of stone, the silence of the dead, ever since that moment in Paphos.

"There was a man named Lazarus," Paul said. "Sick unto death. Laid in a tomb for four days. But when Jesus called him out, he came walking, alive. That is what Jesus is offering you, my friend."

Epaphroditus steadied his breath. "You're saying Adonai is stronger than Aphrodite? That He can protect me?"

"Adonai is not an amulet. He is Creator and Sustainer, holding all things together... even you." Paul tapped his finger on Epaphroditus's chest.

He met Paul's eyes. "Then I ask the same question as the jailer: What must I do to be saved?"

"And my answer is the same." Paul's features eased into a look of hope. "Repent. Be immersed."

"I repent," he said, voice low but firm. "I renounce Aphrodite, and I choose Adonai... alone." He turned to Lydia. "Will you take me to the stream?"

Lydia's hands rose in praise. "Let us go at once!"

They left the house in a chorus of songs and rejoicing, marching out of the city gate and along the path to the river. The stream widened near the Gangites, its current cool and murmuring over stones.

Epaphroditus stood at the edge, feet planted,

eyes fixed on the water. His heart pounded. He was strong enough to walk against the flow, but memories surged: the Aegean swallowing him, the weight of drowning. Water had nearly taken his life once.

Paul stepped into the current and held out his hand. "Don't let fear keep you from obedience."

Epaphroditus exhaled. Reached. And stepped forward.

The chill struck first, biting into his legs. But Paul's hand steadied him, and they moved together toward the center. Paul raised one hand to the sky, the other bracing Epaphroditus's back.

"I immerse you, Epaphroditus, my brother, in the name of Jesus."

He nodded, ready.

Paul pressed his shoulder, and Epaphroditus covered his face and let himself fall back.

Water roared. Then silence.

Everything slowed. His pulse. His thoughts. Only the icy water and the grip on his back remained. Then, something burning... inside. Something burning away every dead thing and igniting a living fire within.

When he broke the surface, shouts greeted him. Paul clapped him on the back and helped him toward the shore.

Luke reached for him. "I prefer this way of getting you out of the water to the last one."

A warm laugh rumbled from his chest, the smile unstoppable. "Me as well." He lifted himself from the water, wrung out his short toga, and slapped water from his sandals as the crowd surrounded him. One by one, they embraced him, congratulated him. Only Shira held back.

She met his eyes, leaving a respectful space between them.

"You may speak freely," he told her.

She bowed her head. "I only wish Priscilla were here to see this. To see what Adonai is doing in Philippi."

"Priscilla?" Paul stepped forward. "Of Rome?"

Her eyes lit up. "You knew her?"

"She and her husband, Aquila. They're dear friends, serving in Corinth, last I heard."

Tears gathered on Shira's lashes. "Praise Adonai. I thought they were lost."

"They were exiled," Paul assured her. "They're still barred from returning to Rome."

"I was sent away, too." She nodded slowly. "I don't know if I'll ever go back."

Epaphroditus cleared his throat. "Paul, as much as I'd have you stay, the magistrate demanded you take your leave. Where will you go?"

Paul looked at Silas. "We'll travel the Via Egnatia westward, toward Thessalonica. Timothy will remain here to help Lydia. She'll need all the support she can get."

Something tugged in Epaphroditus's chest. "We'll miss your presence among us."

"I'm sure we'll meet again. But you have much to do in the meantime."

"Such as?"

"For starters," Paul said. "Your family should hear of your decision."

Epaphroditus nodded. There was much to share.

"And Silas and I should be on our way." Paul clasped his shoulder. "We have much ground to cover and many still to reach."

Epaphroditus turned to Shira. "Let's go home."

She followed quietly beside him as they returned to the villa.

Once inside, he gathered the household.

He told them everything. The quake. The jailer. Lydia's house. Paul's words. He watched their faces as he spoke of the stirring within him.

His mother listened in silence, her expression unreadable. Calliope's eyes sparkled, like she was eyeing gemstones in the marketplace. Enoch and Isaiah nodded, hands folded. Shira stood quietly, her hands clasped tight. Talia kept her gaze on her sandaled feet.

Epaphroditus stood tall. "As head of this household, I declare our new allegiance. From this day forward, we will worship Adonai alone."

Calliope moved toward him. "We will follow."

She lifted the golden lunula from around her neck and placed it in his open hand.

Closing his finger tight around the amulet, he nodded. He turned toward the altar of Aphrodite. The carved figure caught the lamplight, eternal beauty locked in clay.

"No more idols," he said. "No more gods of wood and stone."

He lifted the statue. "We will worship the Living God and devote our lives wholly to Him." He handed the statue to his mother.

"A new beginning," she whispered.

The others left to search the house for any other idols to dispose of.

Epaphroditus caught sight of Talia still sitting near the table. "Talia?"

She rose and walked toward him, keeping her gaze down, and stopped in front of him.

"Talia, I don't know what gods Remus and Calvus made you worship, but I want you to know that in this house, we will worship Adonai together."

She nodded, her dark hair a thick veil between them.

"I don't believe in using force." His shoulders eased. "But I will not allow any other gods to be worshipped in my home. Is that understood?"

She nodded again.

"I'm glad we understand each other." He went to

step away.

"Lord Epaphroditus, I have a question."

He bent to catch her vision. "Please, don't call me Lord, but you may ask your question."

"Forgive me." She turned away. "But what was the name that short man used in his spell to get rid of the demon?"

Images of Paul's frustration and Talia's convulsions flooded over him. "That was no spell. Paul rebuked the spirit in the name of Jesus, and it obeyed."

Talia lifted her head. "May I worship Jesus?"

Epaphroditus caught light shimmering in her eyes. His chest ached with a burning. "Yes, Talia. We will worship Jesus."

Her head dipped to one side as she averted her gaze. "But you said only Adonai."

"I did." He nodded. "But Paul says they are one and the same." He rubbed the back of his neck. "I don't fully understand either. We will have to ask Lydia about it."

She slowly raised her head again. "I can go to Lydia's like Shira?" Youthful excitement clashed with the burning fire in her eyes.

"You will be welcomed, and we will ask her about immersing you as well."

Now when they had passed through
Amphipolis and Apollonia, they came to
Thessalonica, where there was a
synagogue of the Jews.
Acts 17:1

Epaphroditus tore off a piece of bread and passed the broken loaf to the young man on his left. The crust crackled beneath his fingers, still warm and fragrant from the oven. Clement, the city baker and newest face at Lydia's gathering, gave a grateful nod. A faint dusting of flour clung to his tunic, and his fingertips bore the proof of a morning spent at the ovens.

Paul praised Lydia for her meetings by the river, but suggested the group gather indoors on Sabbaths to share a meal and encourage one another. Epaphroditus had been glad when Lydia agreed. He far preferred sitting in the comfort of her villa, cool stone walls and shaded porticos shielding them from the sun's harsh gaze, to being exposed outside the city gate in full view of passersby.

This was their first meeting indoors. Platters crowded the low table: roasted figs with honey, salted olives, smoked fish, and Clement's fresh loaves. Lydia opened a jug of her finest wine. Its dark, fruity perfume curled in the air as she lavishly filled each cup. She poured out Paul's words with equal generosity.

Light chatter occupied the open space, mingling with a breeze drifting through the windows. White linen curtains fluttered at the edges. The clink of cups and platters and the occasional burst of laughter gave the gathering a gentle pulse.

Everything remained pleasant until one conversation rose in pitch.

Euodia's voice, sharp and unrelenting, cut through the others. Her hands carved the air with growing intensity, her brows drawn in fierce determination. Syntyche wagged her head and shut her eyes tight, as if she could drown out the older woman by sheer will.

Shira sat to the right of Epaphroditus, Talia on her other side. The two bickering women sat across from them.

Epaphroditus leaned near Shira's ear; the aroma of olive oil and juniper wafted from her hair. "What's got them stirred up?"

She didn't look their way, only sighed and reached for a cluster of grapes. "They're arguing over what Paul meant when he said Jesus had to die on a tree." She popped one grape into her mouth, then idly twirled another between her fingers. "Syntyche says it was as a Jewish sacrifice. Euodia insists it was to bear our curse, that's why it had to be a tree."

"What does it matter?"

"I agree." Shira finally glanced at them, her gaze flint-sharp. "Paul's words are confusing enough. Fighting over them only muddies the waters." She turned back to him. "But try telling those two that."

Their voices rose, drowning out the rest.

Lydia tapped the table lightly with her fingers, and the noise fell away. "Ladies, please." She waited until Euodia and Syntyche looked at her. "We can disagree peacefully, or not at all in my home. Your choice."

Syntyche lowered her head.

Euodia bit her bottom lip.

Epaphroditus looked down at Shira. He had plenty of quips ready, but decided not to add fuel to the fire Lydia had just doused.

At that moment, one of Lydia's servants entered. She bent low and whispered something in her mistress's ear.

Lydia straightened. "Send him in."

The servant bowed and disappeared.

Epaphroditus scanned the room. No one seemed to be missing. He caught Shira's eye.

She lifted one shoulder in a shrug.

The servant returned with a familiar figure.

Dust clung to Timothy's sandals and tunic, and sweat glistened on his brow, streaking dark lines through the grime of travel. His steps were slow but purposeful, as if every movement carried the weight of miles behind him.

Lydia rose at once. "Many blessings to you, Timothy." She kissed his cheeks and embraced him. "Please, join us." She gestured toward the low table.

Epaphroditus shifted to make room between himself and Clement. The scent of earth and sweat mixed faintly with the lingering aroma of wine and fresh bread, a testament to Timothy's journey.

He sank into the cushion, rubbing a hand over his face as if trying to scrub away the weariness. "Smells good." He sniffed the air, then nodded his thanks to Epaphroditus. "I looked for you all by the river but figured you'd be here."

Lydia resumed her seat. "What news do you have of our dear friend, Paul?"

"I left him in Thessalonica." Timothy reached for a boiled egg, biting it in half, chewing slowly as if savoring the small comfort. "He's started a gathering there, but it's been a struggle."

Epaphroditus pushed a platter of cheese closer to him. "Why?"

Timothy swallowed hard and broke off a piece of cheese before answering. "He's dividing his time between teaching and working. The new believers are mostly poor, barely able to support themselves, let alone a traveling teacher."

"He's only been gone a week." Epaphroditus shifted to get a better view of the younger man. "It shouldn't take much to support a traveling teacher."

Timothy slipped the cheese into his mouth, speaking over his bite, "It takes more than you think to lay a foundation in a new city."

Syntyche hissed through clenched teeth. "Not all of us are wealthy either."

Epaphroditus caught Lydia's subtle frown, her lips pressed tight as if holding back a sharp reply.

Timothy met Lydia's gaze with a knowing nod. "I know many here aren't rich, but you're far more blessed than you realize. Traveling with Paul... it's changed my perspective, on the world and on money." He sighed, eyes distant. "The foundation is fragile. Every coin counts."

Perspective. The word stuck in Epaphroditus's mind. He hadn't traveled far himself, only once to Paphos as a boy and, more recently, with Luke to Troas. Both journeys only confirmed his desire never to leave Philippi again. People were people, rich or poor, here or in Thessalonica.

Lydia lifted her cup. "Then we'll do what we can to support our friend."

Syntyche stretched toward her. "But—"

"The God of Israel has blessed us here in Philippi," Lydia said, her gaze fixed on Syntyche. "I'm sure each of us can make room in our hearts, and in our money pouches, to support Paul's mission."

Syntyche looked down.

Across the table, Luke shifted, reached into his tunic, and drew out a few coins. They clinked softly as he laid them beside the bread. "Let me be the first." He turned to Epaphroditus. "And I suggest Epaphroditus oversee the rest of the collection."

"Me?" Epaphroditus frowned. "It was Lydia's idea."

"You've managed your family's accounts and increased them. Without travel, might I add."

"But Lydia owns two homes and two businesses," Epaphroditus countered. "Surely she's more capable."

Lydia nodded gently. "I agree… with Luke." Her words were gentle yet edged with quiet authority, leaving no room for argument. "Epaphroditus, would you bless us by securing the funds and ensuring Timothy receives them before he leaves?"

Epaphroditus looked around. Every face turned toward him. Their expectation settled over him like a heavy wool cloak.

He sighed. "If that is the will of the gathering."

"Splendid." Lydia patted the table. "And I expect each of you to give as if you were giving to Jesus." Her gaze lingered on Syntyche for an extra moment.

The next day, Epaphroditus set out at first light, the warm sun casting long shadows on the narrow streets of Philippi. With a leather pouch secured at his waist, he moved from home to home of known believers. He spoke softly but clearly, sharing Paul's urgent need and their gathering's desire to send aid. Some faces lit with joy, offering coins freely, as if each gift were a seed planted in fertile soil. Others hesitated, lips pressed tight, hands trembling as they reached into worn purses. A few, overwhelmed by poverty or sorrow, could only offer prayers and tearful apologies.

Epaphroditus accepted every gift humbly, the weight of hope settling as he tucked each coin into the pouch, adding his own to the growing sum. He thought of Paul's struggle to build faith in Thessalonica, and the fragile roots that needed nourishing.

When he completed his round of the city, he placed the pouch into Timothy's hands and gripped his forearm. "God go with you."

He watched Timothy vanish down the dusty road out of town, then whispered a prayer.

The following Sabbath, Silas joined the gathering in Lydia's villa. Without prompting, more coins appeared, small tokens of commitment.

Epaphroditus gathered them gladly and placed them into Silas's outstretched hand. "Tell Paul we're praying for him."

Lydia laid her hand on Silas's arm. "And tell him to write if he needs more."

*Now after these events Paul resolved in
the Spirit to pass through Macedonia
and Achaia and go to Jerusalem, saying,
"After I have been there, I must also see
Rome." And having sent into Macedonia
two of his helpers, Timothy and Erastus,
he himself stayed in Asia for a while.*
Acts 19:21-22

AD 54, Four years later

Lydia's gatherings that once occupied the riverside
now spilled into the courtyards of her villa on a
weekly basis. As she traveled between Philippi and
Thyatira often, she left the community's care to
Epaphroditus and others when she was away.

Epaphroditus often welcomed small groups
beneath the thick shade of his olive grove during the
sweltering hours of the day. There, beneath rustling
leaves and a speckled canopy, he recited Paul's
teachings and did his best to explain them.

While the others came as often as they could, today the most faithful were gathered to hear from him. After he finished his recitation, an urge to speak came over him. "Those who joined us recently brought forward a need I must share." His eyes moved over the semicircle.

Clement sat cross-legged. Euodia knelt beside him with her sandals tucked beneath her. Syntyche leaned against a tree, twisting bark between her fingers. Shira leaned forward, elbows on her knees. Luke stood behind them, poking absently at the ground with a twig.

"Some among us are suffering," Epaphroditus continued. "A few widows are starving. We've had traveling believers in need. Shouldn't we help them, just as we helped Paul?"

Luke let his twig fall and reached for his belt pouch.

Euodia drew a soft leather bag from her tunic. She placed it in her lap, her hand resting on top. "I'm willing to give. But I want to be sure the funds reach those truly in need."

Luke turned to her, brow arched. "Do you question Epaphroditus's integrity?"

"I would never." She placed her hand over her chest. "But the visitors to my home carry heavier grief. I see it firsthand. I don't want them overlooked."

Syntyche kept twisting the bark between her

fingers. "We should prioritize need over familiarity."

Euodia's eyes narrowed as she leaned toward her. "Are you questioning my motives?"

Arms crossed, Syntyche stepped closer, her shoulders stiff. "I've seen who enters your home on Sabbath. They drip with wealth. You claim aid for them while those who visit me come barefoot and carrying children with skin so thin you can see their bones."

Epaphroditus pressed his fingers to his temple. "Ladies, please."

Both turned toward him, eyes sharp.

"Our grace cannot become a matter of clientship," he said. "Need should not be measured by connection. All kinds of people could benefit from our support. We must be just."

Luke stepped between the women. "This is why Lydia trusted Epaphroditus from the beginning. And we should, too."

Epaphroditus dipped his head in silent thanks. A flicker of movement on the path behind them drew his eye. Two figures approaching fast. His body tensed, feet already moving before the thought caught up. "Timothy?"

The younger man approached and clasped Epaphroditus's forearm. "Good to see you, brother. Paul sends greetings from Corinth." He gestured to the man beside him. "This is Erastus, director of public works in the city. Paul asked us to check on the gatherings in Macedonia. He hopes to pass through here on his way to Jerusalem."

Epaphroditus clasped Erastus's outstretched arm. "Any friend of Paul's is welcome here." He turned slightly to indicate the others. "Our sisters in the faith, Euodia, Syntyche, Shira, and my dear friend Luke."

"Ah, the physician." Erastus inclined his head toward Luke. "Paul speaks highly of you."

Luke stepped forward. "What news do you bring?"

"Have you heard Emperor Claudius is dead? Poisoned, some say by his own wife. Nero rules now."

"That boy?" Luke rubbed his chin. "He hasn't seen twenty harvests."

Epaphroditus studied Erastus as they spoke. The man carried himself with the quiet authority of one accustomed to power, yet his eyes revealed a weariness far beyond official duties. As director of public works in Corinth, Erastus was no stranger to heavy responsibility, but here, beneath the olive trees, he seemed less a ruler of stone and streets than a weary traveler seeking refuge.

"Most of our news is grim." Timothy shrugged. "They killed Philip in Phrygia. Persecution is spreading fast."

Epaphroditus froze. A dull ache settled beneath

his ribs. Philippi had remained peaceful so far, but for how long?

Timothy met his gaze, as if hearing his troubled thoughts. "Is Lydia here?"

"She's still in Thyatira."

"Shame." Timothy adjusted the strap of his pack. "Paul hoped to call on her generosity again. The Corinthian gathering is growing fast."

Epaphroditus looked at Euodia and Syntyche; both bristled at the mention of another collection. "We were just discussing the fair distribution of aid among our own." He turned back to Timothy. "But of course, we will send help to Paul."

A soft scoff sounded behind him. He didn't turn to see whose.

Luke moved quietly, bridging the gap between them. "I'd be honored if you two would stay with me while you're here."

"A good plan," Epaphroditus said, patting his shoulder. "Make sure they eat and rest." He turned to the group. "That concludes today's gathering. I'll collect funds tomorrow and see they're used rightly."

Euodia and Syntyche dipped their heads and drifted off, footsteps soft on dry grass as they departed.

Epaphroditus nodded to Shira. She rose and silently joined him.

Their walk home was quiet but not strained. After teaching, answering questions, and more recently, mediating disputes, he craved silence. Shira never pressed into that space. She understood; she always had.

So much had shifted in the four years since Paul's arrival.

His thoughts drifted to Calliope and her new role as wife to Felix. Though he'd been hesitant to fulfill the obligation of the betrothal after committing his family to Adonai, Felix had not only grown into a hardworking young man, but one who faithfully attended their weekly gatherings. Though his labor often kept him from attending the meetings in the olive grove, his faith had grown right next to theirs. Epaphroditus was proud to unite their households.

During the same time, they'd buried their mother, and Melody's womb remained empty. Joy and sorrow seemed inseparable.

Calliope's recent wedding had removed another set of hands from the villa, but Shira rose to fill the gap. Over the years, she diligently trained Talia, who served Melody and the villa just as faithfully. The two women almost filled the emptiness in Melody's life. Almost.

The three women and two male bondservants occupied the large estate with Epaphroditus. He frequently welcomed fellow believers to stay at his home and often hosted meals for Philippians impacted by Paul's teachings. His family's villa, once full of kin, now hosted more servants and fellow believers than family. It was a strange twist of fate.

Through it all, Shira had become indispensable, serving with quiet grace. Something Epaphroditus never imagined that day he met the defiant, bound exile from Rome.

Their time together beneath the olive trees and at gatherings had only deepened their bond. Her questions had grown more thoughtful, her care for others more expansive. Looking at her now, she seemed as close as Calliope, as close as a...

Epaphroditus stopped mid-step.

Shira paused beside him, her eyes searching his face. "Is something wrong?"

He turned toward her, uncertain. The thought hit like thunder, sudden and overwhelming, yet bright with possibility.

"Shira," he said slowly, "do you regret coming to Philippi?"

Shira paused, her expression tightening. "What do you mean?"

"Being brought here. Do you wish things had been different?"

Her shoulders dipped, not with defeat, but with remembrance. "There were days." Her voice was quiet. "Days I wished the flames that had taken my family would have taken me too. Days I wanted to run." She met his eyes. "But if Paul taught me anything, it's this, my body may be enslaved to

Rome, but my soul and mind are free. If that kind of freedom required chains, then no, I don't regret it."

His expression softened, the tight knot in his chest unraveling bit by bit. "Enoch and Isaiah should be inside. Would you fetch them and Talia? I have something to say to all of you."

She studied him, then gave a nod and disappeared through the door.

He lingered in his courtyard, pacing, lips moving in silent prayer for strength and wisdom.

When the four entered, he straightened. "Thank you for coming. I have something I must say."

The men exchanged a glance. Shira remained beside them, hands folded. Talia kept her gaze lowered.

Epaphroditus took a breath. "All of you have served my household with honor. But that service ends today."

Isaiah stepped forward. "Master, what are you saying?"

He raised his hand. "From this moment, I am not your master. You are no longer bound to this house. I'm forgiving all of your debts."

Cautious hope lifted Enoch's shoulders. "We're free?"

"Yes. Free to choose your own path. To travel, to build homes, to start families if you wish."

A long silence stretched. Enoch looked at Isaiah,

then back at Epaphroditus. "Would you hire us?"

His mouth hung open with words that wouldn't come, then a gentle smile broke through. "It would be my honor."

"Then," Enoch said, nodding to Isaiah, "with your permission, we'd like to return to the grove."

Epaphroditus nodded, throat tight. "Your wages begin today."

They bowed and left.

Shira and Talia didn't move.

He stepped closer, his voice soft. "While I can't free Talia since she belongs to you, I am freeing you. Shira, you're free. You could return to Rome. Build a life of your choosing." He leaned over to the younger woman. "Take Talia with you. Show her a life beyond Philippi."

He waited. Quiet hung between them, but for the first time in years, it was uncomfortable. "Shira?"

"I heard you." She glanced up, holding his look for a heartbeat before turning away. "But I'm also home. I have no other. Here, I'm safe, I'm cared for, and I'm free to worship Adonai." Her gaze drifted to Talia, and she reached over to squeeze her hand. "When you go to file the dismissal of my debts, I would like to forgive Talia of hers as well."

Talia yanked Shira's arm and violently shook her head.

Shira patted the top of her hand. "Paul taught me that when one is forgiven much, they should also forgive much. But I know you don't have a safe place." She turned to Epaphroditus. "If Melody will have us, I wish us to remain here in your service."

A firm warmth settled deep inside him as he glanced between the two of them. "You'd both be welcome as long as you wish."

Sisters.

*There he spent three months, and when a
plot was made against him by the Jews
as he was about to set sail for Syria, he
decided to return through Macedonia.*
Acts 20:3

AD 56, Two Years Later

Epaphroditus first saw the split while standing
between two homes, a breeze stirring dust at his
feet.

To his right, the sounds of gentle activity,
children's laughter, the rhythmic thump of a loom,
the murmur of voices, wafted from Euodia's home.
The courtyard swelled with women whose
distracted smiles barely met his gaze. One man lifted
a hand in welcome but avoided his gaze. From
within came the sound of voices in song, a psalm of
deliverance, bright with conviction.

To his left, Syntyche's doorway stood open,
warm lamplight reaching for the fading sun. The

scent of rich wine mingled with frankincense. Inside, a circle of believers sat with heads bowed. Syntyche stood at the center, her voice calm and deliberate as she recited one of Paul's teachings.

Two women. Two homes. Pulled in opposite directions.

It hadn't always been this way.

Epaphroditus recalled the earlier days, the warmth of shared laughter spilling from Euodia's courtyard, the soft murmur of prayers rising from Syntyche's hearth. He remembered how their voices had blended, each note strengthening the other. Together, they had been pillars, steadfast and unyielding against the growing shadows beyond Philippi's walls.

Now, the distance between them was a canyon carved by silent grudges and unspoken fears. The women he once admired for their strength and grace now wore expressions taut with suspicion and wounded pride.

His heart ached as he stood rooted on the road, torn between them. This fracture was more than a disagreement; it was a threat to the fragile unity that had kept their fledgling community alive. He carried the weight of every prayer whispered late at night, every lesson shared beneath the olive trees, teetering on the edge of collapse. How had they come to this? How could two souls, both so faithful, become such distant strangers?

Epaphroditus clenched his fists, the grit beneath his nails grounding him. He owed them peace, for the sake of the others, those who looked to Euodia and Syntyche not just for leadership, but for hope.

He'd tried to reason with the two women. He visited both gatherings, hoping his presence might bridge the growing gap. But the visits had the opposite effect; each side took his attendance as affirmation. He prayed with them, shared news, and urged unity.

Still, the divide widened.

Frustration burned in his belly as he stood in the road. "I can't do this anymore."

He waited until both homes had emptied, then pulled the women aside.

Under the hush of dusk, the air thick and the shadows long, he opened his hands. "Sisters, we're tearing ourselves apart. Have you forgotten? We are partners, not rivals."

Euodia crossed her arms, her expression strained with restraint. "Peace cannot come through silence."

Syntyche's chin lifted, though her voice remained soft. "Nor through pride."

He let out a long, heavy breath. "Help me understand. How did we come to this?"

Silence.

He looked at them, two women whose names meant good journey and good fortune, now walking opposite roads, risking both grace and direction if they continued this way.

"If you two cannot reconcile," he said quietly, "what hope remains for the others?" He exhaled slowly, his shoulders tightening. "I won't choose between you. Christ hasn't."

They parted without another word.

That night, Epaphroditus returned home heavy with weariness. He fell asleep praying for wisdom, his words clumsy and broken.

The next day brought new light and an old friend.

Paul arrived in Philippi without flourish, only dust on his cloak and a fire in his eyes. Epaphroditus was among the first to greet him at the gate.

Embracing Epaphroditus, Paul stepped back, studying his face. "You've aged, my friend."

"So have you."

Paul laughed, bright and familiar, like his favorite song. "Come. Tell me everything."

Epaphroditus led him toward his villa, speaking of all that had unfolded since Paul's last visit. He spoke of the split gatherings, the subtle tensions, and the undercurrent of legalism creeping into their meetings.

Paul listened without interruption, his expression growing darker with each detail.

When Epaphroditus mentioned whispers of the Judaizers, men insisting Gentiles must bear the full yoke of Moses to be saved, Paul's jaw clenched.

"They're here, then," he muttered. "I thought they might come."

"They haven't declared themselves outright, but their teaching spreads."

Paul nodded grimly. "They infected Galatia. Tried to twist the Thessalonians, too. They come with scrolls and certainty, but they bring chains, not freedom." He laid a firm hand on Epaphroditus' shoulder. "You've stood well. I know this work wears the soul thin."

Epaphroditus gripped Paul's arm in return. "Seeing you refreshes my soul. Lending me your ear reminds me I'm not alone."

They walked on together in quiet.

After a moment, Epaphroditus spoke, "I'll gather support while you're here. Even divided, the believers still give joyfully to your work."

Paul hesitated. "You've already given more than most." His hands clenched briefly at his sides. "I can't accept anything this time. Let the other cities bear the weight now."

"We won't hear of it." Epaphroditus stood firm. "It is our duty... and our joy."

Paul's eyes softened. "I'm ever blessed by you, my friend."

Word that Paul was in Philippi spread like a hungry flame. Before the day's end, gifts began arriving: bread, oil, wool. Even coins found their way into his hands from those who could barely feed their own children.

In the little time Paul remained in the city, Epaphroditus drank deeply from the well of his encouragement. The night before his departure, Paul called for a small gathering in Lydia's house.

Epaphroditus sat in her courtyard, his stomach full, his heart heavy. Paul's departures grew harder each time.

Paul paced before them. "There's been a plot."

A hush fell over them.

"They're waiting for me," Paul went on. "Men tied to the circumcision party. They've learned of my plans to sail from Neapolis to Syria."

Epaphroditus stiffened. The sea route was the fastest and the most exposed. Once the ship left the coast, there would be no place to flee.

"They intend to intercept me," Paul said. "Perhaps worse. I don't intend to find out."

A murmur rose, half-prayers, half-curses.

Epaphroditus clenched his fist. He'd seen zealots wield the Law like a dagger. Even in Philippi, their influence was seeping in like rot beneath the soil.

"We'll go north instead," Paul said, raising his voice above the unrest. "Back through Macedonia. The land road will slow us, but we'll have ground under our feet."

"And eyes to watch the path," Timothy muttered.

"Exactly." Paul nodded. "I won't go alone. There are faithful men who will travel with me, Sopater of Berea, Aristarchus and Secundus from Thessalonica, Gaius of Derbe, Tychicus and Trophimus of Asia…"

Epaphroditus knew the names, loyal men, tested and unafraid of long roads or hard truths.

Across the table, Luke stirred. He had been quiet all night. Now he stood. "I'll be counted among them."

Epaphroditus looked up sharply. "You can't. You heard Paul, men are hunting him." He turned to Paul, almost pleading. "You already have a guard. Tell him he's not needed."

Luke didn't flinch. "How can I stay?"

Epaphroditus heard the ache beneath the reason.

Luke stepped closer, his voice low. "You'll hold the others together. You're the anchor. But me? I need to go."

Something twisted inside Epaphroditus, grief, fear, or both. He wanted to protest, but the fire in Luke's eyes outshone every word. He reached out and clasped Luke's forearm. "Then go with my prayers."

By morning, the travelers were ready. Low clouds threatened rain. The air smelled of livestock and wet earth.

Epaphroditus stood at the edge of the road. One by one, they passed, some clasping his shoulder, others offering quiet smiles.

Luke lingered, eyes tired but intent, holding Epaphroditus's gaze a moment longer. "Take care of Melody."

Epaphroditus gave a single nod.

"And the others." Luke's mouth lifted at one corner. "They need your strength." He turned to catch up with the other men.

Paul tarried. "Stand firm, my brother. We shall see each other again."

Words failed. His throat burned. He reached out, clasping Paul's forearm, tight and brief. Then let go. Praying against all odds, this would not be the last time he set eyes on his dear friend.

He watched until the dust of their departure settled, his soul as empty as the road before him.

Could the believers in Philippi survive, torn as they were?

Not without prayer.

He bowed his head. *Not without You, Lord.*

And when it was decided that we should
sail for Italy, they delivered Paul and
some other prisoners to a centurion of
the Augustan Cohort named Julius.
Acts 27:1

AD 60, Four Years Later

Epaphroditus scrubbed dirt from his hands and face. The grove was flourishing despite a short drought. He only wished he could say the same for the believers in Philippi. Though their numbers continued to increase and some individuals matured in their faith, the gathering had fractured into scattered assemblies across the city. Lydia, once the heartbeat of their fellowship, had remained in Thyatira because of her failing health, and eventually passed in her home, surrounded by her family.

Epaphroditus tried to step into her sandals, but her steps were wide, her faith vast. His own steps faltered. People weren't olive trees; they didn't take to tending so easily.

Shira entered the kitchen, fingers white around a scroll. Uncertainty hovered in her gaze.

He wiped his hands on a cloth and pointed to the letter. "Who's it from?"

"Luke." The name left her lips uneven, sweet with longing yet taut with worry.

He held out his hand. "Let's hear it together."

She released the scroll to him.

Epaphroditus unrolled the parchment and read aloud:

> *Luke, humble physician and friend,*
>
> *To the esteemed Epaphroditus, brother in the faith,*
>
> *Grace and peace be multiplied to you from God our Father and the Lord Jesus Christ.*
>
> *It seemed good to me to write to you concerning the journey which has brought us to Rome by the hand of the Lord.*
>
> *When Paul was arrested in Jerusalem and it was determined that he should be sent to Rome for a trial, he was entrusted to a centurion named Julius of the Augustan Cohort. I was permitted to accompany him, as was*

Aristarchus of Thessalonica. Though we set out with hope, the winds soon opposed us, and the voyage became perilous.

Shira gasped and curled her fingers to her lips.

Epaphroditus lowered the scroll slightly, steadying her with a look before continuing.

Paul, perceiving what was to come, warned that the journey would end in loss, but his counsel was not regarded. A great storm struck, and for many days we saw neither sun nor stars. All hope of survival was nearly gone. But the Lord sent a divine messenger to Paul, assuring him that though the ship would be lost, not one life would perish.

Our ship wrecked on an island called Malta. All 276 souls were brought safely to land, though the ship and its contents were lost to the sea. The islanders received us with uncommon kindness, even after some whispered that Paul was a god, after he survived a venomous snake bite and healed the chief's father, along with many others.

After some time, we resumed our journey and have now arrived in Rome. Paul remains under guard yet is permitted to receive visitors and continues to proclaim the kingdom of God with boldness.

I write these things that you may rejoice in the steadfast love of our God, who saves not only from storm and sea, but from death itself.

The believers in Rome greet you.

May the grace of Jesus Christ be with you.

Epaphroditus rolled the parchment closed. His heart thudded. The scroll trembled in his fingers, as if the winds of Malta still clung to it.

Shira reached to steady herself against the wall. "We must do something."

She voiced what he hadn't yet dared to say. He nodded slowly, not trusting his voice yet. Paul had lost everything. They must do something. "Gather the others. We need to pray."

By sundown, word of the letter had spread. A gathering formed in Epaphroditus's courtyard. He read Luke's message aloud, his voice firm despite the tightness in his throat.

When he finished, he added, "We must send them help."

A murmur of agreement rippled through the crowd.

"They've lost everything," Shira added, her voice edged with urgency. "Paul needs resources to survive in Rome. Who knows how long they will keep him in chains before his trial."

Someone mentioned collecting a gift. Another suggested clothing, supplies.

For a moment, the old unity stirred, flickers of warmth on weary faces. But then came the protest.

"Our harvests have barely broken even."

It was true. Famine had wrung the region dry. Cracked soil, empty markets. Families forced to sell their heirlooms just to buy grain.

"We'll give what we can," said Euodia, arms folded tight.

Syntyche stood opposite her, hands on hips. "And how do we send it? No courier will carry that kind of weight to Rome without silver upfront."

Tension reopened like an old wound. The fracture between Euodia and Syntyche had never healed. It had set crooked, like a bone left to mend without care, and could bear little weight.

Epaphroditus glanced at Shira, then stepped forward. His olive grove had done well. His family's fortune was stable. He'd been saving a sum of coins for an expansion that could wait. "I'll front the silver."

Heads turned.

"The gift. The transport. All of it."

Syntyche's brow arched. "All of it? Yourself?"

"Until after the next harvest. The church can repay me… if it chooses to."

A heavy silence settled.

Euodia narrowed her eyes at him. "Why would you do that?"

He scanned their faces, hope dulled by hardship, faith rubbed raw. "How can we hoard what was never ours to begin with?"

Nods followed. Slowly, the tension melted. Coin purses appeared. Pledges were spoken.

Syntyche held out two coins. "We've yet to decide who carries it to Paul. The journey's months long. If it's confiscated or stolen…"

Melody gestured toward Epaphroditus. "He's already paid the price. Let him carry it."

Voices rose, some in agreement, some in dissent.

Epaphroditus turned toward her. "I can't."

"Luke needs you." Her eyes pleaded. "Paul needs you. There's no one I, or any of us, would trust more."

Others echoed her words.

"I can't," he insisted. "You know I can't."

Clement stepped forward. "I'll go with you."

Epaphroditus's chest tightened. "And leave your ovens?"

"Others can carry my burden here. Let me help

you carry this one."

He bowed his head, torn between reverence and dread. "I can't do this," his voice cracked. Tears burned. "It's across the Great Sea."

Paul's words struck through him like thunder. *Don't let fear keep you in disobedience.*

He clenched his hands, then released them.

Melody laid a hand against his cheek. "You must go."

He opened his eyes. In her gaze, he found strength. He had decided. Still, his stomach twisted with the unknown.

By morning, they gathered at the city gate. Clement stood beside him, pack secured. They sold extra supplies for coins, hiding them in wax-sealed pouches and stitching them into seams.

Shira approached with Talia at her side. "I'll pray every day." She held out his cloak. "For strength. And a safe return." Her eyes lingered on him a moment longer before stepping back.

He threw the cloak over his shoulders and bent to meet Talia's eyes. "Take care of your mistress for me. She can be quite the handful."

The corners of Talia's lips twitched. "Of course, my lord."

"Talia, what did I say about using that word?" he asked, unable to keep playfulness from his reprimand.

She lifted her chin. "Jesus is the only Lord." She

met his soft gaze. "I will be praying for you, brother."

"That's better." He set his hand gently on her cheek and pressed a light kiss on her forehead before releasing her.

Calliope handed him a honeyed cake and placed her hand on his chest. "Take courage."

His gaze traveled to her rounded midsection and then to Felix at her side. The fruit of their love had bloomed, and it sent a twisting joyful and envious knot in his stomach. He counted the days of travel ahead and realized he would probably miss the arrival of their new family member. "Take care of your bride and that little one until I return."

Felix ran a hand through his thick hair. "It's odd not taking part in all the rituals. At the wedding and now..." He dipped his head toward Calliope's stomach.

Epaphroditus gripped his shoulder. "There is no need to wake the dead gods when we have the Living One on our side."

Felix nodded. "You'll be in our prayers. May Adonai go with you."

Clement muttered about catching the wind before it turned.

Epaphroditus allowed himself one last look at all of them. He saw not just individuals, but a body, aching, imperfect, faithful. Euodia and Syntyche stood on opposite ends of the crowd. Both bowed their heads at the same moment.

What will happen while I'm gone?

He could do nothing but pray.

He kissed Melody and Calliope's cheeks, then turned toward Neapolis.

The road unfurled in silence, a ribbon of stillness beneath the waking sky. He and Clement walked without words. There would be time enough later. Months of it.

At the harbor, the air bristled with salt and shouting. Sailors barked orders. Children darted between puddles. Gulls wheeled over creaking hulls.

When they reached the vessel bound for Italy, Epaphroditus paused. He whispered a string of prayers and stepped aboard. The planks groaned under his weight.

Clement followed close behind.

As the ship pulled away from the dock, Epaphroditus stood at the rail, watching Neapolis shrink into a blur of stone and green.

The wind caught his cloak.

Arianna's prophecy and Paul's encouragement danced in his mind.

Death waits for you across the Great Sea; your life will be Aphrodite's fee.

Don't let fear keep you in disobedience.

He gripped the rail, knuckles pale, eyes shut against the wind. Obedience. Was this the path to the end he'd always feared, the one foretold long ago?

But I am like a green olive tree
in the house of God.
I trust in the steadfast love of God
forever and ever.
Psalm 52:8

Epaphroditus stood at the bow, gripping the weather-beaten beam as though it might keep him from being swept away. Salt had soaked deep into the wood under his fingers, deeper than it ever would into his own bones. The sea had already wrung him out, his strength, his appetite, even his dignity, spilled into the sea more times than he cared to recall.

The horizon tipped and leveled with each swell. Somewhere below, the captain shouted for fresh line and canvas, but up here, only the wind answered. The sky had turned as pale as bleached linen, and the endless blue-green water mocked his attempt to stay upright.

"Keep your eyes on the horizon," the captain

had told him when the first wave turned his stomach inside out. "Let your eyes find something still, even if your feet can't."

He'd tried. He was trying now. But his stomach betrayed him again. A surge rose in his throat, and he turned just in time to avoid fouling his tunic.

He wiped his mouth with the back of his hand and drew a slow breath, the salt air burning the back of his throat. His fingers hovered over a fold of his tunic. A coin pouch thumped softly against his ribs with every motion of the ship, its weight both comfort and burden. The gift from Philippi... still safe.

If he lived long enough to hand it over.

The wind shifted, catching the sail overhead. The mast groaned. He braced his stance.

The words of the prophetess rose unbidden, coiling through his thoughts like smoke: *Death waits for you across the sea.* He'd been just a boy at the temple, barely tall enough to see over the ship's railing. Arianna's lips had been as red as garnets, and the words she spoke that day had never left him. He carried them like a brand, hidden beneath every prayer and purpose.

Was she right?

The sea churned below him, clawed with white spray. It stretched beyond memory, deeper than fear. If death lay ahead, at least it would come honestly.

A creak in the boards beneath his feet sounded like a groan from the underworld itself. He closed his eyes, steadied himself with a breath, and pressed a palm against his satchel where Luke's letter lay, tucked in a spare linen wrap. The words still burned behind his eyes: *Paul imprisoned. Awaiting trial.*

A shadow passed beside him. One of the crew handed him a clay cup.

"Smooth seas don't make strong sailors," the man said, his breath heavy with wine and salted fish.

Epaphroditus took it with a nod and used a mouthful to rinse the sour taste from his tongue. "I've heard that before."

The sailor laughed and moved on.

The sky stretched wide and pitiless overhead. Days at sea blurred into one long ache. The rocking, the stench below deck, the taste of brine and bile in equal measure, he would have traded all of it for a patch of dry earth and an olive tree's shade.

He rubbed his hand down his face. Was this Aphrodite's revenge? For leaving her temple behind? For bowing now only to Adonai?

He didn't need a priestess to whisper warnings in his sleep. The storm of his last voyage haunted him still. Even now, with clear skies and calm waters, his mind drifted to images of splintered hulls and bodies flung like shattered amphorae into the sea. Every lurch of the ship made his fingers twitch toward the rail.

Clement emerged from below deck, his cloak pulled tight against the spray. "You should eat something." He offered a twist of barley bread and a dried fig.

"I'll pass."

"You've passed every day since Neapolis."

"And yet I'm still upright."

"Barely." Clement crouched beside him, casting a look toward the captain at the stern. "He says we'll reach Leucas before midday tomorrow."

Epaphroditus said nothing. His gaze remained locked on a smudge on the horizon, low hills shrouded in mist. The Ionian coastline. The captain had chosen the longer route, skirting the western edges of Greece. Safer, he'd said. Slower, but less likely to end in a watery grave.

He'd take it slower.

The sun was climbing toward its height when they dropped anchor in a crescent inlet. A scattering of red-tiled roofs clung to the hillside. The scent of cooking oil, seaweed, and wet stone drifted from the shore.

Locals gathered with baskets of lentils, fish, and olive jars near the docks. The clamor of bargaining voices rose above the cries of gulls.

The captain called out, "One night. Trade what you need. Wind changes tomorrow."

"We'll need to stretch every denarius," Clement muttered, fingering the pouch at his waist.

Epaphroditus nodded once. The thought of meeting Paul with empty hands tightened his gut worse than the waves.

They wove between crates and stalls, voices raised in halting Greek as they found an older woman selling dried chickpeas and flatbread near the crumbled base of a Roman milestone.

"Peace to your house," Epaphroditus said. "We seek a fair trade."

She studied him, then gestured to the coin in Clement's hand.

The exchange was swift: two small sacks, a few loaves, and a flask of oil.

They slipped back into the crowd, where the scent of roasting fish tangled with salt and sweat.

Shouts rose ahead. Two men, likely crew from another vessel, argued with a young boy. The child clutched a half-empty basket of salted perch, eyes wide.

"You sold the same fish twice!" one man snarled.

"I didn't—" the boy began, but his voice cracked under the weight of accusation.

A fist rose.

Epaphroditus stepped in before it could fall. "Peace!"

The sailor turned, teeth bared. "He lied."

"Then take the matter to the guards," Epaphroditus replied. "No coin is worth a beating."

The boy trembled, eyes darting toward the alley

behind him.

Epaphroditus met his gaze, the boy's dark eyes stirring a familiar ache. That innocence reminded him of his first meeting with Felix. "Make your trades clean next time. Keep your word."

The crowd held its breath. Slowly, the sailor lowered his hand. The boy fled. Tension snapped like a frayed line in the salt wind.

Clement exhaled beside him. "You handle conflict like a man who's seen his share."

Epaphroditus' thoughts flickered to Euodia and Syntyche, always at odds, their bickering a constant undercurrent that wore at the soul. He had seen their quarrels stretch on endlessly, each one more exhausting than the last. "I've seen enough."

Back on board, they sat near the stern, knees brushing coils of damp rope, and ate modestly. The chickpeas were dry, the bread tough, but it stayed down.

"I keep thinking of Luke's words," Epaphroditus said, his voice low. "Paul is still teaching. Still writing. Even in chains."

Clement broke off a piece of bread. "He'll keep going until his last breath. You know that."

"I wonder if he's cold," Epaphroditus said. "If he's eaten today."

Clement chewed in silence for a moment. "He has Christ."

Epaphroditus nodded, eyes on the rippling

water. "But the body still needs hands. Feet. Comfort. That's why we're going. I need to remember that."

The ship rocked gently in the harbor, groaning like an animal.

At dawn, the sails billowed with the returning wind, and by mid-morning, the coast of Cephalonia fell behind them. The waters turned deep and blue, dotted here and there with signs of life, dolphins breaching, seabirds soaring. The crew moved with efficiency, their rhythm as practiced as a temple rite.

By afternoon, only the sea remained. Italy still waited far ahead, past the volcanic rise of Sicily and the long stretch of the Tyrrhenian coast.

Epaphroditus leaned against the railing and drew Luke's letter from his satchel. The parchment had curled at the edges, stained with salt and use, but the words still held.

Grace and peace be multiplied to you from God our Father and the Lord Jesus Christ...

He read it through again, lips moving without sound. Then he rolled it and pressed a hand over the pouch beneath his tunic.

Wind and wave swallowed his whisper, but still he spoke it: "If my life is to be a fee, at least let me finish this mission."

*And when we came into Rome, Paul was
allowed to stay by himself, with the
soldier who guarded him.*
Acts 28:16

The ship groaned like an old man stirring from
uneasy sleep as it slipped into the docks of Ostia.
After months of raw wind and the ceaseless pitch of
the sea beneath him, Epaphroditus struggled to
adjust to the sudden stillness of land. His knees
wobbled. The planks beneath his sandals seemed
foreign. Beside him, Clement looked no better, skin
sallow, cloak stiff with salt, lips cracked from brine
and wind.

Still, they grinned like fools.

Epaphroditus's fingers brushed the worn
leather strap of his bag, a silent prayer threading
through his thoughts. The Philippians' offering. Still
there. Still safe.

The small satchel was more than cloth and coin;
it was the lifeline of faith and hope from a distant

place, carried across a merciless sea by trembling hands and desperate hearts.

His thoughts flickered to Melody, to the faces of the believers back in Philippi, some joyful, others heavy with burden. How fragile they seemed, stretched thin between loyalty and discord. The voyage had tested his body, but it was his soul's endurance that truly frayed beneath the salt and wind.

A sudden sharp gust tore at the sail above, reminding him how close they had come to ruin. He swallowed the lump rising in his throat. What awaited them in Rome was unknown, yet the gift in his grasp was a beacon, a promise he dared not lose.

Beside him, Clement shifted, breaking the spell. "You look like a man about to face lions."

"More like wolves," he muttered, jaw aching from holding it clenched so long. "Friendlier, perhaps."

They passed through the city gates with the surge of morning traffic, vendors shouting, carts rattling over stone, animals bleating. Ostia struck Epaphroditus' senses like a slap: the stench of fish guts and dung, the clang of metal, the mix of languages striking in the air. Beggars hunched on temple steps, hands outstretched. Legionaries swaggered by in polished lorica, claiming the road with every stride.

The journey was far from over. From Ostia,

they would have to walk the Via Ostiensis, a long, dusty road that stretched nearly twenty miles to Rome. The rising sun would soon scorch their skin, and the relentless pace would steal their strength. It would take the better part of the day to reach the city, a final trial before the streets of Rome swallowed them whole.

By the time they reached the city gates, the sun had begun its descent, casting long shadows across the road. Voices floated up in Greek, Latin, Aramaic, so many tongues in one city, all clamoring to be heard. The air was cooler now, tinged with the scent of evening fires, as the last light of day wrapped the city in a golden haze. They had fought for months for this moment. Still, the Lord had carried them.

They asked their way through half of Rome, traders, beggars, anyone who looked like they might know. Word of Paul lingered in whispers and nods, finally leading them here.

The house on the Vicus Patricius appeared unremarkable, a narrow two-story structure with flaking paint and shuttered windows.

Epaphroditus cleared the salt from his throat and called out, "Greetings to the owner of this house."

The door scraped open.

A sharp-eyed woman studied them, lips pressed in suspicion. Epaphroditus held her gaze, shoulders squared, though weariness gnawed at every joint.

Then she turned and called out, "Timothy!"

Timothy appeared at once, his beard fuller than Epaphroditus remembered, eyes widening in disbelief. "Epaphroditus?"

"In the flesh," he rasped.

Timothy reached for him in a jumble of motion, cheek to cheek, then a grip on his arm. His laugh broke midway, rough with disbelief.

Luke followed close behind, a scrap of parchment in his ink-smudged hand. "I don't believe it. You actually boarded a ship and survived the crossing."

"Aphrodite must've been distracted." Epaphroditus's lips twitched in a hesitant smile.

"And Shira? Melody? The others?"

"All well. They send their love and prayers."

Luke blinked faster than needed, lips tightening. "I miss them too," he said, and pulled Epaphroditus inside.

The room was modest, with a small writing desk, a cot, and a clay lamp flickering in the corner. The soldier stationed nearby shifted as they entered, the chain at his belt linking him to the man seated on the mat.

Paul lifted his head slowly. His beard had thinned and gone whiter since they last met. But his eyes, dark and flint-edged, hadn't dimmed. He rose with effort, the chain dragging heavy across the floor. "You made it."

Their embrace was rough, hindered by restraints and exhaustion, but firm.

For the first time in months, the ache in Epaphroditus's chest eased.

"You endured," Paul whispered, gripping his arm with unexpected strength. "I thank God for you daily."

"I brought a gift." Epaphroditus unfastened the satchel, placing its contents into Paul's hands: cloth-wrapped bundles, sealed pouches, and ink jars tied with twine.

Paul's fingers quivered. He ran his thumb over the worn leather. Then he sat heavily, the satchel cradled like a sacred relic, and wept. "A fragrant offering," he murmured. "A sacrifice acceptable and pleasing to Adonai."

The days that followed settled into a rhythm. Paul dictated in the mornings, rested in the heat of the day, and prayed by lamplight. Epaphroditus copied lines onto parchment with focused care, while Timothy's stylus scratched with speed, and Luke murmured corrections. Clement cleaned the pantry, baked fresh loaves each dawn, and coaxed Paul into eating more than he preferred.

They had returned to a kind of family. The chaos of the world seemed to pause, holding a fragile peace. Epaphroditus allowed himself to breathe in the stillness, the weight of companionship settling like a balm on his weary spirit. The journey had been long and harrowing, but here, in this humble room filled with familiar faces, hope flickered anew, fragile but fierce.

It was only a few days later that Paul asked, "And Philippi?"

Epaphroditus leaned back on the low bench. "We've had joy," he said, choosing the word carefully. "And trouble."

Paul's mouth pulled sideways. "Which wins?"

"Depends on the hour." He exhaled, fingers tightening around the edge of the bench. "It's Euodia and Syntyche."

A deep crease carved itself between Paul's brows as his gaze sharpened. "Still butting heads?"

"They won't speak. They sit on opposite sides of the gatherings, glaring. They've drawn lines, forcing others to pick sides. Use their wealth like levers, giving or withholding to bend the rest into sides. It's... poison."

Paul lowered his head with a slow, heavy sigh. "They've labored hard. Zealous women both. But zeal without harmony..." He stopped, eyes narrowing. "It can burn down a house faster than any fire."

"People are frightened," Epaphroditus admitted. "Not just of Rome, or hunger, or being named among us. They're afraid of each other now. How can we teach unity in Christ when we're fracturing from within?"

Paul stared at the blank parchment beside him. "I will write to them. Not in anger. In sorrow, if that will reach them. They must be reminded, they are citizens of heaven. Not rivals scrapping over scraps."

"And if they don't listen?"

Paul's eyes lifted to his. "Then we keep loving them until something breaks through."

Epaphroditus swallowed hard. He didn't speak the thought that pressed behind his teeth, that maybe the wound was already too deep to mend.

That night, sleep would not come. Epaphroditus stepped onto the narrow balcony, and the cool air kissed his face. Rome sprawled beneath the stars, rooftops glowing in lamplight and shadow. Smoke curled from chimney pots. Somewhere far off, a flute sang a lonely song.

The salt still clung to his skin. The sea still rolled behind his eyes when he closed them. He had survived the voyage, but barely. The wind, the sickness, the creak of timbers above dark waves, he still woke gasping, heart hammering as if he were drowning.

His fingers curled tight around the iron rail.

He had come this far.

But could he return?

I have thought it necessary to send to you Epaphroditus my brother and fellow worker and fellow soldier, and your messenger and minister to my need, for he has been longing for you all and has been distressed because you heard that he was ill.
Philippians 2:25-26

Epaphroditus woke to shivers galloping down his spine. The room was still, save for the faint scrape of wind through the shutters, but his body convulsed with cold. He twisted upon the reed mat, limbs tangled in the linen wrap soaked through with sweat. It plastered his back.

He groaned, a sound low and rasped. Every joint pulsed with fire, every breath scraped like sanded bone. His skin stung where it met the mat. He rolled to his side, willing the pain to abate, but it only shifted and deepened. Heat rolled from his core like bellows fanning a forge beneath his ribs.

Closing his eyes brought no relief.

He was underwater.

Salt scorched his nostrils. Muffled screams pressed in from somewhere distant. His arms moved sluggishly, bound in green cords, no, seaweed, coiling like vines. A light flickered ahead, iron bars yawning in the ocean deep like a waiting mouth. Something waited beyond the gate, teeth gleaming in the dark.

The current dragged him closer.

He screamed and shot upright, a mistake. Pain knotted in his gut, wrenching him back down, and a sour taste filled his mouth. He could only breathe in shallow pants. The linen wrap latched to his chest like drenched bark. His face dripped. He swore he tasted salt.

A hand touched his forehead. Cold. Startlingly cold. His breath caught.

"Burning up," said a familiar voice. Luke.

Epaphroditus squinted, his vision blurred. The room spun, shadows sliding across the walls like waves over sand. Luke's face loomed, carved with worry and weariness. A cup touched his lips, bitter, pungent water. He tried to turn his head, but Luke steadied him.

"Drink. Slowly."

He managed a few swallows before retching it up.

"You're not dying," Luke said, though his voice

didn't sound certain.

Epaphroditus blinked at him, his lips cracked. "I don't think even you can cure this illness, physician."

"We know of a better physician. Yield yourself to His care."

He tried to chuckle, but it came out as a wheeze. "No Daphne tucked away in your medical satchel?"

"Daphne isn't strong enough to save you this time."

He let his head fall back to the mat. The ceiling beams wavered, swimming in and out of view.

Time fractured.

Sometimes he woke in daylight, other times to the dark, with no sense of how long he'd been asleep. Days bled together like ink unraveling in water.

Sounds warped and shifted, soft footsteps became thunder, whispered prayers twisted into howls. At times, he saw faces in the walls, eyes blinking from cracked plaster, watching in silence. Once, he cried out to them, thinking them divine messengers. But they did not answer. Only shadows moved, stretching long fingers across the floor as if to pull him under.

He sweated through each night and heard the voice of the prophetess whispering repeatedly: *Death waits for you across the great sea; your life will be Aphrodite's fee.*

Each time he closed his eyes, the sea took him.

In one of the fever dreams, he sank into a

moonlit tide, drawn toward a silver gate with bright handles and a voice calling from beyond. Not soft. Commanding. *Come out of your tomb.*

He reached toward the gate and woke, gasping.

Luke was always there. Sometimes praying. Sometimes mixing herbs. Once, Epaphroditus glimpsed him turn away, thumb swiping the corner of his eye in silence. A gesture he wasn't meant to see.

"I'm finally worthy to partake of your healing herbs," he rasped.

"I'd turn over every remedy to aid you, my friend," Luke said. "In fact, I've nearly done so."

"Well," Epaphroditus whispered, "if the world-traveling physician can't save me, then I must be too far gone."

Luke didn't answer.

The fever stayed. More days passed. He heard the voices of Clement and others he didn't recognize. Someone recited psalms. The words fluttered past him, never taking root.

His bones were hollow. His arms, brittle twigs of strength. He barely shifted positions without help. When he spoke, it took too long for the words to form, like hauling stones through thick silt.

But his mind didn't rest.

I am a fool. A fool who thought he could outrun a prophecy.

It wasn't dying that he feared the most, not

anymore. What gnawed at him, night after night, was the thought of failing the gathering in Philippi. They'd all trusted him. Sent him across the sea with their coins, their prayers, their hope. He'd delivered it all into Paul's hands, but would he be able to return to them? They needed him. Or rather, he needed them.

Adonai, he prayed in shattered fragments. *Even now... bear fruit from this broken branch.*

Then came the worst night, the fever's cruel summit.

His body trembled with cold he couldn't shake. He heard water dripping nearby, though he could not decipher the source. He reached toward the sound and instead found his own chest, slick with sweat.

Then he was on the sea again.

The ship lurched. But no wood creaked. No sails flapped. Only silence. He was alone on a deck that dissolved into mist. The stars overhead blinked one by one, until only black remained. A woman's shape emerged from the black water. Cloaked in silver light. She wore no face, only blood-red lips whispering fate, coiling around his ribs like a serpent.

Your life will be Aphrodite's fee.

He clenched his fists, mustering the last thread of fire left within him.

"No," he growled through chattering teeth. "My

life is not hers to claim."

Then came the voice, the one that reached him through death's veil.

Come out of your tomb.

And at that moment, he knew: this illness, even if fatal, would not be her triumph.

He drifted again.

When he woke next, the light filtering through the shutters was warm, and his shivers had quieted. His limbs no longer lay heavy like quarried stone. His head throbbed still, but his mind was clearer.

Luke slept slumped against the wall, still keeping vigil. A scroll hung limp in his hand.

Epaphroditus watched him for a long moment, then turned his face to the ceiling. Breathing didn't hurt as much. The bitterness in his mouth dulled.

When Luke stirred, Epaphroditus managed a rasped word, "Still here?"

Luke startled, then leaned over him with cautious joy. "You're not dead."

"Sorry to disappoint."

"You're the most stubborn patient I've ever had."

Epaphroditus's lips twitched in a faint, tired smile, the corners of his eyes folding despite the fatigue. "I'm told that's a gift."

Luke pressed a cool cloth to his forehead. "You're through the worst of it."

Epaphroditus didn't answer at once. He let the

words settle, let the truth of them unfurl inside him like a cautious dawn. Through the worst. Not free. Not whole. But through.

"I thought I wouldn't see the sun again," he murmured finally. "I kept sinking, deeper each night."

Luke gave a soft nod, the kind born from too many bedside watches. "The body suffers, but the soul bears it all."

"I wasn't afraid to die," Epaphroditus whispered. "I was afraid to die unfinished."

He turned his head toward the window. Light spilled through the cracked shutters, and for the first time in days, it didn't sting his eyes. A bird trilled somewhere beyond them. The ordinary beauty of it nearly undid him.

"I prayed," he said. "Not like before. Not with words. Just… with what was left."

"That's when the true prayers rise."

Epaphroditus shut his eyes again. "I asked Adonai to take what was left of me. To use it. Even if I never rose from this mat again."

Silence stretched.

Then Luke said quietly, "That kind of offering… is rarely refused."

Epaphroditus closed his eyes, heart heavy with gratitude, and offered a silent prayer, for both physicians.

Luke's tireless care had become his anchor. The

physician's hands, steady, practiced, unflinching, had checked his pulse, measured his breath, and examined his skin with the practiced eye of one who'd seen illness in every form.

But beneath each remedy, Epaphroditus discovered something deeper, Adonai's mercy, threading through him, knitting brokenness to life. The Greater Physician needed to intervene. Though Luke was a vessel, the healing was God's alone.

*Indeed he was ill, near to death. But God
had mercy on him, and not only on him
but on me also, lest I should have sorrow
upon sorrow.*
Philippians 2:27

Olive oil and damp stone clung to the air, laced with
the sharp tang of bitter herbs Luke used for
poultices. Epaphroditus stirred on the mat, his
breathing steady but thin, an echo of fever still
threading through him.

It seemed the worst of it was behind him, the
weakness and terror of the fevered nights fading like
a distant storm. Yet each motion sent weakness
shivering through his limbs, a sharp reminder of
how near death had crouched. He hadn't expected
recovery to be this fragile, as if strength were
trickling back grain by grain.

Luke leaned over, fingers pressed lightly to his
wrist. "Your strength will return, though not all at
once."

Epaphroditus swallowed against the dryness in his throat. Memory trickled back in fragments: sweat-soaked nights, sea-drenched visions, Paul's silhouette bent in prayer beneath torchlight too dim to catch his words.

"Any more nightmares?"

He caught the inspecting gaze of a physician mingled with the look of a concerned friend. For the last several nights, Epaphroditus had slept peacefully, even weak from the strength-stealing fever, he slept better than he ever had.

His gaze traveled the room. Paul leaned on the low table, murmuring to Timothy, who nodded at his every word. "Where's Clement?" he asked, his voice raw from disuse.

Luke met his gaze and hesitated. "Gone."

"Gone?" Epaphroditus pushed himself onto his elbows, only to collapse under the weight of his own weakness.

"Easy." Luke set a firm hand on his shoulder. "Paul sent him back to Philippi. We were all so worried about you, we thought..." He took in a shaking breath, then cleared his throat of emotions. "We thought it best they know what was happening to you."

"They'll think I'm dead."

"Only that death came close." Luke adjusted the goatskin blanket on top of Epaphroditus. "Clement needed to return, and your family and friends needed to know about your condition so they could pray for you."

Epaphroditus closed his eyes, imagining Melody and Shira's voices lifting in prayer along with the others. Would they weep and fast? He had left strong, full of purpose, a courier entrusted with coin and encouragement. And now?

Now, he was a man who had brushed the edge and lived.

Footsteps sounded, deliberate and familiar. Paul stooped near, eyes brighter than his aging frame should allow. He sat beside Epaphroditus without a word, folding his legs with a quiet groan.

"You should rest," Epaphroditus mused.

"Look at the one telling me to rest." Paul chuckled. "I should do many things. But today, I write."

Tertius, Paul's faithful scribe, settled at a low table next to Timothy, where parchment and ink stood like sentinels awaiting his command.

Paul gave him a simple nod to show he was ready. "I sent Clement back with prayer and a message regarding you." He patted Epaphroditus's arm. "But you... I will send with a letter."

"No." The word escaped before Epaphroditus could temper it.

Paul looked up, his expression sharpening. "No?"

"Let me stay," Epaphroditus said, forcing

himself up on one trembling elbow. "They sent me to serve you. I failed them by falling ill. Let me—"

"You did not fail." Paul's voice sliced through the air like a blade. "You risked your life for the sake of Jesus. That is not failure, brother. That is faith."

Epaphroditus remained still. Paul's words echoed in his chest, louder than the pounding of his heart. Faith. Not failure. It was hard to let that truth in. He had come so far with such certainty, chosen by his community, entrusted with gifts, bolstered by prayers. And then the collapse. The burning. The endless days of sickness that peeled everything away but breath.

Epaphroditus lowered his gaze, fingers tracing the rough weave of the mat. "And yet Clement returned. I remained. What use is a servant who can barely stand?" he muttered, more to himself than anyone else.

"You remained because you nearly died. I sent Clement for their sake, not because you were unworthy." Paul exhaled and leaned forward. "You think the Lord needs your strength? Your perfect obedience?"

Epaphroditus blinked, stung by the words but pierced by their truth.

"He used a shepherd boy to slay a giant. A barren woman to birth a nation. A fisherman to lead His people. And now, He has used your brokenness, your brush with death, to show what grace really means." Paul's hand pressed briefly to his shoulder. "You are not wasted. You are a witness. This letter will let them see what mercy looks like."

Epaphroditus stared at the ceiling beams overhead. Was he truly a witness? Had he not seen Adonai's mercy firsthand? Had he not experienced a God who doesn't favor the strong, but the surrendered?

Paul eased back. "When I visited your city," he said slowly, "I heard people shouting in the marketplace, laughing as they threw dice. They called out 'Epaphroditos!', Favored of Aphrodite."

He paused, letting the words and the familiarity settle on him like dust.

"They invoke her name for favor," Paul continued, "for luck in games of chance. But we call on Adonai, the one true God. He has shown you favor, Epaphroditus, not by the dice of fortune, but by the mercy of His hand."

Epaphroditus closed his eyes. That name, his name, had always been a strange garment to wear. Aphrodite's favor, named by parents who had hoped their son would rise with charm, wit, and success. Yet here he was, shorn of strength, hundreds of miles from the people he most cared for, and no longer in Aphrodite's favor.

Truly, the dice had been loaded. He had not gambled with chance. He had wagered his life on the God of Israel.

And God had answered.

Paul rose to his feet slowly. "It will take days to complete the letter. You will need those days. Your legs are not yet ready for the sea."

Epaphroditus gave a brief nod. He could barely stand, let alone travel. But Paul's words ignited something within him. The return to Philippi would not be one of shame. It would be one of testimony.

"I will write with care," Paul added, leaning over Tertius. "These are not idle words. They are life."

Days once more settled into a rhythm: food reluctantly eaten, strength creeping back in increments, Paul dictating to Tertius while Luke kept a vigilant physician's eye on Epaphroditus.

A few weeks later, Epaphroditus sat at the low table scattered with scrolls and ink, watching Tertius make rhythmic markings under Paul's dictation. Ink mingled with the scent of boiling stew.

Luke entered, arms folded, and studied him for a moment. "I see your strength has returned. Your color is looking better every day."

"Truly?" Epaphroditus asked, searching Luke's expression for any hint of untruth.

"You'll grow tired," Luke said. "But the sickness won't return. The Lord has spared you. It's time you made ready."

Epaphroditus breathed in deeply. The air was

sharper, cleaner, as if cleared by prayer.

That evening, Paul came to him with the finished scroll in hand. He turned it over once, twice, as though weighing not just the parchment but the words it carried.

"You set out with coin," Paul said. "You return bearing grace." He held the scroll out and pressed it firmly into Epaphroditus' hands.

Epaphroditus took it in silence. The coins he once carried shimmered with earthly worth, but this... this letter bore eternal weight.

"Tell them," Paul added, "how their encouragement saved a life, mine and yours."

"I will," Epaphroditus whispered.

Paul's smile stretched wider, etching new lines into his weathered face. "Then go with joy."

The following morning, Epaphroditus set shaking legs on a rocking ship. Sailors barked orders along the dock. Ropes groaned, and the scent of tar, salt, and the faint odor of livestock hung in the air. The scroll rested beneath his tunic, warm against his chest.

No dread gripped him this time. The last voyage had begun in shadow, the priestess' whisper of death trailing him across the sea.

But death had not taken him.

God had taken him instead... and given him back.

He stood at the railing, watching the dock drift

away. The sails snapped open, filling with wind. The ship cut forward, cleaving the waters beneath a rising sun.

Epaphroditus closed his eyes and whispered a prayer, not for safety, but thanksgiving.

Philippi waited.

I have received full payment, and more.
I am well supplied, having received from
Epaphroditus the gifts you sent, a
fragrant offering, a sacrifice acceptable
and pleasing to God.
Philippians 4:18

Salt clung to Epaphroditus' lips as he gazed toward the horizon. Months at sea, and still, no end in sight. The deck groaned beneath him like a dying man, timber joints creaking as the ship rolled under the wind's relentless hand. His cloak, sun-bleached and salt-stiff, flapped against his legs. He clutched it tighter, as though that might still the thudding in his chest.

Beneath the folds, tucked against his skin, the scroll rested, Paul's letter to the Philippians. So light, and yet heavier than the pouch of coins he'd carried from his city so many months ago. He had delivered the gifts into faithful hands, and it had been spent to sustain Paul and the others. But this letter would not be spent. It would be sown.

He closed his eyes. The sea's scent no longer masked the memory of illness, of sweat pooling in the hollows of his collarbone, of Luke's cool hand on his burning brow. He'd hovered on the edge of death then, tossed in fevered visions where iron gates yawned beneath black water, and voices beneath the waves called him forward. The prophecy had come close to fulfillment.

But he hadn't died.

Not in body, at least. Something else had been buried in that illness. A deeper death. Fear. The gnawing dread that he was not enough, that he would fail his Lord, his brothers and sisters in faith, his city. That he would die far from home and leave his family unattended. That was the true death. And he had passed through it.

"Adonai," he whispered as the coast broke the haze. "You have borne fruit from this broken branch."

The familiar shape of Neapolis rose out of the mist. Even from this distance, he could trace the lines of the city, the market square, the temple roofs, the outline of homes built snug into the slope. Somewhere beyond them in Philippi, his wife would be watching the road, praying for his return.

He patted the concealed parchment. A letter filled not with orders or instructions, but with joy, hope, and grace. Words Paul had labored over, each one carefully chosen while Epaphroditus recovered in the shadow of death. It was no small thing to carry such a message.

The ship docked as the sun slipped lower. As he stepped off the gangplank, his legs nearly gave way. Not from weakness, but from the strange gravity of return. The harbor buzzed with life, traders unloading goods, children running with baskets, sailors arguing over coin and catch.

He moved through the crowd like a spirit.

Every sound pressed on him. Every color seemed brighter than he remembered. He had not expected to be overwhelmed by so much all at once.

The path to Philippi was dusty, but the smell of earth warmed him within.

Then, at the city gate, he saw her.

Melody.

She stood cloaked in his favorite olive palla, wrapped so that part of it covered her hair and the other part wrapped around something in her arms. Her eyes fixed on him, as though blinking might make him vanish.

He didn't wait, but ran toward her, enveloping her in his arms. For a moment, there was nothing but the warm, inviting scent of her skin and the sound of her breath.

Home.

"You're thinner," she murmured, brushing his face with her hand. "And you smell like fish."

He laughed. It cracked in his throat. "Better than the scent of a grave."

"Clement told us..." Her lips quivered. "He said you were dying."

"I was." He leaned his forehead against hers. "But God had mercy on me."

She cupped his face, brushing her thumb beneath the tear gathering at his eye. "Thank you, Adonai."

Epaphroditus pulled back when something moved between them. He looked down to catch the face of a baby in the crook of her arm. "Is that my niece or nephew?"

"Neither." Her eyes met his with a softness that seemed to hold every unspoken word of affection. "This is your son."

"Son?" The word pierced his heart with a thousand arrows, allowing a tidal wave of love to pour in. "My son?"

"Adonai has seen fit to answer more than our prayers for your safe return." She traced the lines of the boy's chin. "He sought to pour out His grace upon us."

With trembling fingers, Epaphroditus scooped the baby into his arms. "He's beautiful." He glanced at Melody. "Like his mother."

"And keeps me up at night, like his father."

A loud chuckle escaped Epaphroditus's lips, startling the boy, who made his displeasure known with a wail. He gently rocked him until he settled again.

"I know it's tradition to withhold a name until after their first harvest." Melody stretched to look into her son's face. "But..."

He gazed over her. "Nathaniel."

"What does it mean?"

"Hebrew for 'God has given'." He lifted the baby to his cheek. "Adonai has given him to us."

"Nathaniel Paul."

He looked up at her.

"Well, he needs a strong Roman name too, and I can think of none stronger."

His gaze traveled the face of his son. "Nathaniel Paul, let's go home."

The villa doors stood open when they arrived. Familiar voices drifted into the street.

He shot a glance at Melody.

"They've gathered every evening since Clement's return to pray for you." She took Nathaniel Paul from his arms. "Go on."

As Epaphroditus stepped in, the room stilled. Then, they spoke his name as if in prayer and surrounded him.

Hands clasped his shoulders, touched his arms, and others wept over him.

"We thought you were lost," Clement whispered into his ear.

"Almost," he said, and meant it. "But the Lord

carried me through."

Epaphroditus's gaze settled on Shira and Talia, standing a short distance away. He caught Shira's breath catch, the tension around her eyes loosening like a thread finally given slack. Beside her, Talia's lips curved just enough to catch the light, a quiet flicker of joy, barely contained but unmistakable.

In those shared glances, the weight of the moment shifted. Relief washed through him. He was truly home.

Calliope drifted toward him. A bundle in her arms as well. "It's a good thing you survived your journey." She held up her baby. "So, my son could meet his uncle."

Epaphroditus brushed the boy's round cheek. "Are you waiting to name him?"

"Of course not." Felix came to stand beside his wife. "Our faith lies in Adonai." He dipped his head to the boy. "We'd like to present to you, Epaphras Kastas."

Epaphroditus turned misty eyes on his sister. "Truly?"

"He's named for the two bravest seafarers I know."

He gazed over the gathering, seeing bright faces and there, Euodia, standing stiff near a support column. Across the room, Syntyche, her arms crossed in guarded distance.

A familiar weight settled in his gut. He retrieved

Paul's scroll and raised it. "I bring a letter from Paul."

The gathering fell silent.

Someone brought a stool, and another carried a lamp closer.

The scroll trembled in Epaphroditus's hands as he unrolled it and read:

"'Paul and Timothy, servants of Christ Jesus, to all the saints in Christ Jesus who are at Philippi, with the overseers and deacons: Grace to you and peace from God our Father and the Lord Jesus Christ. I thank my God in all my remembrance of you...'"

The words poured into the room like light through a lifted veil. The letter was alive, not just read but received. He watched as eyes closed and lips moved in silent prayer.

He went on, "'Only let your manner of life be worthy of the gospel of Christ, so that whether I come and see you or am absent, I may hear of you that you are standing firm in one spirit, with one mind striving side by side for the faith of the gospel...'"

He continued through the scroll, breathing out Paul's words with his own breath and prayers.

His eyes halted on the next line, then turned to look at the two women and spoke without moving his gaze, "I entreat Euodia and I entreat Syntyche to agree in the Lord."

Syntyche's jaw clenched. Euodia's lips parted, then closed.

"'Yes, I ask you also, true companion'"—Epaphroditus glanced at Clement—"help these women who have labored side by side with me in the gospel together with Clement and the rest of my fellow workers, whose names are in the book of life.'"

He waited, not with pressure, but with quiet hope.

Lowering his gaze, Epaphroditus finished Paul's remaining thoughts, "'Greet every saint in Christ Jesus. The brothers who are with me greet you. All the saints greet you, especially those of Caesar's household. The grace of the Lord Jesus Christ be with your spirit.'"

Then, with reverent fingers, he rolled the scroll closed. His hands ached with the weight of it. He looked at the two women.

The room held its breath.

Then, slowly, Euodia stepped forward. Syntyche hesitated, then mirrored her. They stopped before him, their hands hanging at their sides.

It was Euodia who spoke first. "Forgive me, sister."

Syntyche's eyes glistened. "And me."

Their hands met in the quiet space between them.

The room exhaled.

Epaphroditus bowed his head and led them in a

prayer for unity and strength and for Paul across the Great Sea.

As the gathering thinned, a few remained behind.

Clement approached him, eyes alight. "You carried it well."

Epaphroditus's lips twitched into a weary smile. "I nearly didn't make it."

"But you did."

He looked down at his hands, marked by travel and fever. Some of Paul's words from the letter echoed through him. "Paul called me his fellow soldier."

"You are."

"I'm not a soldier," he mumbled. "Never have been."

Melody came to his side. "You stood when others would have fallen. You fought sickness, distance, and doubt. You carried out your mission faithfully. If that is not a soldier, I don't know what is."

He turned to the doorway. Beyond it, the city hummed, vendors shouting, children laughing, sandals scraping on stone.

And yet... everything had changed.

He closed his eyes.

He remembered the fever, the heat, the sweat, the ache in every bone. Luke's cool hand, Paul's voice praying in the dark. And beneath it all, the dread, the old whisper of prophecy: *Death waits across the sea.*

But death hadn't claimed him. Instead, death had drowned, dragging fear with it. Death drowned in fever and waves and left behind something new.

Faith.

Epaphroditus looked at Melody, warmth rising in his chest.

The prophecy and the sea had not swallowed him. He had stepped from his tomb of fear... and risen in faith.

WHAT'S NEXT?

In the face of prejudice, Persis clings to the promises of Jesus.

In the port city of Thessalonica, Persis, a daughter of Persia and a bondservant of Aristarchus, is forever changed when she encounters the teachings of Jesus and learns of His imminent return.

Surrounded by a community of believers and drawing strength from Paul's letters, Persis discovers the power of hope while navigating the challenges of persecution and prejudice. Through trials and triumphs, she learns to embrace her identity as a beloved child of God and live out the radical call to follow Jesus.

Join Persis as she struggles to hold fast to the refuge of her newfound faith while uncovering hidden truths about her past. Dare to embark on a journey to discover the boundless depths of grace awaiting those who dare to believe as the letters of 1 and 2 Thessalonians come to life in *Keeping Thessalonica*, Book 2 of the Paul's Patrons series.

MORE FROM JENIFER JENNINGS:

Special Collections and Boxed Sets

Biblical Historical stories from the Old Testament to the New, these special boxed editions offer a great way to catch up or to fall in love with Jenifer Jennings' books for the first time.

Faith Finder Series: Books 1-3
Faith Finders Series: Books 4-6
The Rebekah Series: Books 1-3
Servant Siblings Series: Books 1-3
Servant Siblings Series: Books 4-7
Paul's Patrons Series: Books 1-3
Paul's Patrons Series: Books 4-6

* * *

The Rebekah Series:

Follow Rebekah on her faith journey through life.

The Stranger
The Journey
The Hope

* * *

Faith Finders Series:

Go deeper into the stories of these familiar faith heroines.

Midwives of Moses
Wilderness Wanderer
Crimson Cord
A Stolen Wife
At His Feet
Lasting Legacy

* * *

Servant Siblings Series:

They were Jesus' siblings, but they become His followers.

James
Joseph
Assia
Jude
Lydia
Simon
Salome

* * *

ABOUT THE AUTHOR

Jenifer Jennings is a passionate storyteller who brings ancient worlds to life through Biblical historical novels. A devoted student of Scripture since coming to faith in Jesus at seventeen, she holds a bachelor's degree in Women's Ministry and a master's in Biblical Languages. Jenifer is an active member of Word Weavers International, serving as an online chapter president, and a member of American Christian Fiction Writers (ACFW). When Jenifer's not writing, she's on a date with her husband or mothering their two children, a wise-cracking mathematician and a feisty artist.

If you'd like to keep up with new releases, receive spiritual encouragement, and get your hands on a FREE book, join Jenifer's Newsletter: **jeniferjennings.com/gift**